UNDERCOVER

~ An Austen Noir

YouTube Playlist: https://goo.gl/g5WtO9
Pinterest Inspiration Board: https://goo.gl/hdqSTF

To the readers
who appreciate a steamy
Mr. Darcy mystery
This one's for you!

ONE

November 1952

Everyone in the know acknowledged that El Barrio Steakhouse on 116th Street in East Harlem was frequented by a less-than-stellar clientele. The restaurant was a hotbed of questionable activity both at the tables and upstairs in the proprietor's office. What the general public didn't know was that Oscar, the owner, was the best damn pigeon in the city, even if he did, occasionally, break a few laws. The man had his crooked finger on the pulse of everything going on in New York City's dark underworld ranging from organized crime in the Bronx to petty theft in Brooklyn. And thankfully, for Elizabeth Bennet, she was the only private investigator he talked to.

She supposed it was because of the many times she'd dined at El Barrio, always putting on a good show for his patrons by acting as his dame. Her assets served her well and he appreciated the role playing even if they never actually ended up in the bedroom. She smiled at that recollection of how he had often told her that she was the restaurant's best advertisement. In spite of Oscar's illegal connections and the occasional, necessary political graft, she trusted him—within limits. He was one of the few people in her life, with whom she dared to share anything about herself.

With telephone receiver pressed to her ear, Elizabeth gazed out onto the empty stretch of 44th Street visible from the large picture window of the second-floor office that served double duty as her apartment. Across the way, the red neon sign still flickered above Ruby's Diner, while the interior lights were shutting down one by one as her favorite haunt locked up for the night. At two in the morning, their work was ending as hers was just beginning with an unexpected trip up to El Barrio. At this late hour Spanish Harlem was the last place she wanted to go, but she didn't have a choice. Ten years ago, that neighborhood was safe, but post Second World War, Latino immigrants were opening bodegas and botánicas; encroachment into other ghettos caused turf wars. Everything was changing—except the private eye business.

Delicate fingers ran down the outside of her skirted thigh, reassuring her that her lucky stocking pistol, a derringer nicknamed "Sally" was secured in the holster at the right garter, at the ready should she need it.

"Are you sure, Oscar?" she asked her informant on the other end of the phone.

"Yeah. It was that Wickham fellow. Ten sheets to the wind and cussing like a sailor—"

"Well, he was Navy during the last war," she interrupted, feeling anxious over the information. *Finally! He's back on the radar.*

She lifted the telephone base and walked purposefully to the art deco mirror by the door, stretching the cord to its maximum length. A final application of vivid red lipstick dragged across her bottom lip before she blotted it with a satisfied pop.

"Whatever he was, he had a wild look in his eyes when he left with your sister Lydia about fifteen minutes ago."

"How was she?" Her stomach knotted as she removed a well-worn, black fedora from the coat rack beside the mirror. Cradling the receiver between chin and shoulder, she positioned the hat atop her raven waves, tilting the brim down enough to cover half her forehead.

"She was also smoked and spitting nails. I got a bad feelin' about this."

"Me, too. I'll see you in about twenty minutes. There shouldn't be any traffic at this hour traveling cross-town. I wish you would have telephoned sooner. I haven't had a single lead on that man in over eight months. My client won't be happy about this and I'm sure as hell not delighted that Lydia seems to be caught in Wickham's net."

"Sorry, doll. I couldn't break away to get you on the horn. I didn't realize who the boozehound was at first. That Slick Wick looks different than the last time he showed up at El Barrio."

"Yeah. He's a master at disguise since he left town in February of '51. I'll take down all the information when I get there. You didn't telephone the law, did you?" she asked, sliding her arms into the tan raincoat she always wore on nights like this.

"Whatta you kiddin'? Have this place crawlin' with flatfoots'll put me outta business."

"You're right. Glad you called me, though. Thanks, Oscar. See you shortly."

Hanging up, she chastised herself for not paying closer attention to her wayward sister and fought the urge to redirect her anger at the one person truly responsible: their father. She discounted the idea of telephoning him at this hour even though he was probably awake keeping company with his bourbon. It seemed as though she was the only sibling to care. Her eldest sister Jane (the perfect one) was married in her perfect, wealthy suburban life. Mary was praying her little heart out in the convent of the Sisters of Mercy in Maryland, and Kitty was somewhere in Europe living it up as an "artist" on her sisterly dime, painting from some street corner.

Propping a foot up on the desk chair, Elizabeth adjusted the ankle strap on her shoe then hiked her skirt before sliding a small knife into the sheath attached to the inside of her left garter. It was important to be prepared, especially when she had an uneasy feeling in her bones.

"Lydia, what have you gotten yourself into now? You should have known better than to meet him. Mary King has yet to be found and now you're running with my prime suspect," she fumed turning the light off before she exited the apartment.

Many nights she had gone out alone, stalking her prey, spying and acting the part as femme fatale for clients to get what she wanted: information. Private investigators, especially relatively green ones like her, were a dime a dozen in Manhattan, but none of them could boast 35-21-35 measurements and legs that she prided herself could stop traffic. She enjoyed the fact that maturity and street smarts had developed her into the ultimate man bait for Wickham—if she could find him. Oh, the delight she would have at seeing him again, only to squash him under her three-inch heels and send him up the river.

She exited the old building into the stilled city darkness and stood on the corner of 44th Street and Tenth Avenue barely affected by the chill or the eeriness of the hour. She heard mumbled words from a darkened doorway behind her, but wasn't afraid; that was typical for this street. Besides, she had Sally. Even the steam rising in gray streams from the subway grates was relegated to part of the expected scenery as her mind stayed solely focused on details she knew by heart, those of Mary King's disappearance. Elizabeth prayed that her sister wouldn't meet the same end if Slick Wick was indeed the kidnapper.

This neighborhood was no different than East Harlem, but having lived here for eighteen months, she knew the west side of Hell's Kitchen like the back of her hand. Located not far from Pier 83 on the Hudson

River it was still respectable enough being near the Theater District and just seedy enough to keep her hidden among B-girl prostitutes, bums, and striptease clubs. It was the perfect neighborhood from which to track down murderers and two-bit criminals.

Alone on the street corner, beneath the bishop crook lamplight, Elizabeth's gloved hand swept the side of her coat up toward a hip, displaying a long leg through the skirt's slit. As though out of nowhere, a bright yellow taxicab materialized, stopping before her under the glowing spotlight.

She climbed into the checker cab. "El Barrio restaurant," she directed the cabbie, withdrawing from her pocket a World War Two Navy portrait of George Wickham. The hackie hit the meter.

Holding out the photograph across the seat separating driver from passenger, she asked just as she had done for the last 648 taxi rides, "Have you picked this fare up recently?"

He looked at the photo then glanced back at her over his shoulder. She batted her eyes and pouted, "Please?"

"I don't think I've ever seen him before, but I can think of a few things that might jog my memory."

She snapped the photo back from his grasp. "Just drive."

••

As expected, Oscar waited outside the closed establishment. His well-tailored suit hid the rough-around-the-edges man within, but he was always thoughtful, tempering his brusqueness when it came to her. Perhaps, he was buttering her up for what she'd never give him even if she had explained herself many times. Handsome as he was, no man was going to get that unless she wore a sparkling diamond and it was accompanied by "I do" in a big church wedding but the likelihood of that happening was nil, given her line of work. Both this war and the last hadn't changed society's acceptance of women working in a man's job—particularly as a gumshoe. Apart from Oscar and Detective Christopher Brandon from homicide, there weren't any other men who respected her and what she did for a living.

When the taxi pulled to the curb, Oscar smiled, promptly going back to smoking his cigarette. She smiled back before paying the cabbie, brusquely blowing his off attempt to renegotiate with information she knew he didn't possess.

Several of El Barrio's Saturday night regulars lingered outside the closed restaurant, but neither she nor Oscar paid them mind when he kissed her cheek, snaking an arm around her waist. "You made good time, toots."

"Funny, for a cold night, I caught a cab with no trouble."

"Is it any wonder when you flash one of your gams?" he held the establishment's door open for her.

"You flatter me, pally, but you have to admit a girl has to do what a girl has to do."

"And you do it so well."

She sauntered into the restaurant, removing her black gloves with a tug to each finger. The stench of cigars and liquor hung heavy in the air. Ashtrays were filled with bent cigarette remains, and a half-eaten plate of burritos sat at the end of the long counter. The waitress had left her apron draped over the red padding that wrapped around the bar's perimeter.

Before removing her hat and trench coat, she withdrew a notepad from the pocket and placed it on the edge of the bar, and couldn't help the sly smirk that spread upon her lips when she felt Oscar's stare zero in on her chest. The new scoop neck white sweater and ringlet brassiere displayed her assets just fine. Oh, why did she feel the need to tease him so?

"You know, you're going to be the death of me, Eli."

A glance over her shoulder and a winsome smile caused him to chuckle when she said, "I know. But you're so good for my ego."

She couldn't help tormenting him. Good girl hadn't been her nature for quite some time. The Elizabeth of old started to change in 1945 at the age of 19 when her sweetheart came home from the war with a British bird on his arm and a newborn baby. She had to wake up and smell the coffee pretty fast; post-war was a whole lot different than pre, but when 1950 saw another conflict—this time in Korea—she fell right back into believing in another man, who only caused her more heartache.

"Where did he and my sister sit?" she asked, her eyes scanning the small restaurant as she traversed between tables.

"First the bar, but then they moved to that back table beside the curtain. Wickham ordered a plate of chuchitos."

"Well, you can't blame him for that. Elena's are the best in the city." She circled the table, polished nails skimming the white tablecloth as she examined the stamped out cigarette butts overflowing the ashtray. "Belomorkanal cigarettes?"

"Yeah. Ruskies."

"Any idea where he would come by Russian smokes?"

"Perhaps the Russian Tea Room."

She turned, raising an eyebrow. "No offense, darling, but if he's dining in El Barrio, it's doubtful he could afford the Tea Room."

"None taken. There's a small pocket of Commies down in Brooklyn, Sheepshead Bay area. Low-life scum involved in party recruitment along with black market exports and imported prostitution. As if we don't have enough American broads doing duty as pro skirts in the Big Apple."

"Many of whom you profit from." Elizabeth's red-tipped fingers flipped closed the empty matchbook found discarded under a cloth napkin and joked, "What's the matter, is the foreign talent encroaching on your business?"

"If you weren't so gorgeous, Gorgeous, I might have to silence that smart ass yap of yours."

She smiled in that particular way she knew would unhinge him, and she was right. Oscar winked at her as she pocketed the matchbook from the "Kit Kat Klub," thankful for the two leads that jerk Wickham had left for her. She wondered if Slick Wick was baiting her; she had been searching for him for close to a year and a half after he left her trusting neighbors and her father, who had hired him to work in his garage. He had played on her friends'—and her—sympathies with his charm. Little did anyone from the neighborhood know, the man was a criminal, gone AWOL during the last war and been on the run ever since. That information was compliments of his buddy Denny, who stayed behind after the chiseler skipped out on his debts.

"Wickham is sporting a beard now and he dyed his hair black. He's lost a few pounds since the last time we saw him here at the restaurant. Carmen the waitress noticed a fresh scar at his hairline."

Oscar lit a cigarette, hungrily watching Elizabeth as she bent at the waist to look under the table, her backside on display before his appreciative eyes. This woman did things to him. She had brains but was made for sex; she had a chassis as sophisticated and sexy as a Lincoln and gams for days. Like a tigress in constant heat, she purred "lay me" just by her prowling body movements.

He toyed with his cuff link, his eyes fixed on her bottom. "Eli, what's your *end* game for Slick Wick?"

Elizabeth rose then sashayed back to the bar, examining every detail in her path, as he continued to examine her.

"End game? It's simple: find Mary King then exact revenge."

"I like revenge."

"Yeah. Me too. It's liberating and you know what a true believer I am in liberty."

"You gonna wax him when you find him?"

She raised an eyebrow. "Someone should, but I'm not a violent person."

"Another thing, some highfalutin fella came in just before your sister arrived. He and Slick had heated words, something about the suit's sister. Cautioning him to keep away or else. It almost broke out into a fight but I had my boys at the ready in case we needed to pop one of them."

"You're all class, Oscar. Did anyone else overhear the conversation?"

"Just Julio the bartender, and he ain't gonna be putting his mouth in. He's got trouble with the law already."

"Hmm ... Did you, at least, get the name of this "suit"?"

Oscar leaned back against the bar, resting his elbows on the red padding. He smiled smugly watching her jot down facts in her notepad. "It'll cost ya."

Chuckling, Elizabeth glanced up from her task, their eyes meeting, both knowing that there was only one thing he wanted in exchange for information and there was no doubt in her mind that he wasn't going to get it from her.

She took a step towards him then ran a finger along the lapel of his unbuttoned double-breasted jacket. Tilting her head, her smile teased, her amber eyes searching his, her raspy voice scratching his overdue itch.

"How about next week we take in a show at the Copa together and you can pretend all you like that you're getting *that*?" she offered.

"As usual, doll, you know how to work me. The suit's name was Darcy, that's all I heard. He had Park Avenue written all over him. The boys tell me that he drove off in a Caddy Coupe de Ville."

"Thank you. Anything else you can tell me? How was Lydia?"

"Lacquered and lit up like a Christmas tree. They were drinking rum then switched to cheap whiskey when the dough ran out. Jose heard her mention Cuba a couple of times and she didn't sound happy about it."

"Cuba?"

"Yeah, must'ave been the rum talkin'."

"Well, let's hope she found her way back to Queens and the safety of my parents' house. It's too late to track her now. After a few hours of shut-eye, I'll head out there and check on her, maybe even subtly grill her about Wickham if she's in an amiable mood. She'd clam up if she suspected my interest in him or Mary King."

"You got yourself a handful with her."

"You're tellin' me. Between her and my parents, I'm ready to take a Mickey Finn just to get the hell out of New York."

She settled the fedora back on her head, assuring in the reflection of the bar's mirror the tilt was just right, her voice taking on an optimistic hint of hope. "LA sounds exciting and the weather is divine year round."

"Eli, you know as well as I do, that with your New York bowling ball-sized *cajones*, the only place you'll ever be happy is Gotham with a legit man by your side."

"I guess you're right, but what are the chances of me meeting Mr. Right in a city of seven million people, especially when half the men are fighting it out in Korea?"

"There's always me. I'm here; I'm at the ready."

She pulled a twenty from her purse and laid it on the bar then placed a used glass upon it, forming a wet ring over Andrew Jackson's face. "Thanks. I'll remember that." Brushing past him toward the restaurant's door, she grabbed her raincoat then glanced over her shoulder. "You didn't say what this Darcy looked like."

"It was dim, tough to make out the eye color or the details from where I stood, but he appeared to be just your type. Tall with dark hair and a brooding puss."

"Dealing with Wickham can make any man brood. It's the smolder that I look for."

••

Two

Everything felt the same as the day before, particularly since the narrow glimpse of visible sky was dreary gray. Rain splattered against the window of Elizabeth's small bedroom, waking her with the gradual realization that she had, once again, overslept. She groaned, covering her eyes with her forearm, barely alert after having finally gotten into bed at five that morning. The radiator clanked, pushing out heat even though the apartment already felt like a hundred degrees.

Stretching, she winced from the tug of brassiere against her flesh, remembering how she barely had enough energy to remove her clothes and forewent disrobing from her undergarments before falling onto the mattress. Though the garter belt and stockings remained, Sally and the dagger were carefully ensconced beneath the empty pillow beside her.

"Another winter day and a trip to Queens. Oh joy," she groaned, and then strained to look at the clock on the wall. Two o'clock in the afternoon seemed to be par for the course for this night watchman, and she still had to plan tomorrow's busy day: people to telephone and a "highfalutin fella" to track down through some of her contacts at the *New York Herald* or her police friend. *Tall with dark hair. Brooding.* She would leave no stone unturned until she found the man who picked a fight with Slick Wick. As soon as she was coherent enough, she'd search the City Directory for this Darcy.

She leaned to her nightstand and flipped the radio on. "Hold me, Thrill me, Kiss me" filled the small room occupied mostly by an antique bed left by the former occupant. Before placing her bare feet on the wood floor, she considered that a phone call could save the long train ride to Jackson Heights to check on Lydia. She picked up the heavy telephone receiver and listened, as was standard practice, before attempting to dial her parents' house. Yes, her party line buddy was discussing her gallbladder again.

"Excuse me; I'd like to use the telephone, please. You've had those gallstones for eight months now," she said before hanging up then dragging a hand through her shoulder-length, messy waves. She felt the puffiness to her eyes and then remembered that she hadn't removed her mascara and lipstick before bed.

From the opposite side of the thin wall, she could hear the four girls who shared 2F in the boarding house next door to her apartment. They, too, worked at night, a couple of cocktail waitresses and the other two, thespians.

"Coffee. I need coffee."

The daily pound upon her apartment door made her groan for the third time, and she slid her arms into a short kimono, padding through the somber living room toward the office at the front of the three-room apartment. Even the red roses she had purchased from the pushcart lady two days ago failed to brighten the space. The rain-streaked picture window and the ominous clouds beyond gave the room an eeriness that suddenly chilled her bones in spite of the heat.

"I'm coming, I'm coming," she said entering the office through a connecting door. She could see her friend's silhouette through the frosted window pane of the entrance. Before sliding back the chain lock, she opened the door a crack confirming that it was Charlotte from across the hall, doing mouth exercises. Elizabeth rolled her eyes. Since cast as a chorus kid in "Wish You Were Here," the woman was obsessed with her stretching and vocalization.

Blonde, petite, and adorable, Charlotte must have just awoken, too, because she stood at the threshold wearing nothing more than a man's cotton pajama top.

"Hi, doll," Charlotte sang with a brightness that contrasted the dreariness surrounding them. She brushed past Elizabeth as soon as the door opened wide enough. "I'm outta coffee. Can you help a girl out on this Sunday morning?"

Elizabeth laughed when her friend strolled through the office then plopped down onto the sofa in the living room, unfazed that she wore no undergarments below the pajama top.

"Don't you ever go to the grocery, Char?"

"Why should I? I have you, and besides, I just don't have time with rehearsals and all." She lit a cigarette, then leaned back onto a decorative pillow beside the vase of flowers. "You're up late today. Do you have a gee in your bedroom? Some lover who brought you these roses?"

"No. I had a late night, working on a case and I bought the flowers."

"Ooo!—a case. Anything exciting?"

With a disingenuous shrug of Elizabeth's shoulder, turning her back, she hoped her girlfriend would get the hint. Theirs was a friendship of very little sharing of confidential or personal matters.

"Oh do go on. I love a good caper: murder, mischief, mayhem."

"Trust me; it's nothing exciting. Just a twenty month-long case that I refuse to close."

"Say, when are you going to change the name on your door to read 'Eli'? It's not like anyone calls you Elizabeth."

Elizabeth smirked. "I know, but Elizabeth sounds professional. No one wants to hire a female private dick with the name Eli."

She struck a match and lit the stove burner before placing the filled coffee pot down and turning to lean against the tiled countertop.

Folding her arms, she eyed the once Miss Coney Island up and down. "I'm wondering, in the social circles you run with, have you ever heard the surname 'Darcy'?"

Charlotte took a long drag then blew a few practiced rings from her lips, exercising them still. "Sure. He's a dead politician."

"Hmm ... would he have a son?"

"Oh. Yeah. The dreamy Fitzwilliam Darcy. War hero or something. He and that actress Martha Roarke used to be a hot item until he dumped her at the Stork Club."

"Interesting. Is that all you know?"

"About him, yeah. If you have hours I could fill you in on Martha, a real gold-digger, that one."

Elizabeth settled into the chair opposite the sofa and propped her bare feet on the coffee table. "Have you ever heard of the Kit Kat Klub?"

"Know that, too. It's over on 52nd off Fifth."

"How on earth do you know all this?"

"Honey, in my line of work you meet people, who associate with people—and everything is in *Variety*, not just billboard headlines, but good old fashioned gossip. It would save you a lot of hoofing around the Big Apple if you just read it."

"What kind of place is the Kit Kat?"

"It's a gentleman's nightclub. One of the understudies in my show used to perform as a bump-n-grinder at that joint. It's a little sleazy, but she made some good dough to pay for her voice lessons."

"Do you think I could get in?"

"I don't see why not. I'm sure a few Commie lesbians are regulars there. It's off the radar of all this McCarthyism mumbo-jumbo. Could be a good cover for you, but not tonight."

Elizabeth twisted her lips in consideration. On Sunday nights, Gotham's establishments serving liquor were locked up. Well, except for the Stork Club, but it sounded like the Kit Kat was no high society place. Her visit would have to wait until tomorrow.

"Is it burlesque or striptease?" she asked.

"Strip. Why? Is PI work not paying? Are you looking for a little action on the side? It's quite provocative. Missy used a boa constrictor in her act and with a figure like yours you'd be headlining in no time."

"Ha. Ha. I do just fine by keeping my clothes on. I don't need *that* gimmick to get the results I need."

"Not *all* the results you need."

Determined to put an end to this conversation before it went any further, Elizabeth abruptly rose then walked toward the bedroom to make that call to her parents. "Darling, *that* kind of result only comes with trouble."

"There's no trouble with a man who can deliver results. It's the coming part that can destroy a girl's career, but that's why they make rubbers."

"Abstinence is much more effective and less damaging to the heart." Elizabeth turned, facing her friend, closing one of the French doors. "I'm sorry, hon. I've got to make a call. Make yourself at home and enjoy the coffee, but you'll have to let yourself out."

"Eli, one day you will have to let me in. We are best girlfriends, you know."

"I do let you in—I let you in every morning when you need to mooch off me." She grinned, glad that Charlotte didn't read into her comment anything more than the playful retort it was. But a pack of cigarettes flew toward the door anyway.

Elizabeth picked up the Chesterfields then shut the door, giving her friend one last wink.

••

The rain fell in sheets and the sky lit with flashes as Elizabeth sat at the edge of her bed dialing the phone. The storm felt like a prophetic omen of the day to come, particularly when her father answered.

"Yeah?"

"Hi, Pop. Is Mother there?"

"Whatsa matta, you don't wanna talk to your old man anymore?"

"No, that's not it. I just, um, need to discuss feminine issues with her. Unless of course, you can answer some questions I have about my menstrual cycle."

Elizabeth could hear his labored breath as he considered her words; problem drinking did that to him. "Hold the line. I'll get her." The expected bellow "Frances!" caused her to hold the receiver from her ear; his grumbled followed, then a cough instigated by those Pall Malls he's smoked for the past thirty years—then finally another "Frances! Get the hell over here. It's your daughter!"

Her mother's shrill came through the receiver like a derailing train whistle, "Which one? Is it my beautiful Janie?"

Elizabeth sighed in exasperation when her father said, "No, the other one."

That wasn't the booze talking; that was his familiar scorn for her leaving eighteen months ago to be a career girl when she opened Bennet Private Investigations. Apart from Lydia's presence, they were on their own now, with only their perfect daughter, living on the wealthy North Shore of Long Island with her perfect husband, and a grandchild on the way to provide parental satisfaction. But that was another story, one she refused to think of today. She and her elder sister hadn't spoken in years—not since Wickham had arrived in town.

"It's about time you telephoned your family, but I'm listening to "The Answer Man," Frances greeted. "Are you coming to Netherfield for Thanksgiving?"

"I hadn't planned on it. I have business affairs to attend to."

Another thunderous peal shook the brick building, followed by an immediate lighting crack.

"You're a bookkeeper for Macys, Elizabeth. What could you possibly have to work on over Thanksgiving? You never worked on the books over the holidays for your father's garage. Will you be at the parade?"

"No. I just have to work, that's all." It was a lie. Her world, with all its criminal activity, smoky bars, and surveillance, was her refuge from the Bennet family. There would be no holiday meal with relations, especially at Jane's over-done mansion, not now, not ever. No amount of turkey could entice her to sit through their condemnation of a twenty-six-year-old unmarried woman living alone in the city. Spinsters should be at home, taking care of their parents.

"Mother, did Lydia come home last night? I thought I saw her uptown at a restaurant and I just wanted to be sure that she got home safely."

"Tom! Is Lydia in her bedroom?" the woman yelled out, competing with the game show blaring from the radio. Elizabeth could tell that she, too, had begun her evening imbibing earlier than usual.

"What would Lydia be doing uptown? You must be mistaken," Frances stated, once again disbelieving that her other perfect child could be up to wrongdoing.

"I think I saw her with George Wickham."

"Now I know you're mistaken. George is overseas, serving his country in Korea. Before his re-enlistment a few months ago, your father received a letter from him asking for a postponement to pay back the money he borrowed."

Dumbfounded, Elizabeth's jaw dropped. That correspondence might have had a postmark, could have been a lead. However, her parents didn't know that, didn't know that she was a private eye, not some number cruncher at a department store and that the man, proven to be a scoundrel, was feeding them his usual malarkey. Pop would never see a dime of the three thousand Wickham stole and most likely Mr. King would never see his daughter again.

"Borrowed? You mean embezzled."

"Look, missy, it was a simple accounting error."

"Mother, I was the bookkeeper and I don't make errors. He stole that money, and Pop should have called the authorities when I brought it to his attention. Look, is Lydia at home or not?"

"Your father says no. She must have gone to the movies. You know how she loves those Saturday matinees."

"Today is Sunday."

"Then you should be at church."

The sinking feeling in the pit of Elizabeth's stomach increased, and she did something she hadn't done in nine months—lit a cigarette. Lydia was God knows where on a Sunday afternoon—and it wasn't at church. That was for sure.

••

THREE

"M y answer is no, Georgiana. I absolutely forbid it," Fitzwilliam Darcy stated, walking to the bar to fix himself a gin and tonic.

He tried not to let his sister see his current frustration after foolishly confronting that thug two nights ago up in East Harlem. He was in no mood for her cheeky attitude. It was bad enough that he was angry at himself for having taken the risk of being seen threatening a man, even one like George Wickham.

"Forbid?" She chortled, mocking his established authority in this household.

With a drink in hand, he abruptly turned to face her, liquor sloshing above the crystal rim.

Standing in the center of the drawing room of their suite in the Dakota Apartments, Georgiana looked the picture of graceful femininity in spite of her brazen challenge. "Brother, you may at one point have been my guardian, but as you well know I am no longer that child and you have very little control over my actions. I was only informing you out of *courtesy*. I leave tomorrow morning." A delicate hand petulantly clutched her slender waist.

He felt the burn of anger rising in his cheeks as he eyed his defiant sibling up and down. From her blonde coiffure and cultured pearls to the elegant ensemble she wore, she was, in fact, a grown woman, who obviously had a mind of her own. He could no more control his baby sister than he could his temper—but he could try to tame at least one of the two.

"Control? You need more than control! I will not have you trotting off to Cuba for a wild holiday in the sun. Do you not understand how your actions affect my reputation if the press gets wind of unguarded behavior while you're playing in the Caribbean? And Cuba of all places! It's unstable there."

"I understand perfectly that you think a holiday with a few of my Barnard sorority sisters is unladylike, but I assure you, I am going, no matter how "unstable" you deem it. Unless, of course, you can give me a better explanation than my following the so-called acceptable mores of proper etiquette or your own ambitions for the political ring."

"Barnard friends? I want their names and their fathers' political party affiliations. I won't have you associating with any pinkos." He turned his back to her, unable to meet her heated gaze as she stared him down, her blue eyes flashing in anger.

"Fitzwilliam, are you trying to protect me or is it that you don't trust me? It's unlike you to think only for yourself and your political aspirations. So don't try to twist it that way. I am not to be caged or tethered as if I'm some wild creature. What is at the core of this?"

"I have my reasons."

"Does this have to do with my telling you about running into your Navy buddy last month at the 21 Club?"

His lips pursed before answering. With a harshness he couldn't help, he threatened, "My caution to you stands regarding that man. I forbid your association with him, but there are several reasons I will not allow you to travel to Cuba."

"Reasons? What other reasons can there be? And don't say one of the reasons is because I need a chaperone."

"That thought hadn't even occurred to me. Yes, you need a chaperone."

"I'm not that child you left in the care of Mr. and Mrs. Reynolds."

"For that, I had no choice after I withdrew from college to serve in the Pacific," he said.

"Well, then surely, you will agree that now that I am twenty-one I can care for myself. Many of my girlfriends my age are already married."

He closed his eyes, defeated by his beautiful sister's keen understanding of him. He was afraid for her, always intending to protect her for the rest of his life, up until the *right* man could be entrusted—a man worthy of her.

Darcy sighed. "No, you're not a child as you were then, but '42 was a different time. Father was not far, down in Washington and you were just an adolescent at the time—not someone whom people would try to use or gain favor with. But Georgiana, as of four months ago, you became one of the wealthiest socialites in the city. It was splashed all over every newspaper. Without your realizing it, you are man bait for the worst kind of Lotharios."

She walked to him and placed a hand on his forearm, halting the drink before it rose to his lips. "I promise to be cautious if that will make you feel more at ease but I cannot live in this gilded cage, shut off from the world and 'real' society because of my wealth—and your fear. My life needs to be more than lunching at the Colony Club."

Had she really felt that way? Isolated? He smiled tightly and stepped away to the fireplace where he leaned, looking into the flames.

"I hadn't realized that you felt like Mother had ..."

"I do. Please, Brother, trust in me. Let me prove to you that whether at home or in the Caribbean, I am not only a woman with a moral compass but one who can hold my own in this ever-changing, challenging world."

Although that sounded like rehearsed malarkey, he turned and his heart melted, anger dissipating as he observed the frown upon her lips. A wipe to his brow preceded his comforting smile. When had she grown to be so eloquent, so elegant, so matured? Yet still, in many ways, she remained a naïve child and he desired nothing more than to hire a bodyguard to watch over her wherever she traveled. However, he knew that would not instill *her* trust in *him.*

Breaching the space between them, he searched her face, the soft slope of her cheek, the proud chin, a tentative smile of hopefulness upon her lips.

"Then go with my blessing. I trust you, Georgiana."

His eyes locked with hers and then he saw it, embedded in her blue pools—she was up to something. Damn.

"But, know this, little sister—if you deceive me, if I read in the gossip column even one iota suggesting that your behavior was not that of a lady, you'll be treated with the same disregard as you treat my trust. You will lose my respect."

She laughed. "Don't worry so, Fitzwilliam. I am fully aware that once your good opinion is lost, it is lost forever."

"I am not truly that unyielding."

"Then why are you still single?" She raised an eyebrow.

"That's a very strategic detour from a conversation about *you.* I'm single because, just as you, yourself, should be concerned, I don't care to be sought after or trapped for my wealth or position."

"Hmm ... indeed. God help you if someone does pursue you in spite of your irascibility. You'll never trust her enough to believe that she wants you and not your money."

He grunted. "Where are you headed on this Monday night?" he changed the subject, walking to the door.

"Oh, just out with the girls to make some final plans for our trip. The Stork Club is having the most divine entertainment."

••

Four thousand square feet felt an interminable prison before Darcy's late-night venture to another dark side of town, Strippers Row. Even the temptation of Eddie Bracken's humor on television was an unwelcome diversion, so he chose to wait in silence. He sat in his dimmed study, listening to the grandfather clock's pendulum tick with each passing minute before his leaving undercover into the black of night. Georgiana had been gone two hours and their driver, Andrews, assured him that he witnessed her kiss the cheek of Katherine "Kiki" Kavandish, one of her sorority sisters before entering The Stork Club. In fact, there was some big headliner performing. So, she had told the truth—for now.

He rotated in the desk chair and faced the elegant portrait of their mother above the fireplace in the study. That antique Kashmir sapphire necklace was now Georgiana's, bequeathed to her before her debutante ball. He reflected on his sister's life, how the death of their parents, years before her coming out, affected her. His face darkened recalling Wickham's manipulative ways, hoping that the man took his warning as more than a gum-flapping, empty threat the night before. Georgiana would be the perfect victim to fall for the man's easy manner and charisma.

Thoughts traveled to all those people George Wickham, his commanding officer at the time, had used and abused while screwing his way through every port stop in Central and South Pacific. Remembrance of the cruel streak in the man, who went AWOL in the Philippines in '44 to escape the brig, sent chills up his spine. Good-bye, good riddance. Slick Wick's downfall and eventual disappearance, served as Darcy's wake-up call. The once moral Darcy—society's pinnacle of gentlemanly behavior—had been given the opportunity of redemption, to focus on the man he really wanted to become.

Darcy lit a cigarette as his admiration of the portrait became a hazy stare when his thoughts moved into the present.

He knew Wickham had resurfaced when Georgiana came home after lunching with Kiki at the 21 Club three weeks earlier. Very few things shook him to the core, but that did. That run-in prompted a telephone call to another Navy buddy, Wentworth, who last heard that Wickham had settled into a false persona. Word had it that the deserter had been working in Queens, no doubt chiseling money and favor from a fresh field of dupes and more than likely seducing every woman he set his sights on. But that lead was long cold. The grifter had left behind a string of bad debt and broken hearts twenty months ago. It appeared that in the eight years since last he'd seen the man, little had changed.

Then, four days ago, a hand-delivered letter came to his office at Darcy Investment Associates. Apparently, the man was well-informed, most likely having read of the probable political candidacy. The missive was simple: Fifty grand or he'd talk to the press. He'd give them an earful about just what type of candidate was running for federal office; tell them all the sordid details of the nineteen-year-old Navy seaman, the rebellious, idealistic son of an anti-war, isolationist senator. Wickham suggested a face-to-face meeting in East Harlem for the money exchange, and that was a lucky break, afterward following him and a floozy home to a derelict tenement in the Bronx.

He recalled the heated conversation at El Barrio, subconsciously flexing his hand, then balling it into a fist. God, he wished the Navy had caught up with Slick Wick before the war ended. The man should have been killed a long time ago. Maybe someone would do the job.

A Saturday night at El Barrio Steakhouse looked like one of those gin mills in a low-budget crime film. Dimly lit for a reason, the obnoxious stench within was a mixture of Latin food, booze, and stale cigars. The bouncer in the cheap suit gave him the once over when he walked into the joint. Darcy supposed his Brooks Brothers overcoat and fine felt fedora were an obvious giveaway that he was lost on the wrong side of town. Wickham sat at the bar, a half-filled bottle of Bacardi Rum at the ready. He was a shadow of the strapping man he served under. Although only three years older than Darcy, he looked middle-aged. The days of hard living and running from death at the end of a military rifle for desertion hadn't been kind to him, but based on the way the waitress was chatting him up, he still had that slick suave that all the women went gooey-eyed over.

The boozehound looked up, a drunken smirk played upon his lips at the sight of his quarry standing at the end of the bar. "Guess you got my letter," he sniggered. "Take a seat, let's talk turkey."

"No thanks. I see you're still living in the gutter where scoundrels belong."

"And I hear you are following in your father's footsteps. Shame; you had promise, Fitzy." He slugged back the shot glass full of rum then asked, "Did you bring the money?"

Standing to his full 6' 2" height, Darcy took two steps toward his nemesis, his narrowed eyes locking with the smaller man on the stool. "No I didn't bring the money but I have come with a warning. I came to tell you that I don't respond well to blackmail. Keep away from my family, my friends, my life. Disappear back into that hole you crawled from."

Darcy watched as Wickham lit a cigarette, tossing the matchbook toward the rum bottle. A black cat and the words Kit Kat Klub were clearly visible on the discarded cover.

"What'ya gonna do, run me outta town? You ain't the law."

"No. But I will inform the military—Slick Wick—where they can find you for your long overdue court-martial and firing squad for desertion."

"And I'll let them know about the son of a senator and that little bar fight we had in Nouméa," Wickham threatened, playing what he knew would be his trump card.

Nouméa, that port in the South Pacific on Grand Terre. He had never forgotten what he did. His hands were forever stained with the blood of a man—a Marine—no less, no matter the boozing circumstances that precipitated it. All his endeavors at atonement: massive charitable donations, financing the Fort Hamilton Veterans Hospital, contributions to the American Legion would be raked through the mud.

"Or maybe I'll just let your sister know that her brother ain't such a saint after all."

Darcy clenched his fists at his side in a struggle to control his rage. Anger flared in his eyes. "Stay away from my sister or I'll come after you with a vengeance like you've never seen!"

"Oh yeah? You think you can wax me so easily?"

"Whoa, you fellas better pipe it down in here or I'll have Jack over there take you outside. You're disturbing the other patrons," *the bartender cautioned.*

Neither man acknowledged him, but Darcy lowered his voice. "There won't be any money to silence your empty threats. You can take that to the bank, Wickham."

"We'll see."

"You have no proof of any actions I may or may not have performed. Exposing me will only be your own demise, and I have way more power than you in this town."

Wickham laughed. "There's that Darcy pride I liked so much. Like I said, shame. You had real guts, real potential back then."

An enraged turn on his heel was all Darcy could do to keep from popping him one in the kisser. That, for sure, would have crossed the line. It was bad enough he allowed the bum to push his buttons to the point of threat.

"See you around, Fitzy," *Wickham called after him.*

••

Four

The Kit Kat Klub was exactly as Charlotte had described: seedy and risqué—and that was only the exterior of the establishment. The neon sign jutting out from the brick façade rose, at least, ten feet high; it's red and black flickering lights called all pussy lovers to the joint with its distinctive black cat logo. At eleven o'clock on a rainy Monday night, this was just Elizabeth's type of dive—easy to disappear into the corners and alcoves of the dark club as she stalked her prey.

Dressed in black, a straight skirt and form-fitting sweater, she sat at an outlying table, far from the bar and the barflies. Her ebony waves, Rita Hayworth lush, blended into even more black beneath her tilted beret. She referred to this look as her bohemian ensemble, suggesting every bit one of those Commie lesbians Charlotte had mentioned, especially since the woman currently on stage was disrobing. She had never knowingly met a femme or a butch before but was determined to act the part. Concealed in the shadows of the lounge and wary of discovery, Elizabeth watched for the only person she came to observe: Slick Wick.

And she had no doubt that he'd be here, philanderer that he was.

Only the color of Elizabeth's lips defied the assumptions of the midnight ensemble: vibrant red because her own femininity would never allow her lips to be unpainted, no matter her evening's costume. She took a deep drag of a cigarette as her left hand clutched a glass of soda water, eyes scanning the audience of mostly older gentleman. Her gaze attempted to remain focused *above* the tables. She'd seen more than her share of shocking things in her line of work, but some of tonight's adult entertainment was happening below the tables. Nearly slack-mouthed, she observed several patrons' indiscreet actions to their private parts as they delighted in the curves of Miss Cherry Blaze on stage.

For forty minutes, Elizabeth remained in this posture. A split second before she was about to withdraw the snapshot of Wickham from her purse to ask the cocktail waitress for information, he strolled in as if he owned the joint. Her heart almost stopped dead at the first sight of that characteristic cocky swagger, conveying the man's hubris in every facet of his life.

Her hand trembled slightly. She didn't expect to be this nervous. Twenty months of searching and here he was right before her.

Eyes narrowed in disdain as his good-looking profile illuminated when passing through the floating dust particles in the beam of spotlight directed at the stage. He made his way to a reserved table. Another time, a more naïve Elizabeth's breath would have hitched, recalling how she had once hung on every word the silver-tongued devil spoke. This was the first time she had seen Wickham since he'd skipped town weeks following their one-night indiscretion—and thank God for that. She could easily have ended up like Mary King, another one of his conquests from her neighborhood. Lord knows, after the police ruled Mary's disappearance a runaway, Mr. King did something her own father probably wouldn't have done—he'd hired an eager gumshoe.

Wickham's suave manner of dress was in keeping with the other patrons at the Kit Kat. Always fastidious, his single-breasted suit flaunted his trim physique well.

As though a regular, he settled into his seat at stage left and ordered a cocktail from the scantily clad waitress. Seconds later, a cigarette girl came to his table and he purchased two packs, most likely those Belomorkanals. Having asked when she arrived, she knew they sold them here.

Elizabeth hesitated, torn between confronting him outright or laying low, watching then tailing him in the hopes of leading her to Mary. She wanted to scream at him, slap him then threaten him with Sally for information, but violence wasn't her nature.

Her attention may have remained riveted upon Wickham's every action if it wasn't for the man who had followed him down the steps into the sunken lounge. Although preoccupied with her prey's presence, and the nervous energy coursing through her, the PI in her—and the appreciative woman—didn't miss the entrance of the tall, impeccably dressed man also passing through the beam of light then immediately turning away toward a table in Siberia. Late twenties, dark hair, proud chin. He glanced in the direction of her darkened booth. *Smoldering.* Fleeting shadow and light played across the angles of his face as he moved. *Strikingly handsome.* For a flash of a second, she considered that this could be that Darcy Oscar had mentioned.

The dreamboat sat on the opposite side of the club also in the back. He, too, seemed to have eyes on Slick Wick and she wondered if he was also a PI. His concealment in the shadow could only mean one of two things: surveillance or self-gratification at the sight of those shimmying tasseled bosoms. Shame if the suit needed to resort to his own hand, a task she would have considered managing for him on another day—in another life. Charlotte was right; she was ablaze like a pussy on a hot stove and definitely needed to get off soon.

Handsome quickly disappeared into the pitch of his booth; all she could see was the burst of a match flare, then the brief glow of flame against his chin when he lit a cigarette. She felt drawn to him and his mysterious concealment. No sir, he was no ordinary Monday night patron hoping to forget his troubles at the Kit Kat Klub; he was here for another purpose.

Wickham slugged back his whiskey then glanced over his shoulder toward where the man sat. Yellow and orange embers lit in the darkness when the man inhaled his smoke, and she could tell how the object of her investigation looked uncomfortable, even edgy. By nature, Wickham wasn't one who concerned himself with being discovered at a striptease club, so what was the cause of his figure eights? Was it the mysterious watchman?

A slow saxophone riff signaled the headlining performance of Angela the A-bomb, billed as the best grinder in the Big Apple. Her provocative dance drew Elizabeth's attention, and she couldn't help admiring the artistry of movement and the pleasing lines of her figure. When the stripper removed her brassiere, she wondered if the man in the shadow was captivated by breasts the size of melons. She herself had melons. She glanced over to him, imagining his hands upon them, bared and ready for his lips.

Goodness, this show was highly erotic, tantalizing her, and she shifted uneasily wondering if lesbians reacted with the same fluttering need as she did. Her eyes drew, again, to the enigmatic man. His dark energy was palpable even from across the lounge, as though she might be the subject of his scrutiny. The heat had just turned up in this joint, and even the cool soda water would not be able to extinguish the man's affect to her body.

After taking the last drag of her Chesterfield, she snuffed it out, noting that Wickham seemed to have settled into a comfortable position, admiring the stripper with obvious lust. Considering his current preoccupation, she'd risk losing him to alleviate the burn to her sex and slid from the booth to use the powder room.

Darcy couldn't tear his eyes off the seductress now exiting the booth on the opposite side of the lounge. She had sat virtually cloaked in darkness, nursing a drink and a cigarette, but for a few fortunate moments of illumination from the meandering stage lights, he could see the fleshy pucker of kissable red lips surrounding the filter or the rim of the glass. He suddenly felt no remorse for crossing the threshold that separated him from the respectable life in which he lived. Not just an affluent financier and member of the best society, he was now a sleazy voyeur—and stalker of the man who proudly wore that low-life distinction.

When the dame rose and stood at the edge of the booth, his eyes traveled the length of her well-formed body silhouetted in a tight-fitting skirt; his gaze lingering on that shapely bottom of hers until she turned to face his direction. Knowing that she couldn't see him, he smirked then took an appreciative drink of both her and his gin. His stare remained fixed on the exaggerated sway of her hips as she drew closer to the spotlight, legs that reached the stars sauntering provocatively with each step in alluring stiletto shoes. Her vixen body awakened his repressed, hungry need, but her stunning beauty took him by surprise. An exotic vision with light-colored eyes so in contrast to her midnight allure that he was lost adrift in her storm even if she was more than likely a lesbian. Forget Wickham for the moment; his only desire was to observe her. The performer on stage had nothing compared to the allure of this siren calling his name. His hands flexed at the very thought of squeezing her ample assets, pointed prominently, ready for his mouth …

Focus on why you are here! You are not that foolish young carouser you were during the war.

The woman was an incendiary bomb. His arousal twitched, his craving growing. *Good God, man! Stop this!* He shifted uncomfortably in the booth.

As she took the four steps up toward the powder room, he delighted, again, in the rise and fall of her bottom until she was out of sight.

Think of your reputation. Just being here puts you at risk!

But, truth was, keeping his sister from the clutches of his former Navy buddy superseded all personal concerns for his own welfare. He'd risk destroying his career to protect her reputation, fortune, and future. His attention drew back to the degenerate man, once his commanding officer, who had shown him the seedier side of life, manipulating the then wholesome son of a senator to do things he'd never dreamed of doing before serving in the South Pacific. Smoking and a tattoo had been verboten until the USS *Stevens*, then a girl and hooch whenever he could get them, not to mention the bar fights. Was it war or was it Wickham that made him do the things he'd done?

Darcy took another drink attempting to clear his mind of those mortifying recollections of a young man unfettered from the reigns of good society's expectations. Maybe Georgiana was feeling the same need for liberty, but she better not act on it with Wickham. He'd follow this man every night to make certain that she was not with him.

His eyes studied his nemesis, fully illuminated by the light coming from the stage. The chiseler seemed on edge when he repeatedly glanced at his watch, probably stolen.

A lone figure walked to Wickham's table, slid out a chair and seated himself. Obviously without the intention of staying to enjoy the show, he still wore his hat and coat, ready to do business then leave in haste. The two men spoke, both leaning across the table toward the other. Darcy could see a particular smile spread upon the blackard's lips when the stranger removed a white envelope from his coat, its crinkled thickness apparent as it was pushed across the table.

Wickham laughed and slid something back. They spoke no more when the money man rose and made his way toward the steps leading to the exit.

What was he up to? Perhaps it was a good thing that Georgiana was headed to Cuba for four days, far from those scheming clutches.

Elizabeth witnessed the transaction as she exited the powder room. Now focused, she immediately recognized the style of hat the newcomer wore: a black Russian cossack. Thank goodness for the opportunity to work a case with Detective Christopher Brandon from the 8th Precinct. He'd taught her a few things, even if he'd had a one-track mind.

She and the Ruskie crossed paths nearing the stairs, she preparing to descend, he ascending. Employing her man bait walk, a seductive smile of ruby red met his appreciative stare. With perfected execution, she feigned a caught heel on the carpet and fell forward, straight into him.

The man instinctively grabbed her, as she knew he would. Her right hand pressed against the shoulder holster below his overcoat, and her left hand slipped into his coat pocket, fishing for the item Wickham had given him minutes before.

The thug's paws remained fixed around her waist, their bodies hugging each other on the narrow steps. Elizabeth's manicured fingers grasped a piece of paper and a slick snapshot within the pocket.

"Oh, pardon me. I'm so sorry," she cooed, seamlessly slipping both leads into her skirt pocket.

"It is no problem," he replied with a tell-tale Russian accent.

Quickly glancing over his shoulder, she could feel the smoldering stare of the dreamboat, and noted the glowing cigarette embers. Wickham, too, watched the exchange, and she knew then, it was a matter of minutes before a confrontation happened if he recognized her. In this act, she had blown her cover, but may have gleaned more information than she might have in a more discreet manner.

When the Russian's hand traveled to her back, sliding down the curve of her bottom, she reacted as any true woman of substance—or a gumshoe who needed a getaway would—she slapped him, pulling from his hold. Storming toward the coat check, she fought the rising panic, forcing a calm that came with the knowledge that Sally always had her back.

••

The vixen is good, very good, Darcy noted to himself as he watched her hand slip into the man's coat. She must have been at the club to watch Wickham, too, seizing the opportunity to find out this man's connection. Was the dish a scorned lover? Or worse—a PI, whose investigation would lead directly to him and information about the things he did in '43 that would ruin a future politician's career? Would she uncover Wickham's recent blackmail?

That purposeful gait of hers to the hat check was as sexy as her saunter, as provocative as her sashay. Although he hoped that he'd never see her again, the thought of shacking up with her wearing nothing more than that little beret was an engaging imagining.

This visit to the Kit Kat Klub had been a payoff, indeed. And judging by the way, Slick Wick was readying for the next stripper, he doubted Georgiana would be joining the man here. His undercover surveillance for the night was over and now he had a few things to turn over to the military. It was time to go home with a raging hard-on for a woman who was as intriguing a mystery as Marilyn Monroe and Philip Marlowe wrapped in one.

Elizabeth breathed a sigh of relief when the Russian exited out onto the deserted 52nd Street then hopped into an old jalopy parked at the curb, driving away.

With heart thundering and hands trembling, she hailed a taxi back to the safety of Hell's Kitchen and Ruby's for a late night snack before falling onto her lonely mattress. Sitting in the back of the taxi she reflected that the night hadn't been a total bust. She now knew where Wickham frequented, had a solid lead in her skirt pocket, and had her fancy tickled by unknown eyes in the corner of a strip club.

••

FIVE

Palm branches on the verdant trees gently swayed in the invigorating breeze as Georgiana Darcy paused atop the open threshold of the Cubana de Aviación plane. Below her, percussive Latin American music floated in the air of the José Martí Airport in Cuba—a proper welcome for tourists to the island's playground of the rich: Havana, the capital and Rome of the Caribbean. Paradise.

Before descending the air steps, she took a moment to inhale the sweet tropical aroma mixed with aviation fuel as she shielded her eyes with a gloved hand against the brilliant sun. Her heart leaped and her tummy fluttered at this first taste of absolute freedom. She coveted this unique thrill of doing something so daring as traveling unaccompanied in absolute defiance of her brother's rigid standards of propriety. Although she was a Darcy, she was a modern woman and more attuned to being her mother's child than her father's and, by extension, the responsibility of her brother. Once her girlfriends had disembarked in Miami for their little getaway, she'd changed planes and, alone, continued onward to a different kind of fun in the sun.

With mink coat draped over her arm, her yellow dress waved in the wind with each step downward, but her hat remained secured by the heirloom mother of pearl pins. Each step toward the tarmac felt liberating; a woman her age, on an island known for excitement and romance would have a memorable time. Of course, being escorted by one of the most dashing, eligible men of Philadelphia's Social Registry, a decorated naval hero, to boot, would assure it.

She waved, holding back her absolute excitement when she spotted him amongst the crowd of men sporting white Panama hats and the women in colorful dress awaiting the airplane's arrival. He held a bouquet of white flowers and beamed the most winsome smile she had ever seen. Her heart raced, joy bubbling over. George Wickham was positively creamy!

••

At eleven in the morning, Elizabeth awoke, naked and alone, laying on her back and perspiring in the excruciating heat of her bedroom. She groaned, craving coffee and a smoke. Damn!—Her addiction was back full force after chain smoking at the Kit Kat Klub last night to pass the time. She twisted her head to look out the window. Once again—rain. Why did it seem that news of Wickham always accompanied a violent storm? Still, she had to feel satisfied that at least she had a trail to Mary.

As one arm reached above her on the pillow, the other hand instinctively slid down her slick chest and abdomen when her body undulated in a stretch, the sensation of which caused her to think of the enigmatic man at the club. If she hadn't been a principled woman (and undercover) she would have shacked up with the suit—had he offered. He might have made her rethink that Eli Bennet doctrine. Of all the men who had made passes at her, his would have been the one she welcomed and accepted. When he had glanced in her direction her breath caught. Tall, mysterious, and handsome, his brooding smolder was hard-boiled through and through. His body was trim, his fashion sense impeccable, and each cloaked inhale of his cigarette felt like a lengthy seduction of fire and ember, stoking and building.

Her small hand slid down to her pubis and her mind flickered to what his hand would feel like—his mouth doing things to her, but she abruptly retracted her itching fingers, ending the fantasy as quickly as it had begun.

Rolling to the edge of the bed, a turn of the radio knob was followed by a light to a Chesterfield and a long drag. She sat there, half listening to the newscaster report that the hydrogen bomb's first test had been successful. It seemed all they spoke of these days was "the bomb." That and Communist spies. Until last night at the Kit Kat Klub, she hadn't cared about either, but the recollection of the Ruskie handing what she assumed was an envelope filled with dough over to Slick Wick got her attention. Had Wickham gone Red? What was his game now? And who was the classy blonde in the photograph that she pickpocketed from the Russian. But most importantly, was Lydia involved in his plans and schemes? She'd have to telephone her parents today, again, for the third time.

Thankful that this hour of the morning was too early for Charlotte and her mooching, inquisitive visit for coffee, Elizabeth rose and donned her short kimono. "Strong coffee," she said before crushing her barely smoked cigarette in the ashtray beside the photograph of her and her best friend, Mary King at a U.S.O dance in '44.

Two hours later, dressed in her Sunday best (although it was Tuesday,) she closed her umbrella and circled through the revolving door of the Horn and Hardart on Fifth and 59th Street. Unbuttoning her raincoat at the entrance, she scanned the automat for the person of interest she was meeting. Eyes lit with humor when she spotted Detective Brandon talking up a woman six inches taller than he was at the sandwich selection doors. The man was doll dizzy but the smartest flatfoot she knew, *and* he respected her street-smart professionalism. In his forties, he was a bit paunchy around the middle and not the best looking man of her acquaintance, but he was always willing to help a girl—and a gumshoe—out. With Brandon, she never needed to put on airs because, as a good homicide detective, he had her number.

Elizabeth took a seat at a table beside the rain-streaked window and removed her coat and gloves, waiting for him to join her with that lopsided smile that softened his rough and tumble cop manner. She grinned, truly happy to see him as he walked toward her carrying a sandwich and a piece of pie.

"How's tricks, kid?" he greeted in Brooklynese with a wink. "When the desk sergeant told me that you telephoned late last night requesting a lunch date, I couldn't believe my ears."

"I told you I'd be in touch."

He sat opposite her, framed by a backdrop of heavy rain and a passing double-decker bus on the avenue. Scanning her face, he smiled, nodding slightly. "You're a sight for sore eyes on this miserable afternoon."

"Thanks, Chris. You're looking swell since last we met. What was it—the Benson suicide back in June?"

His first mouthful of egg salad on white bread didn't keep him from responding. "Yeah, that's right. I hoped I would've heard from you months ago."

"I know. I'm sorry. I've been busy. It seems everyone has a cheating spouse these days."

"And here I thought I scared you off."

"You? Scare me? Never!" She laughed.

"What can I do for you today? You and me gonna work a case again or is it that you want something else?"

With a smile, she signaled the waitress to come fill the empty coffee cup on the table.

"Something else as in—*only* information—no hanky panky from this PI, Detective."

"A man can live in hope, right? Say, can I buy you lunch?"

"No thanks, just the coffee. A girl has to keep her figure if she's going to work information out of an over-eager cop. The coffee and the information are the only manna I need."

She reached into her purse and withdrew the snapshot and the piece of paper where she tucked them the night before when she'd stopped off at Ruby's. "I'm looking for information on this woman?"

"She's a looker. Obviously not from our side of the tracks. Can't put my finger on it, but she looks familiar. I'll have to do some fishing around the station to get you a name."

"No, that's all right. I'll keep digging on my own. I don't want the law involved in this. I only came to you because I trust you and with you being on the force for so long, I took a shot, figuring you know everyone in this town."

"Not everyone—only the two-bit crooks. Is this that cold case you've been working on for the last year and a half? What was the mugg's name?"

"Yes, that's the case and never mind his name. If he even gets wind that the police are looking for him, he'll slip my clutches again and then where will I be? He has a history of that—vanishing like a ghost. What I will tell you is that I think he's dealing with the Soviets."

"Why do you think that?"

"I witnessed a conversation at the Kit Kat Klub."

"Well, that would make sense. That dive is lousy with Commies. Word is that the Kit Kat's a hot spot for subversive activities and party recruitment in the Big Apple."

"Who says? McCarthy?"

"No, that's an honest to goodness fact from the Red squad at the Central Investigation Bureau (CIB.) The Reds hide behind all sorts of organizations, even striptease clubs."

"Well from what I saw, everything—and I mean everything—was out in the open, including the patrons if you know what I mean."

"The real question is ... what were *you* doing at the Kit Kat?" He raised an inquisitive brow, his lips drawing into a smirk.

She sipped her coffee before replying, letting his imagination to run wild.

"Not what you think—or hope, wise guy. It was solely surveillance."

"You weren't attending any secret meeting there were you? Tell me you didn't sign anything when you went in?"

She laughed and shook her head. "No. I finally got a lead on that bad hat I've been searching for. He was there, so I naturally watched his every movement. After about fifteen minutes, he met with a Ruskie, exchanging money for this snapshot and piece of paper."

Brandon quickly swiped his egg-smeared hand on a paper napkin from the tabletop dispenser, took the folded note and read the notation aloud. "Hotel Nacional de Cuba."

"What goes on at the Hotel Nacional de Cuba?" she asked, already anxious that Lydia had been overheard in El Barrio discussing Cuba.

"Playground to the rich and famous in Havana. My guess is that this society dame in the photo is going to be at this hotel. Looks like your pal just crossed the line into international waters. Cuba might be an island paradise, but right now it's a hotbed of Soviet and Mafia activity. Don't you read the papers, Eli?"

"Obviously not as much as I should. When I became a PI, I just thought the occasional missing person or extramarital affair would fill my days and nights with excitement as I continued my personal case. Heck, my last case was right up my alley doing account auditing for embezzlement. But, now ... I don't know, Chris—politics and organized crime?"

"Why not? You're a smart cookie since, obviously, you have a head for numbers. Let me help you out on this one; consider it training for the next big case. Maybe a few murder investigations are in the cards for you down the road."

Now that made her smile. Her heart danced. Yes, Brandon was real cream, a true cream puff when it came to her.

"Yeah?"

"Yeah." He handed Elizabeth a fork and the two of them dug into the piece of apple pie, sealing the deal.

With a mouthful, she said, "Then take the snapshot; this young woman may be in trouble and Lord knows the smooth-operator I'm tracking has a history, even if it's unproven, of hurting women. I promise that once I get to the point where I need you to put the arm on him, I'll telephone."

She sliced another bite of the pie. "There's another thing. Where can I find a Fitzwilliam Darcy?"

Brandon sat back in his chair, chuckling. Wiping his fingers on the napkin, he joked. "Business or pleasure?"

"Why? Are you jealous?"

"Just ribbing you, sister. Darcy's big money. Owns half of Gotham and manages the dough for the owners of the other half. A real J.P Morgan-type. Darcy Investment Associates' office is downtown on the corner of Wall and Broad Streets."

"See, you do know everyone in this town."

He snorted. "You could, too. If you're gonna succeed as a lady dick in this city, you really should pick up a newspaper every once in a while. At the very least a City Directory or something."

"Ha. Ha. I'll have you know, he's not in the directory, but I will have to start scanning newspapers *and Variety*. Apart from Darcy's money, what's so special about him that he'd make the papers?"

"Son of a former senator and considering a run for a congressional seat. It's pretty accepted that he's anti-union, and a dyed-in-the-wool conservative with whiffs of agreement in McCarthy's search for Reds."

A breath of defeat left her lips. "Politics, again. I hate politics."

"You and me both. Is this business that's making you ask? All dolled up like that, you two could be the talk of them society pages, the perfect couple. He'd be tripping all over himself just to be seen out on the town with you."

"If you don't mind, I'd rather not go into detail about Darcy, but if it makes you feel better, it's not my nature to step out with a politician or a moneybags."

"Now *I* have a question for *you*," Brandon stated, moving closer and resting his elbows on the table, his crooked smile showing one-half of his teeth.

"Shoot."

"Is Sally tucked in your garter belt?"

Elizabeth laughed and tossed her napkin at his face. "I'll answer if you drive me downtown in your squad car to this Darcy's office."

••

Six

With each ding, the elevator neared Elizabeth's destination: Darcy Investment Associates on the 10th floor of 15 Broad Street, one of the tallest buildings in the world. Brandon was correct: this was big money. Even the elevator car was mahogany paneled with polished brass trim and a gleaming, well-oiled safety gate. Not to embarrass herself in front of the uniformed operator, she resisted running her fingers over the shiny trim. Instead, clutching her hands together in a poised posture, head held high with false assurance she stood as though she belonged there. She wondered what the office suite was like if the elevator was this magnificent. Further, she speculated about the man she was to meet. According to Charlotte, Fitzwilliam Darcy was one of the city's most sought-after bachelors; according to Brandon, he was loaded. Hence, the attraction for every unmarried woman in the Big Apple.

"Have a good day, Miss," the attendant said with a smile, moving the handle of the crank again, stopping at the door labeled 10th floor.

"Thank you," she whispered feeling unusually apprehensive, her tummy suddenly clenching in anxiety. Sally always gave her confidence, but this place wasn't Sally's forte (even if she was tucked securely above her garter.) Here the Elizabeth Bennet of old had to be called upon.

Isn't that why she dressed the way she did today? Sophisticated elegance right up to her fashionably tilted pillbox hat.

The young man slid back the inner gate, then released the door.

"Lizzy!" Jane's husband, Charles Bingley, proclaimed when the elevator door slid back fully.

Shocked, she halted her exit abruptly. *Damn!* Her worlds had suddenly collided.

"Charlie? What are you doing here?" she exclaimed, regrouping as she stepped into the lobby followed by a kiss on his cheek, her hand resting upon the lapel of his cashmere topcoat.

"I'm visiting with my banker."

Yes, Jane had done well for herself. Not only was Charlie an amiable sort of fellow, fair-haired like her sister and good looking, but also wealthy—and too good for Jane. She smiled as warmly as she could muster; it wasn't his fault that Jane and she had a falling out. He hadn't even been in the picture yet when sibling rivalry for Wickham's affections caused the irreparable rift. She'd never forget her vain sister's cruel words. *"I'm the beauty, not you. What would George want with such an ugly duckling? He'd never go for a girl whose own boyfriend married another."*

"You look wonderful, Lizzy. Macy's must be treating you well," Charlie complimented.

"Thank you. Um ... how is Jane? Is everything progressing nicely in her pregnancy?"

"Everything is fine. Between her ladies group pinochle games at the country club, Janie's been busy with the nursery. Won't be long now before you're an aunt. You know we'd love to have you for Thanksgiving and I'm sure your sister would love to see you."

"Maybe. I'm sorry, Charlie. I really need to meet with someone." She kissed his cheek again. "I'll telephone you."

He furrowed his brow. "Do you have a meeting with Darcy?"

"Well ... um ... not quite. Do you know him?" *Don't go there, Eli! Don't inadvertently involve him in your investigation!*

"Of course, I know him. He's my best friend. Had you come to the wedding, you would have met him. In fact, I think you two would have gotten along smashingly."

There was that word: smashingly. She hated when he said it. Old money did that, made one use hoity-toity words that the rest of real society wouldn't be caught dead uttering. She audibly chuckled thinking how the world of a private eye had altered her vocabulary, too. She'd have to be careful around him.

Charlie took the closed umbrella from her hand, dropped it into the brass stand beside the elevator, and grasped her hand in his, tucking it into the crook of his arm. "C'mon. I'll introduce you."

"N ... no ... no really, that's not necessary."

Her protest died as she took a step with him. That grin of his was so earnest she couldn't possibly deny him. *Damn.*

Together they walked down a marble hallway, passing the prim and proper secretary, who gave her the complete once over, from pillbox hat to leather high heels.

A knock on the closed office door adorned with a brass plaque inscribed *Fitzwilliam Darcy* prompted a deep response of, "Come in."

Charlie eagerly swept open the door revealing a seated executive behind an organized desk, signing and flipping over documents one by one before methodically re-stacking them into a pile.

"Darcy, you'll never believe who I ran into exiting the elevator onto your floor."

A grunt escaped the man below a dark head of waves as he continued to sign.

"Jane's sister, Elizabeth Bennet."

Darcy looked up, instant identification nearly causing his jaw to drop along with his fountain pen. It was her—the woman who had tormented his sleep the night before, the one whose shapely body had driven him nuts with desire. And by God if that pillbox hat she wore wasn't even sexier than the black beret from last night.

He abruptly stood, attempting not to knock over his chair or look the nervous wreck he felt. Coming around his desk, their eyes locked on each other. Mutual recognition infused her expression, apparent by the way her lips twisted into a kissable little quirk.

Does she recognize me from the Kit Kat? She obviously does if she showed up here at the office. Damn, I was so careful to remain in the shadow. He didn't know whether to be happy about her visit or not; he was certainly intrigued. She looked somewhat amused by the meeting, or perhaps by the shock he was trying so hard—yet failing—to conceal.

Holding out his hand, he bridged the space between them and took her gloved hand in his, shaking it. Hers was no timid shake. It was purposeful and confident, just like those flecks of gold dancing in her topaz eyes.

"Miss Bennet, it's a pleasure to meet you."

"The pleasure is mine, Mr. Darcy. I hope you don't mind my stopping by without an appointment, intruding like this, but Charlie didn't feel it would be a problem."

Her throaty voice was pure seduction from the moment she purred "Mr. Darcy." He felt his cheeks flush from embarrassment at the shameful thought of bending her over his desk, enjoying her moaning his name over and again.

"It's no problem." Like an idiot, he continued to hold her hand but she made no move to relinquish it.

"Isn't she a beauty, Darce? Just like my Janie."

She smiled at Charlie's compliment, and that, too, left him spellbound. He silently disagreed with his friend. Elizabeth had spades over house-Frau Jane and her wholesome role as the dutiful wife and homemaker. That uptight woman Charlie had married surely needed an uninhibited, hard lay to set her inner female free. No, Elizabeth was nothing like Jane. The intoxicating dame before him already dripped sex like honey from a hive. Taking her to bed would, no doubt, set *him* free. Those cat's eyes of hers told him straight away she could never be domesticated. She was pure feral pussy through and through. She was no lesbian femme—more like femme fatale.

"Well, you two have business to attend to." Charlie turned toward the door. "Don't forget to telephone, Elizabeth. We hope you'll join us on Thanksgiving!"

"I won't forget. Nice to see you, Brother."

Darcy said nothing as Charlie walked out of the office only to peek his head back in.

"Oh and Darcy, she's a real whiz kid with numbers, so there's no need to explain everything like you do for most of your lady clients. She's no dumb Dora."

Regrettably, the vixen slowly withdrew her hand from his then provocatively removed her gloves one finger at a time with a tug.

"Oh? And what is it you do with your figures that makes you so accomplished, Miss Bennet?" Darcy couldn't help baiting, teasing her.

"I'm a bookkeeper at Macy's."

"Of course you are. I appreciate *figures*, too."

"Yes. You obviously do." She smirked and he resisted the urge to slam his lips against those taunting cherry bombs. This was Charlie's sister-in-law for Christ's sake!

Her slender, manicured fingers began the seductive removal of her trench coat. Each measured movement, beginning by untying the belt was stimulating, as their eyes remained fixed upon each other. Inching upward, her fingers rose to the top button, wrapping around it until it slowly released from the hole. She set the next button free with the same tempered technique, like the striptease he'd imagined following his first eyeballing her at the Kit Kat. She was teasing him—opening each descending button, artfully revealing luscious curves encased in tweed. In vain, he struggled against imagining her figure below the trench coat, but was aroused already. And judging by the look on her face, she knew it.

"Will you take a girl's coat, Mr. Darcy?" she asked, turning to give him her back, easing the tan fabric from her shoulders.

Yes, he wanted to peel everything off her. Never had a woman affected him this way; he was quickly becoming unhinged, unable to resist inhaling the fresh scent of her raven tresses. His heart thundered; his mouth watered. His johnson grew just from disrobing her outerwear when his fingers brushed her concealed bicep as the coat slid from her frame.

She glanced over her shoulder and smirked again, batting her long lashes. "Very gentlemanly of you, Mr. Darcy."

Good God, he couldn't help his own smirk. He would be no damn gentleman in the bedroom.

She wore a sophisticated ensemble of brown and white tweed, the belt around her narrow waist accentuated her curvy hips and ample bosom, and he had to regulate himself and shake off these salacious thoughts. *Why was she here?*

Turning to hang the coat on the rack beside the door, controlling his voice, he stated, "It's a small world, you meeting Charlie today."

"It is. I haven't seen him in months. Have you been friends with him long?"

"Since I returned home from the Pacific."

"Ah, I see."

"You are very different from your sister."

A delightful little chortle left her lips. "Yes, Jane and I are polar opposites—right down to our choice of suitors. Although ... once, before Charlie showed up at my father's garage with a flat tire, we were in agreement. She's very happy with her life on Long Island, and he's a good man."

"That he is. Yet you didn't attend their wedding?"

"Had I known I would have the opportunity to meet the handsome son of a former Senator, I would have attended."

He said nothing to Elizabeth's deliberate evasion of the subject or the compliment (one he'd heard a thousand times) and took a seat on the opposite side of the desk, sliding the stack of documents toward the edge.

"What brings you to Darcy Investment, Miss Bennet? How can I be of assistance?"

Barely able to control her expressions, manner, or desire, her confidence dissipated. Seeing Darcy on the other side of the desk had caused her heart to hesitate when she entered the office. Not only was Fitzwilliam Darcy the man at El Barrio but also her brother-in-law's best friend! Further, he was responsible for last night's erotic dreams. In the light of day, this enigmatic man was one fine piece of beef—and at night, in the shadow, he stalked Wickham—just like her. He clearly had noticed her at the Kit Kat, and her assumption then had been correct: he had been undressing her with his eyes from across the lounge and was doing so again this afternoon. The man was raw heat and those indigo blue eyes of his seemed to read her soul as the corners of his desirable lips marginally lifted, invitingly.

Her hands trembled, unable to play the cool private eye she was known to be. Suddenly she didn't know how to begin, not wanting to scare him away with her standard straightforward approach.

"Well, Mr. Darcy, I have it on good authority that you could help me invest the money I have saved, nothing too risky mind you. Without a husband, a single woman needs a nice nest egg to fall back on." *Why did you just say that?* "And I don't want to squander it on a flimflam scheme. I need something safe."

He sat forward, the slight smile expanding at the transparent information she had imparted. "My usual clients must have at least two-hundred thousand in liquid assets. Do you possess that much?"

"No. Is there any way you can help a girl out?"

"There are several ways I can help you, Miss Bennet."

She thrilled at his flirtatious double entendre and how he folded his hands before him. Opening her purse, she removed her PI notebook and pencil.

"Oh? I have one particular way in mind," she baited.

"Yes? Tell me what you'd like for me to do to take care of your needs."

"I need some information about a man of our mutual acquaintance."

Met by his suddenly furrowed brow, she continued. "Mr. Darcy, last night when I saw you at the Kit Kat Klub, I—"

"I wasn't at the Kit Kat Klub," he interrupted, folding his arms across his broad chest as he sat back in his chair.

"I did see you at the Kit Kat; I'm sure of it."

"I don't think so. They say everyone has a twin. That must be who you saw."

Stop smirking and lying, you smug bastard. "Believe me, I've only seen one man who fills a suit like you, even in the dark."

"So, it's safe to assume that you're not visiting my office today because of your *head for numbers?*"

"That's correct. Truly, I'm sorry for the ruse, but I'm looking for information about George Wickham."

Tapping his pen, his answer flowed too quickly, poker face in place. "I can't help you. I don't know this George Wickham you speak of."

"Please, let's not play this game. You and I both know that we saw each other last night. It's vital that I find out where he hangs his hat these days; where he has been residing for the last year and a half? What can you tell me about his past; his years in the Navy? You served in the Pacific. Did you know him during the war?"

She watched as an impenetrable mask darkened his face, transforming it into expressionless stone. No longer the playfully teasing man who had removed her coat with such seduction, Fitzwilliam Darcy now controlled his rage. He was a politician hiding something.

Damn. She had pushed too hard, too fast, but the man had unbalanced her from the start.

"I can also assume that you don't work for Macy's either. Are you a newshawk?"

"No. I'm not a reporter, just someone in need of information. The man ... could be conspiring with the Soviets."

Clearly that got his attention when he raised an eyebrow then lit a cigarette, using the pause to mull over her last statement. Foregoing common courtesy, he hadn't offered her a smoke, but she rectified the deliberate oversight by rising to reach for the pack. Removing one for herself, she leaned toward him, placing the filtered end between her lips, at the ready for his reaction. The gentleman in him couldn't resist his well-bred nature to light it for her with a click and whoosh of his gold lighter as her free hand wrapped around his to steady the flame and the pounding in her chest.

"As I stated. I don't know this Wickham character."

She sat back then seductively exhaled. "I think you're lying to me. You spied on him from your darkened booth at the club, and I am sure that your attention to him wasn't of a sexual interest. You had another subject for that intense stare, and Angela the A-bomb on stage didn't appear to be your object either. As focused as you were, I definitely noticed your, shall I say, ardently, heated gaze in another direction."

His intent focus locked onto her, eyes examining her playful insinuation. He was angered by her accusation, but he wore his passion for her blatantly. In those expressive eyes, he concurred he was attracted to her as she to him.

"Miss Bennet, we can go on all day like this, but my answer will always be the same. I wasn't at the club you speak of, not now or ever, and I do not, or have not, ever known this person you are seeking."

"Then why were you confronting the man about your sister at El Barrio in East Harlem this past Saturday night? Are you following him all over town? Do you know where he lives?"

He abruptly stood.

"Please, Mr. Darcy. It's important."

Heading toward the door, he ignored her plea, his lips tightened to thin lines of displeasure, his manner unyielding.

She'd gotten this type of brush-off from stonewallers many times, especially those who knew something. But she was surprised by his rude dismissal when he lifted her coat from the rack then held it out to her, signaling the end of the meeting.

As poised and classy as Elizabeth Bennet knew how to act, she rose, attempting to tamper down Eli and all her moxie—but failed miserably in that endeavor. She wasn't that demure woman any longer. So sure that his gaze was fixed on her body she leaned over the desk and stamped out her cigarette in the ashtray. A sudden glance over her shoulder confirmed his anticipated stare when their eyes met.

"And how do you know this Wickham, Miss Bennet? Why are *you* so interested in finding him?"

Her expression immediately transformed, reflecting his own stone visage as she purposefully walked toward him. "And that's *my* business."

"Well, then we seem to understand each other perfectly."

"Is that an admission?"

Darcy held open her coat and her arms slid in. She closed her eyes at the faint encounter of his fingers when they brushed against her neck, righting her collar.

Turning within his almost embrace, their faces were mere inches apart. Her breath became shallow from his nearness, as her legs weakened being so close to him. She resisted grabbing onto his jacket lapel to pull that parted kisser down to hers.

Breathy words escaped her lips as she covertly slid a business card from her pocket into his. "Mr. Darcy, Thank you for your time." The chemistry between them was like a powerful H-bomb, even if his abrupt manner was the fallout. Unable to resist his thermal energy, her lips nearly puckered to meet his. "I'm sure I'll see you again."

"I don't think so."

"Don't be so sure of that. I do think our paths are destined to cross again. Whether it be at the Kit Kat or here, across your desk, my proficiency with figures and digits just may leave you breathless. I've been known to coerce a confession or two with my particular skills."

He said nothing, but oh, how she did enjoy watching his pupils dilate at her suggestive invitation. Yes, she was sure she would see him again. The man had information she needed.

••

Seven

Although it was evening outside, within the posh Hotel Nacional de Cuba, Georgiana Darcy's once ivory complexion burned brightly from overexposure to the blistering tropical sun. Neither the wide-brimmed hat nor sunglasses she'd worn that afternoon had shielded her from its unrelenting torment when George took her out on a powerboat. What a gas! If the girls could have seen her, they'd never believe their eyes. If her brother had seen her, he'd have been fit to be tied.

Always being mindful of Fitzwilliam's admonishment to act the lady hadn't precluded her from having a good time this afternoon, and although George tried to have his way with her the previous night, she'd held fast. That type of activity was reserved only for her husband, and only after their vows. Perhaps he would propose tonight under the full moon as a backdrop with romantic Cuban music and kisses stolen under a palm tree; he had already told her that he loved her. Well ... she might be amenable to sleeping with him after an engagement.

Like the Tropicana nightclub the evening before, the casino around her hummed with excitement. Music from the small salon carried over the rapid clicks of the roulette ball circling the wheel beside her. The energy within the hall made her giddy. Tonight was their second to last night in paradise. In two days, she would touch down, alone, in New York, back to her cold, gilded life.

Georgiana pushed that thought away, focusing on the exotic night ahead and how she felt every bit the society globe-trotter, privileged by affluence, unafraid to live high and fast. She wore a Christian Dior cream lace evening dress, but had forgone showcasing the new diamond Rivière necklace she purchased yesterday from the Salon Vedado in the lobby where only Havana's wealthiest families shopped. She instead chose to wear her mother's exquisite Harry Winston sapphire necklace.

Two tables away, Ava Gardner and her party laid their bets for the roulette wheel they surrounded and Georgiana nearly squealed in delight. She, Miss Darcy, daughter of a former senator was rubbing elbows with one of Hollywood's most beautiful women! Kiki and Caroline Bingley would be green with envy!

Lost in her thoughts, she stood with crystal champagne flute in hand, staring down at the hypnotic rotation of the nearest roulette wheel until the feel of George's arm snaking around her waist snapped her from her delightful musing.

Her heart slammed, feeling an unfamiliar thrill when he whispered in her ear. "Are you enjoying yourself?"

"I've never had so much fun in all my life, George. Fitzwilliam is always so concerned with our family image. Thank you for this decadent diversion from my ho-hum life."

"We'll have to do it again."

"I admit I'm feeling a bit of wanderlust now, having a taste of absolute freedom. Where shall we go next?"

"How does Paris sound?"

"Absolutely scrumptious!"

George bent, placing a stack of chips on black seventeen, and she couldn't help admiring his eloquent profile and dark wavy hair. Even the pink scar at his hairline fascinated her. He was the most handsome and humble man she had ever met, always refusing to talk about himself (including the scar) and his old line family in Philadelphia. Instead, he remained attentive to her every word—the true mark of a gentleman of society.

"Yes, you mentioned that your brother is focused on his career."

She chortled. "Focused is correct. He's determined to rid America of what he refers to as pinkos."

"So I've heard. Our society needs men like him in political office, protecting our interests, protecting us from the working man and their overblown claims of oppression."

She didn't know anything about Communism, and didn't even understand her brother's reference to pinkos, but it seemed that George was in the know. Of course he would be; his family owned steel mills around the nation. He was educated at the finest schools and a successful businessman even though he didn't need to work.

A shout went up when the roulette ball fell into number seventeen black on the wheel.

"You won!" she exclaimed, her cheeks feeling a burn from the intoxicating combination of excitement, champagne, and the sun. And, of course, romance.

"You're my lucky charm, Georgiana!" He scooped up his winnings, then pocketed the chips into his white dinner jacket.

Feeling suddenly woozy, her gloved hand grasped the edge of the gaming table and her footing stumbled even as she remained in place.

George's quick response kept her from falling to the floor when her knees buckled. She felt weakened, suddenly like jelly in his arms.

The tender man searched her face, concern etched upon his brow. "Are you okay?"

"Just a bit overwhelmed by the excitement, I think. Have I mentioned what a swell time I'm having?" She gripped his bicep, steadying herself, white lights from the glittering chandelier flickering in her eyes like stars falling from the sky.

"Twice. Would you care to leave, my dear?"

Her head began to spin, and she felt strangely uninhibited, unable to think clearly, but she trusted the dreamboat supporting her. "I think ... yes, I'd like that."

Taking the empty champagne flute from her, he seductively said, "Let's go back to your room, Georgiana."

"My room? I think ... that's a good idea. I'm feeling rather ... free."

••

Neither Wickham's apartment building, nor a survey of El Barrio restaurant produced any trace of the man. Even the Kit Kat Klub was a dead end tonight, same as it had been the night before. The latter locale also failed to produce Miss Elizabeth Bennet, not that he was looking— or hoping—well maybe a little of both. He wanted to see her again, close.

His midnight search uptown ended downtown at two dives Wentworth suggested, both being a waste of time and cab fare. Not that his search mattered since Georgiana, now relaxing in the Caribbean, was far away from the man's clutches, but he couldn't help the growing obsession to keep an eye on Slick Wick and his activities. As quickly as the grifter had materialized on his radar, he had disappeared, again. Something wasn't right; he could feel it in his chilled bones.

At one in the morning, he stood at the subway entrance stairwell on 60th and 5th Avenue, smoking a cigarette, the collar of his coat upturned against the wind, fedora pushed low, covering his eyes. He waited in the shadow of the nearby building, watching the comings and goings of patrons at his last resort for the night: the Copacabana. Wickham enjoyed things with a Latin flare, but Darcy couldn't help the rising panic thinking that Cuban flavor could also be up his alley, too. Only a couple more days and his sister would be home, sheltered back inside the Dakota.

A car's horn jolted him from his thoughts in time to hear snippets of conversation from a passing couple. Something about the nearest fallout shelter for a different kind of duck and cover.

He shook off the image. This hour, even in the cold, bared the naked city.

Feeling every bit the solitary fool, without a gorgeous dame on his arm, he entered the nightclub below its illuminated awning. He hadn't been to the Copa since stepping out with Martha months ago. To her and her publicist, being seen with a man who owned the city had been a career booster. To him, she was a shallow dalliance from the boredom that often plagued him. Unfortunately, she was as dull as the controlled life he led. He dumped her at another nightclub and she moved on to Mickey Mantle and his baseball bat.

The vibrant club entrance and the invigorating music within were a dichotomy to the eerie feel of the late night city, particularly the sea of black that cloaked Central Park right across the street.

Again, his mind drifted to Elizabeth Bennet, having found her business card in his suit pocket following their meeting on Tuesday. He sighed. It was just as he had figured: she was a private investigator, living in the shadows just like he had been doing for the past week. The woman was a focused career girl—class, smarts, spirit and a vixen rolled into one killer dame, but she knew too much, was searching for answers about a man who would unearth his past and bury his and Georgiana's future. He hated to admit it but Elizabeth was intriguing and instinctively he knew she would be good for him. He shook off the image of that fire in her eyes, conceding that she came with a warning label and a family of lushes from the wrong side of the East River. *Why was she searching for Wickham?*

As he paid his $7.50 admission, Jules Podell, the owner greeted him with a hearty, "Mr. Darcy! We haven't seen you in some time. Welcome back to the Copa."

Forcing a smile, he lied. "It's nice to be here. Who's the headliner tonight?"

"Xavier Cugat. You missed the ten o'clock show but we're still celebrating in Cuban style."

Great. Was that a portent of something? Damn. He removed his coat and fedora, placing both on the counter at the hat check before palming his ticket and slipping it into his pocket.

"Well, enjoy yourself, Mr. Darcy. There are plenty of dishes available tonight and I don't mean on the menu. The Copa Girls have a new act since last you visited."

"Thank you, Mr. Podell. I'm looking forward to the evening." He paused before entering through the green painted door, remembering that Podell once ran on the seedier side of life. "Say, have you seen this fella tonight?" Darcy asked removing from his suit pocket a snapshot of Wickham resurrected from the bottom of his Naval sea bag.

"Not at the Copa, and I never forget a mug."

"Thanks."

"Sure, Mr. Darcy. Have a good time."

The club seemed to be even more decorated in Brazilian flavor than he remembered, and even at that late hour the place appeared filled to capacity. Partiers danced on the small floor below the towering white palm trees to the Latin beat of the orchestra and its lead singer. Glasses clinked and laughter rang out in bold guffaws from every corner of the establishment. A party was taking place on the second level where a crowd, two deep, surrounded a round table. Most likely it was Joe DiMaggio and his new squeeze Marilyn Monroe, or another famed ballplayer and some actress. The Copa was the nightclub to be seen at, a classy place to let one's hair down, something he hadn't done in a long time.

He navigated through the crush of mink-clad females and men in expensive suits at white-clothed tables too narrowly spaced, in an obvious effort to seat as many patrons as possible. Most of the faces he passed were Gotham's movers and shakers and, given the music, they were, indeed, shaking it up, along with the bartenders' cocktail tins.

Settling at the bar, he ordered a gin and tonic then turned on the stool to examine the crowd for Wickham, eyes scanning every man on the dance floor until the bartender placed the much-needed drink in front of him. A deep quaff followed and his worried thoughts drifted to Georgiana (even though her earlier long distance telephone conversation conveyed her health.) He became hypnotized by the liquid and ice, mindlessly mixing the lime within with a black swizzle stick. Memories of Nouméa surfaced, gnawing at the back of his conscience. Then the unavoidable recollection of the leggy Elizabeth Bennet shook his gentlemanly composure. *Telephone her. Don't telephone her. Ask Charlie about her. Don't go near her.*

A cacophony of laughter rose from the party table and the surrounding horde parted, making way for the "it couple" to exit onto the dance floor as the brass and violin collided, ushering in "The Wedding Samba."

In shock, the rocks glass stilled at Darcy's lips. He blinked. It was her again—with the owner of that sleazy steakhouse in East Harlem. So that was how she knew he had been at El Barrio. A stab of jealousy pierced his chest as he watched the suave man place his hand upon the small of her back, guiding her down the steps then toward the wood floor.

Elizabeth beamed, obviously having a wonderful time as the center of attention both at the table and in that man's affections. The red number she wore was all class. The sparkling brooch above her bosom, elbow length gloves, and high heels completed the look. Her luscious lips matched her dress— sheer perfection. She was quite the picture and he allowed his imagination to travel to satin unmentionables. She looked as though she was torn from the pages of one of those fashion magazines Georgiana read. He couldn't help staring at her as she and her date held each other, laughing and moving through the crowd of dancers until they found their spot near the bandstand.

The Latin percussion had quite an effect on the way the woman under his scrutiny swiveled her hips. He took a drink, envying her partner's hand resting upon that seductively swaying rounded hip of hers. Spellbound by the way she danced to the beat of the tambourine and bongo drum, all Darcy could do was stare. His reason for being at the Copa in the first place was relegated to the back of his mind. When Elizabeth threw back her head in mirth, he'd had enough. He finally gave in to his base instinct, rose from the stool and then made his way through the crowd.

Before he knew what he was about, he tapped her partner's shoulder. "May I cut in?"

Elizabeth stopped dancing. Her heart seized.

Oscar chuckled and was about to say something, but she forced a smile, slapping his arm playfully. "Yes, you may cut in," she quickly answered silencing her date with a look. She knew exactly what he'd say. Something about tall, dark, and smoldering being her type—just as he had predicted four nights ago.

"If you can keep up with her, she's all yours, bub," Oscar said placing her hand into Mr. Darcy's with a wink before vacating the floor.

After his rude brush off days earlier, she was surprised to see him— surprised he'd want to dance with her. She, too, couldn't resist chuckling, but it was nerves that made her do so. Why was the suit here? Was this a coincidence? Who cared? The man was an absolute beefcake dressed in fine wool and a silk necktie as blue as his eyes.

"Miss Bennet," he said, placing his hand on her hip; her own clutched his muscular bicep, enjoying the firmness below her fingers.

"Mr. Darcy. I wouldn't figure you as a Copa sort of gee."

"It's been a while, but I assure you, I won't step on your feet if that's your concern."

She delighted how their bodies moved together in syncopated tandem, feeling the energy sparking between them. He was right, he could dance. She enjoyed how his hand held hers as their hips mirrored one another mere inches apart.

"Are you following me?" she asked.

"I thought I was leading."

"And you do it so well, but that's not what I meant." She raised an eyebrow.

"I'm not following you. It's purely coincidental. I think it's as you stated, perhaps we're destined to meet." He smiled an honest to goodness grin that reached his eyes. "In fact, I'm happy to have run into you tonight. I regretted my rude behavior on Tuesday and was hoping to redeem myself. Will you forgive me?"

"Perhaps. I admit, I was too forward, as usual. I'm only just learning the fine art of the delicate extraction of information, covertly."

Her regard for him based on the ending of their meeting and his affiliation with Wickham softened slightly when she noted how his eyes danced when gazing upon her. There was no condemnation or anger as he had demonstrated in his office, but one of question—maybe even concern. Whatever that expression was, there was sincerity in it. The fact that he wanted to dance was a sure indication that a feeling man lurked beneath that brooding exterior.

They didn't speak again until the song ended, both a little winded from the fast rhythm and its suggestive repartee of body movement.

He retained her hand, their palms clasped together as he led her off the dance floor. "Miss Bennet, would you like to have a drink with me? I promise to be more amiable than our first encounter."

Flips. Her heart did wacky flips. "I'd love to, but just soda water for this girl."

When they settled at a small table close to the bar, Darcy signaled the nearby waiter then ordered. The orchestra continued its Latin Samba and the songstress took to the stage for a ballad.

"Don't you drink or are you working tonight?" he asked, reaching into his breast pocket, removing a gold cigarette case.

"Working?"

"As a private investigator." He lit two cigarettes, then handed her one. "That is what you do at night, right?"

So he found my business card and still wants to talk to me. He's not as unyielding as I thought. "I'm not working, just holding up my end of a bargain. I owed Oscar a favor. As for drinking ... I haven't for a couple of years now. It dulls the senses, and I prefer being in control of my environment. A single girl could easily be taken advantage of if she's not careful."

No, thank you. She was no longer that lollipop and not likely to make that mistake twice in her life. No doubt, Mary King had regretted it, too.

"That's very wise of you. Advice I often give my sister."

"Me too, but it falls on deaf ears. My youngest sister is too headstrong for her own good."

She changed the subject reminding herself that silence about all things Elizabeth Bennet was always the best course. Having attended Jane and Charlie's wedding, Darcy had already been exposed to her not-so-stellar upbringing.

"Do you always come to a nightclub without a date, Mr. Darcy? I'm surprised there isn't a leggy dish on your arm."

"Oh, but there is." He flirted, moving toward her to give her all his unabashed attention. "And please, call me Fitzwilliam."

"Fitzwilliam? I don't know ... how about Darcy?"

He smiled. "Sure thing."

"Well, Darcy, when questioned on your whereabouts tonight, will you deny being *here at the Copa,* come the morning?"

"Who might be asking me in the morning?"

Their eyes fixed to each other's as she inhaled deeply from her cigarette then slowly prolonged her release. She knew what he was implying but she didn't respond. As tantalizing a thought as that was, this man and the secrets he held about Wickham made him off limits by the very association.

He smiled wistfully, his deep voice lowering an octave. "I know you have questions about me, Elizabeth, but not tonight. Please. As you said, you're not working on a case and, frankly, for the second time this week, I'm more than a little enchanted."

"Oh?"

"You captivate me. I've never met a lady dick before, particularly one as stunning as you."

She laughed, unable to stifle the little snort she occasionally made. "Such a charmer. I'll have you know, I'm not so easily swayed by sweet nothings—especially by propositions of pillow talk in the morning."

"It's not sweet nothings, just honesty. I want to get to know you. The pillow talk can come later, much later if you prefer."

"Well, since you want to know about me, then you will have to share something about yourself in return."

"So, you'll make me work for your affection?"

Startled by his intent, she held her expression at bay. "Affection? Of course, I'll make you work for it. How else would I know if you're real cream?"

"You'll just have to trust me."

"No dice, Darcy. Like I said, trust has to be earned. A little love-making isn't going to sway me." *Particularly since you have a history with Wickham that you are concealing.*

"I guess not trusting a man is a result of your occupation. Well, you may ask questions but I may choose not to answer them."

"That's rather obstinate of you," she teased.

Toying with her, a corner of his lips raised. "Then you only get *one* question that I will answer. So make it good. I'm not that easily charmed either. I'm no cream puff."

"We'll see about that." She gazed into his eyes, examining him, curiously warming to the man. "Now ... about that *first* question ..."

Her fingers touched his resting on the table. Darcy's smile was different than Wickham's; it was earnest. Like the one he gave her on the dance floor his soul lit his eyes, and set hers aflame. Yeah ... kitty on a hot stove. Sizzle.

A myriad of flirtatious questions rapid fired through her mind: *My place or yours? Do you prefer top or bottom? Are you the marrying type? Left or right side of the bed? Would you bring a girl like me home to meet your family? ... And where can I find Wickham?*

The orchestra began to play "Maria Elena" prompting the most important question for that moment. With a twist to her lips, she said, "My question to you is: Would you like to dance again? They say it encourages one's affection."

Humored, he furrowed his brow then chuckled. "That's your question?"

"Yes, but be prepared because tomorrow, in the light of day. I'll ask you all about Wickham. I may even use some charm—and my digits— to get answers."

"Is that before or after pillow talk?"

"I'll let you in on a little secret, Darcy. I may put on a good show, but I don't give *that* up to just any man."

••

The romantic music floated around them on the dance floor, and Darcy was oblivious to the crush of patrons butting up against him. His arm firmly encircled Elizabeth's waist for the slow dance and he pulled her closer to him, swaying back and forth in a tight embrace. There was no doubt, their sexual chemistry was explosive, but there was more to the attraction on his part. The woman was absolutely brilliant. Not only could he get lost in those amber eyes and the scent of her cascading raven locks, but the thought of spending hours listening to her sultry voice discuss the ramifications of the Red menace in America was enough to drive the hot-blooded Republican in him nuts. He wondered if she had known his views on the subject before they began their discussion over cherries flambé; she seemed simpatico to his every opinion. Intriguing verbal intercourse was almost as enticing as her siren's lure for vigorous intercourse of another manner.

"So tell me, what's a doll like you doing as a lady dick?"

"Leave us to do the thinking, sweetheart. It takes equipment," was her reply with a twist to her plump lips.

He laughed, immediately knowing the quote. "Philip Marlowe in Chandler's *The Little Sister*."

"I'm impressed. You read crime fiction, Darcy."

"I adore it. I'm a big fan of Sam Spade, too. I remember reading *The Maltese Falcon* as a boy and I was hooked. Once I thought I'd like to be a police officer, but I gravitated toward a career in law instead."

"That began it for me, too! Such a small world. I loved the movie and then later listened to it on the radio. That line from *The Little Sister* became a source of irritation and I always imagined that I had the smarts *and* the equipment to pull off an investigation just like Marlowe."

Yes, she did.

"Yet, I can't extract information from you, so surely, I am lacking somewhere."

"My sister says that I am unyielding," he admitted.

"I'd have to agree, but just as ice melts and stone can be chiseled, no doubt even Fitzwilliam Darcy can be buttered up."

He pulled her closer to his chest, his eyes scanning those sparks of gold within hers, lit with humor. His mouth lowered to hers, hovering. "You can try, Elizabeth."

"Oh, I plan on it." She playfully taunted with an alluring half smile.

He laughed breaking the intensity of what he felt. She was chipping away at his façade faster than he would allow any person to do so, and he would not allow the kiss. "You didn't set out to be a private investigator, did you? I would assume that your parents had other aspirations for you."

He turned her under his arm and she sprang back into his tight frame, her delicate hand landing upon his bicep.

"Of course, they did. They had one plan only for my sisters and me: marriage and children. Jane is the only one to actually achieve such *esteemed* success. Instead, I took a secretarial course and learned to keep books, passed my exams, then went to work in my father's garage."

"And do they know about your change of profession?"

"Not on your life! In spite of my parents' penchant for the booze, they are quite sanctimonious. Go figure. And what about you ... what about that dream of becoming a lawyer?" she deftly changed the topic.

The song was coming to a close and he turned her again, followed by a strong dip in his arms. The smile on her face undid him. This woman was the perfect partner for him.

"I need a drink for that story." His fingers thread with hers and he led her back to their table, now cleared from their late-night dessert.

"So you're willing to answer a second question then?"

"I told you I'm not so unyielding—not such a sourpuss."

••

EIGHT

Darcy rarely ventured to Hell's Kitchen, but when he did it was always by design: to buy or sell property. But tonight, at three-thirty in the morning, standing on the corner of 44th Street and 10th Avenue, he noted how this part of the Big Apple was home to many who kept early morning hours. For ten minutes he leaned against the lone lamppost, staring up at Elizabeth's darkened office window as he gathered courage. Her gloves smoldered in his pocket like the fire in her eyes had burned into his heart. He wondered if she had deliberately left them on the counter of the hat check before he'd escorted her to a cab ninety minutes ago. Probably just wishful thinking on his part. He couldn't get her out of his head. Apart from the forgotten gloves and an unmistakably intense attraction between them, she gave him no other indication that she desired his company tonight. His gentlemanly offer to escort her home in a cab had been refused, albeit politely. He was operating on a hunch and two Old Fashions. After all, a man needed courage for a dame like Elizabeth. But that damn Philip Marlowe quote gave him fortitude as it repeatedly rolled around in his brain: "Alcohol is like love. The first kiss is magic, the second is intimate, the third is routine. After that, you take the girl's clothes off."

Barely able to discern the painted lettering on the glass of "Bennet Private Investigations," he acknowledged what a smart cookie she was to hide her career from her family. No doubt, they wouldn't accept her dangerous life and definitely couldn't understand; he barely did, but he understood the appeal of the profession. He had set aside his curiosity for the evening, never asking her what her interest was in Slick Wick. They instead, talked about their common interests and he did the unthinkable, talked about his father. Elizabeth did have skills in extracting information from him. She was an eager and sympathetic listener, making him feel like the only man in the room—scratch that—in the world.

And they had danced the night away, almost every dance. That Oscar fellow took the hint and took a hike, early on.

It was the best damn time he'd had in his life. Honest to goodness fun and exhilaration brought on by her laughter and keen wit, her attention and fine footwork. The babe was quite a hoofer. In spite of her particular career, her obvious undercover work to find Wickham, and, not to mention, her low-class family—he had fallen for her like a ton of bricks. The evening had confirmed everything he already knew: She was brilliant and not afraid to live life on her terms. He admired her. Unlike her sister Jane, who married up attempting to make something of herself, Elizabeth was out there on her own working hard for a living, making her way in a man's world. And using what she had to get what she needed. She was good at it, too.

With a snap of two fingers, he flicked the cigarette into the street, then breathing in the cold night air, walked to her building.

••

Still wired from the Copacabana, Elizabeth laid awake in the dark staring at the ceiling until rolling to her side to switch on the radio. Nothing good was ever played at this late hour, but whatever random song came through the Zenith was, at least, company to her restlessness. Of course, not the kind of company she needed. She kicked the bed linen from her legs and tossed yet again, attempting to cool off on the vacant side of her bed.

What a night. What a man. What a mess.

Turns out *she* was the cream puff. Hook, line, and sinker she had fallen for Darcy. Only he was shrouded in mystery—maybe even mayhem. But mischief? She couldn't quite believe that. A would-be politician with a suspect past, a member of high society with a bankroll larger than City Hall was not her type of guy, but maybe he could be. He certainly had everything she looked for in a man. She couldn't deny that they'd had a wonderful time tonight, dancing and laughing. Under that brooding puss and expensive suit, he had a wicked sense of humor and she was surprised when he spoke a little bit about himself, sharing his defiance to his influential father when he joined up to serve in '42 versus remaining sheltered at Columbia University.

Her palms cupped the lower swells of her bare breasts, moving up to brush over her taut nipples. Oh how she wished he were her guy, even just for the night. She burned for his touch. Those slow dances below the palm trees made her knees go weak. It felt like pure seduction each time his hand slid down her back like an electrical frisson along a tense wire when he'd held her in his arms.

She closed her eyes imagining his hands doing other things and her heart rate sped, the pulse within her sex increasing just from the thought of his lips. Her head spun as it floated in the blissful pleasure of her imaginings, the radio fading as Darcy's suggestive voice became more prominent in her memory. "Let's do this again, Elizabeth."

There was a knock on the office door.

Damn. She was just getting to the good part.

Three thirty in the morning. Charlotte, did you lose your key, again?

Slipping into her kimono, she tied the sash tight. Nude wasn't something she did in front of her girlfriend, even if Char was uninhibited.

A second knock on the door sounded, a little more forceful this time. For that she needed Sally. That wasn't her friend's typical signal. Tiptoeing through the apartment, and then the office in the dark, she kept her pistol poised and at the ready. Through the frosted glass of the door, a man's black silhouette was backlit from the illuminated hallway. His hat sat tilted in a familiar fashion, the expanse of his shoulders exactly as she had been just imagining.

"Yes?" she asked with her ear close to the glass, confirming that it was Darcy.

"Elizabeth. It's me, Darcy. You ... um ... left your gloves at the Copa."

That made her smile. Smart man; he took the bait. Like she said—hook, line and sinker—both of them.

She cracked the door, peering through, the barrel of Sally peeking out below the chain lock. Darcy's tie was partially opened, his cheeks flushed from the cold, the smile on his lips so damn adorable.

"Don't shoot. I'm not dangerous." He joked waving the gloves.

Containing her own smile, she slipped the gun into the robe's pocket.

A slide to the chain preceded her opening of the door, making sure that she stood at the threshold with hand on hip and a sly twist to her lips. "Yes, you are, Mr. Darcy. You're very dangerous and a dope to show up here at this hour. I could have shot you."

She wanted to laugh at the way his eyes traveled over her half silk-clad body. What a picture she must have presented to his hungry libido. God how she enjoyed teasing him, loved how he responded to her.

"You shouldn't have come."

He took a determined step to her, his arm sliding around her waist, his mouth hovering over hers. She fixed on the expression in his eyes and her breath caught. *Damn.*

"You wanted me to come."

"Yes," she breathed. His smolder tore straight into her soul and his boldness made her heart thunder.

Starved, full lips crashed against hers, consuming her, assailing every sense with their intoxicating movement. The coolness from his cheek did nothing to quell the immediate burn traveling through her body. Wet, hot kisses that tasted like sweet liquor deepened when he pulled her into him, his firm hold.

Her head spun, intoxicated by him as he stepped into the dark office, slamming the door closed behind them before tossing his hat across the room. Their lips never separated, connected by need.

"Wait. Wait," she panted when his delicious mouth descended to her neck, willing her to give him greater access with a tilt of her head. He clutched her so securely in his arm that there was no escape.

"I can't wait. I want you, Elizabeth. I couldn't stop thinking about you."

"Then kiss me again," she demanded, her breath ragged, the throbbing between her legs escalating.

All restraint dissipated with the intensity of his kiss, their mouths molding perfectly. She couldn't stop her hands from pushing off his overcoat as his steps progressed toward the office desk, leading her to lean against it in the sliver of moonlight through the picture window. Faint strains of music from the radio carried through the apartment.

Darcy was a man on a mission, ravishing her lips and she met his every foray with equal hunger.

His hands gripped her waist lifting her to sit upon the desk. Settling himself between her spread legs, the edge of the kimono separated revealing her inner thigh but she didn't care. Visions of him penetrating her sex raged through her imagination straight to her pearl, increasing the throbbing.

He dropped the silk from her shoulder and the fervor of his kisses slowed into worshipping caresses, their tongues dancing in languid exploration. The gentle stroke of his hand upon her neck gliding downward to her shoulder reached a place she would never have imagined—her heart. There was tenderness and reverence in his touch. So very different than that "other man" she had given herself to. Darcy was seducing her with emotion.

She held onto him, one hand clasping his firm bicep, the other gripping his hip. In her mindless euphoria, her palm itched to move the inches to touch him intimately.

A soft kiss deposited upon her nape only increased her need, and she dropped her head back. A second suckling one to that sensitive place sent her to the zenith and she lifted a leg, wrapping it around him, pulling his body closer to hers. Love bites trailed down her shoulder, alternating with lingering kisses as he leaned her back onto the desk.

Unable to control her desire, her hand boldly slid across to his rigid arousal, tempted to release him, to finally surround his thick girth with her fingers and stroke him but she held back.

The feel of his large hand gliding up her bare thigh caused her to shudder, especially when he pulled her body closer to the edge of the desk. His throaty moan in tandem with his kisses to her collarbone nearly caused her to cry out. This enigmatic man was completely under her skin now.

Oh God, how does he know ... how could he possibly know how to set me aflame?

She could feel papers under her back shift, heard items fall from the desk, but that was all insignificant. All she cared for in this moment was filling the emptiness in her body and her soul with him—all of him.

"Elizabeth, you are so beautiful," he whispered when one side of the robe fell lower, baring her breast to him.

She eagerly arched her back, inviting him and those luscious lips of his. Her aroused nipple waited anxiously for his trailing kisses. This was just as she had dreamed these many nights since the Kit Kat.

That first delicious sensation of his mouth surrounding her tautness left her breathless followed by pants of rapture. His lips sent sparks to her womanhood—increasing the throbbing, the wetness. *Oh God!*

His talented lips suckled her nipple. She writhed below him when his tongue slowly lapped, circled, and flicked her before sharing his attentions with her other craving breast. She arched further, meeting his every arousing indulgence.

"Darcy," she begged, grasping onto his jacket lapel, lifting herself up, inches from the desk, delighting when he straightened for a moment, untied the sash of her kimono, completely baring her entire feminine body to him. His hand caressed her waist, then slid to her hip where it held her tight until traveling again. Long fingers brushed through her pubis—so close, so eager to explore her folds, yet still, tentative.

He leaned down again, nibbled her peak and she purred, "Oh, yes."

She needed more from him and reached for his bulging arousal. So stiff and large against her palm, again she fought the urge to release him, struggling with her desire to guide his hips to slide his length into her, to allow him to take her right there on the desk. Her body strained at the immediate need for his pounding thrusts.

He bit her nipple and the sparks came ... increasing, building ...

She shuddered—reeling in ecstasy, her sex clenched in rapture, ready to explode. "Yes, oh yes ... Darcy." *Touch me there,* she wanted to demand but stopped herself, feeling a loss of control. She reached for the desk, seeking an anchor and accidentally knocked the pen holder to the floor.

Reality suddenly crashed upon her with the loud noise. Drunk on passion and these unbridled emotions would cause her to do foolish things. She couldn't allow this to continue, even if he was masterfully bringing her to heights she had never experienced.

"Darcy."

Threading her fingers through his hair brought his gaze upward to meet hers. His expression was filled with desire, his lips well-loved.

He whispered in the darkness. "What do you need, Elizabeth?"

"You know what I need."

"Is that what you want? Tonight? Tomorrow and the next? From me? From only me?"

"From only you, yes. But not tonight. I can't." She shook her head, and with a glimmer of disappointment he smiled wistfully before kissing her nipple then covering her with the silk. Taking her hand, he helped her to sit up followed by an ardent kiss. His hands cupped her face endearingly and her heart leapt. He was a gentleman; he was no Wickham. Yes, Darcy was real cream on that account.

Her body cried, her heart rejoiced, her soul swelled. This surprising man had found his way in, his way past the wall, and she smiled, but she had to be honest with herself. What could become of them? Nothing. Although they had many things in common—in the essentials—their worlds were entirely separate and he was connected to Wickham. That had never changed. No matter the evening they'd had or the intimacies shared, the man was hiding something and she didn't run with liars—or politicians.

He stood between her legs, one hand smoothing the hair surrounding her face, the other clutching her hip. "I'm sorry if I pushed too fast."

"There's nothing to be sorry for, but you should go. Someone like you shouldn't be seen on this side of town at this hour."

"I'd like to stay, even if—"

"No. You need to go."

"Will I see you again?" he kissed her, and the sweetness of the sentiment nearly made her cry.

"Only for business. Only at your office when you tell me about Wickham."

Darcy dropped his arms and took two steps back from her, his expression changing. "Was that what this was tonight? Just a means of extracting information from me?"

She righted her kimono then stood. Crossing her arms over her bosom, her anger reared, raised by pure moxie. "Of course not! You came to me, remember? I was perfectly satisfied with the way we left things at the Copa. I won't deny that we had a good time tonight, but come tomorrow, I'm right back to my investigation."

"Yes, finding that low-life chiseler."

"See. You do know him. If sleeping with you was part of my entrapment then I wouldn't have put a stop to your seduction. I would have gotten what we *both* needed then waited for pillow talk. I told you before, Mr. Darcy, I'm not that kind of girl."

"So what was this then—between us—just now, if not your skill at using your digits and figure?"

She looked away, unable to meet his gaze and whispered in the moonlight. "It was an erotic dream, a fantasy, nothing more."

"You led me down a primrose path, didn't you?" His face contorted in anger, and he shook his head and bent to pick up his coat from the floor. "Answer me one thing, Elizabeth. Were you *only* interested in me as a lead for your investigation? Was this, and those *supposed* feelings that went along with it just part of your act?"

"Why? Is there something else you want from me? Something more than to shack up with a leggy dame? Someone you assume is a floozy because of my profession, my upbringing, believing that I'd scratch your uptown itch?"

His scowl nearly burned her heart as deeply as his touch had scorched her flesh.

"A moment ago I had thought there was more between us, but now I'm not so sure. That tongue of yours is as dangerous as the Communist Manifesto. My showing up here tonight was for so much more than to get you into bed. I should have listened to my initial reservations: The inferiority of your family, you being a career girl, and the very fact that you obviously know George Wickham."

Dumbfounded, she watched as he reached into his coat pocket and withdrew the gloves, placing them on the table beside the door. "I suppose I should be grateful that you're the first woman who didn't want me for my money, only information. Don't bother contacting me about the man. Consider me—and any future with you I may have thought possible—a dead-end, as dead as I wish George Wickham was."

He stormed out, leaving her standing in the office with arms still folded across her chest, his fedora forgotten, lying on the floor.

Damn!

••

NINE

The sun had barely risen, but Wickham was already on his way back to New York City—a full day earlier than his society companion had expected. He sniggered, congratulating himself on his clandestine departure. Georgiana Darcy was still unaware of anything that had occurred after the Mickey Finn he'd slipped her six hours ago.

The ride from the Hotel Nacional de Cuba to the airport was brief, but long enough for him to appreciate the relief that coursed through his veins: his job was complete. A Moscow-trained member of the newly-organized underground Third International in Cuba's People's Socialist Party was his escort. The thug was there to ensure that he got on the waiting Cubana de Aviación plane. It was part of the deal: contriving Georgiana's arrival in Havana and arranging for her doping and disappearance. In return, the Reds were gonna pay him $15,000: 3,000 clams up front, the rest on his return to New York. They had already forged for him a new identity, and assured safety back to the States before the law had a chance to hang a red light on him.

Fifteen thousand was no peanut change. That, along with Miss Darcy's jewels tucked in his pocket, was enough for him and Lydia to skip out on Gotham forever. That is ... after he got home with his tail between his legs and ponied up those two necklaces into her gold digging fingers. Lydia had been madder than a hellcat when he told her he was flying off to Cuba with a flossy doll who had $20 million in the bank. She didn't like his "plan B" following Fitzy's arrival at El Barrio—without the money and making threats of his own.

As much as Wickham enjoyed Havana, he didn't want to be anywhere near the fallout when the wealthy socialite came up missing and her lollipop brother capitulated to the ransom. Nope, he ain't no dope. In a fast four hours, his alibi would be waiting for him back at La Guardia Airport, sure to go wacky over his new clean cut disguise—and the jewels.

"Are you sure nobody's gonna finger me for this? The law better not come lookin' for me," he cautioned the Commie dressed in all black.

"There is no worry. Measures have been taken."

"I ain't gonna be no fall guy if things go south."

"It is none of your concern. You did your job and you will keep your mouth shut."

"I still don't think you'll get what you want. Darcy is too straight-laced, too loyal. There ain't no way he's going to denounce McCarthy's political supporters, no way he'll be your inside stooge."

"We will see. Family is a most effective means to an end."

"And if he doesn't run for office or get elected?"

"That is no problem. We will assure it. We have friends."

"And another thing, he ain't got the moxie to set up these flimflam offshore accounts you people want."

"Silence! It is none of your concern."

George fidgeted in his seat. Rubbing a hand across his clean-shaven chin, he looked out the window at the passing view. The tranquil ocean waves lapping onto the nearby shore brought to mind memories of the South Pacific. He would miss the Caribbean, but not these Soviets. When he got back to New York and its freezing rain, he and his chippie would fly to Rio or somewhere far from these Ruskies, far from Darcy and his threatened promise to turn him over for that long overdue court-martial. No doubt, when Georgiana came up missing, he'd be first on Fitzy's radar, and second—on the Navy's.

He chuckled again, enjoying the memory of the port town of Nouméa and his then subordinate Seaman Darcy.

••

Backdropped by the picture window in her office, Elizabeth sat at her desk opposite her newest client, Mrs. Carter of Gramercy Park. The dear older woman was sure her husband had a mistress. There were a lot of these cases lately, and most of them did corroborate the suspicion. Wives always knew, as did *most* sweethearts.

Heck in that last year of the war, Johnny's letters had come less frequently but those that had come lacked his usual ardor—even sentiment. She suspected something was amiss. A man in battle should have missed his girl more, but she attempted to discount his coolness as a result of war—certainly never expecting that he'd get hastily hitched to a foreigner during a furlough.

Feeling empathy for Mrs. Carter, she intently listened, leaning forward in the same manner as Darcy had just days ago in his office—manicured fingers placed lightly upon the desk. *The* desk. Concentration and sympathy gradually became supplanted by visions of the night before: his hot kisses, his arousing nibbles, their heavy petting on that very desk. She was mortified recalling herself exposed, spread, and so eager for his touch. Mortification quickly turned into anger at herself for allowing it, provoking him in the first place with her flirting and unchecked desire. Where had her good regulation and deference for respectability gone? She knew where: she couldn't resist Darcy's magnetism. He had said he wanted more from her, thought there was more between them. What could he have meant? Surely not a future—surely he couldn't have felt the same lightning love bolt as she'd felt.

Her cheeks flushed and she sat back in the chair, refocusing, shifting uncomfortably in her seat, willing herself to fully focus on her client and the rain pelting against the window. Yes, it was raining again, and yes, love at first sight did exist.

"I want photographs, proof," Mrs. Carter stated, trailed by a vulgar expulsion from her nose into a lace-trimmed handkerchief.

"Not to worry. I just purchased a Kodak Medalist with a range finder."

"Is that good?"

"Only the best for Bennet Private Investigations. I assure you; if Mr. Carter is having an affair, I'll find out about it and so will you. You'll have the proof you need—if, in fact, he is cheating. For now, we'll assume that he isn't." She jotted a note in her PI book.

"I came to you because you're a woman, Miss Bennet. Your appearance, your manner. As a lady, you understand these things ...

The waterworks turned on, again. She always hated this part of her job, but worse was, too frequently, delivering the blow at the end of a case. Mrs. King had those same tears when she and her husband initially came to see her after she'd first settled into this small—at the time, rundown—apartment.

Elizabeth smiled wistfully. *Poor woman.* "I do understand, Mrs. Carter. Thank you for your confidence. You have my word that, to the best of my ability, I'll employ everything within my arsenal and I promise you I'll keep buttoned—absolutely discreet."

The client nodded then blew her nose again.

"Now, can you tell me the names of a few establishments where your husband frequents?"

"The Oak Room."

Yeah. She knew that restaurant. It was in the Plaza Hotel.

"And what does he do for a living? Perhaps he's wining and dining clients in the Oak Room."

"Robert is an actuary. He doesn't have clients."

All Elizabeth could manage was a nod. Already the gee's goose was cooked in her experience.

The telephone rang and she hated to answer it, hated to disturb this moment, but every call was essential in the private eye business, any possible client or lead could not be overlooked. *Maybe it's Darcy.*

"Excuse me. I must answer this ... Bennet Private Investigations."

"Hi, Doll. It's me, Brandon."

"Oh hi, *Detective*. Were you able to get that information for me?" She greeted putting emphasis on "detective" to let Mrs. Carter know she had connections. It obviously worked when the woman nodded in satisfied approval.

"That's a fine how do you do? Yeah, I got what you need, but that ain't why I'm on the horn."

"Well, then how can I help you?"

Another nod.

"Did I wake you? You decent enough to get in a cab in this rain?"

"Of course. It's two in the afternoon and you know I'm not put off by a little bad weather." She deliberately said that, too.

"You have another white night last night?"

"Yeah, very little sleep for this private investigator."

"Remember when I said I'd let you in on my next murder case? Well, kid, I got a doozy over in the next room that you may want to take a flutter at."

"A homicide you say?"

"Yeah. Whataya got a client sittin' before ya? Are you trying to impress the bankroll?"

She swallowed to suppress a laugh. "Yes."

"Well listen, tell him to scram so you can get down to Stripper's Row before the coroner gets here. You know how it is; stiffs get colder by the minute than an arctic blast in December."

"Stripper's Row?"

"That's right. One of your haunts." He laughed. "The Kit Kat Klub."

"Right. I'll be there as soon as I can. Thank you for telephoning, Detective Brandon."

She tried to act composed but could hear his laughter as the receiver traveled to the cradle; a little smirk played across her lips. Like she said, he had her number.

The Kit Kat Klub seemed to be where all the action was these days.

••

Elizabeth exited the cab in front of the Kit Kat just as the sky opened up with teeming rain beating down against the entrance awning. Two police officers wearing standard issue NYPD rain slickers stood sentry. At the curb, the coroner's ambulance was just arriving, maneuvering through the scattered row of black and green police cars.

Placing her hand on Darcy's fedora (now her fedora), she passed several newshawks and their flashing cameras. She'd never seen so much attention given to a crime scene before. The coppers and the press made it difficult to pass but she withdrew her private eye badge from her pocket then flashed the one weapon in her arsenal that always worked: a brilliant smile. Heads turned, the crowd separated, and she could feel the stare from every hot-blooded man upon her when, chin held high, she strode past them with confidence.

"I'm Private Investigator Elizabeth Bennet. Detective Brandon telephoned me to consult on this case," she said to one of the cops flanking the door.

His eyes raked over her, settling on her legs as he spoke. "Sorry, sweetheart. No one's allowed out or in and that's from the top brass, especially no keyhole peeping dame."

"It's alright, Donovan; the doll's on the list. Brandon says so."

She steamed but grinned. "Thanks, boys. Keep up the good work standing at the door in the rain while we detectives get all the fame and glory."

The joint was a hive of activity; sections in the lounge were tied off with police tape while other alcoves and corners were filled with corralled patrons getting interrogated by the detectives. Near the stage, men huddled around the crime scene, but Elizabeth couldn't see the victim from her perch at the top of the stairs. In the light of a dreary day, without the safe cloak of darkness, the seediness of the club was exposed: the carpet, dingy and stained; the red tablecloths dirty, most with cigarette burns. She kept on her rain-soaked trench coat for protection, thinking of all those male patrons and the fruit of their one-handed labor. Their actions gave the word "seedy" a whole different meaning. Her stomach turned at the recollection of recently sitting at a booth in Siberia where aroused men hid far from curious eyes; she shuddered.

Brandon waved to her from the stage where he finished chatting with one of the robe-clad performers. Snapping his detective pad closed, he looked over at the dead man on his right and shook his head, moving toward her.

"That poor slob didn't see it coming."

"Hmm ... he's certainly drawing a big investigation. I've never seen so many flatfoots at a crime scene before. Is he someone famous?" she asked.

"Nah, just some G.I. who got waxed. There's another stiff in the far corner over there."

"Two? No wonder you have this place locked up so tight."

"Follow me, toots, and don't touch anything. The boys are still dustin' for fingerprints."

"Yuck, I wouldn't want that job. You can be darn sure I won't be touching anything. So, about that name, Chris? You know, the snapshot I gave you at lunch?"

"Yeah. I figured you'd start off with that." He removed the photograph from his breast pocket then handed it to her, its condition now, far more crinkled than he had received it days before.

"I thought I recognized her from the papers, but I did some askin' around to be sure. Her name's Georgiana Darcy, sister to that moneybag you went to see. Just inherited her trust fund and now has more dough than Fort Knox."

Nearly gasping aloud, her eyes widened in shock. *Oh God! Darcy's sister!*

"Say, whatever happened at that meeting down in his office?" he asked.

She stared at the photograph, trying hard not to tip her hat to her turmoil, and answered. "Nothing came of it—a real sourpuss, that one. But I guess I'll have to go back downtown to warn him. Any girl that my grifter knows is a girl in trouble." *Even Lydia!*

"Do you want me to go with you?"

"No. I definitely think I should go alone. Fitzwilliam Darcy might not be happy to see me, but he'll listen to me. Our last meeting didn't end so well. We both wanted something the other wasn't willing to give."

She knew he immediately saw through her response when he raised both eyebrows. "Is that how you ended up with a man's expensive hat on your head?"

"No comment."

"C'mon, let's get to business. I'm not gonna harp on you about your love life. I might get jealous." They stepped over an evidence box and walked around the gurney that the coroner had just carried in, navigating to a spot directly before the first victim, slumped over to his side, lying on the booth seat. A coagulating pool of blood surrounded his head and dripped down the red vinyl.

Brandon held out his hand. "Eli, meet Viktor Volkov, card-carrying Commie with a knife wound to his jugular vein. Poor shmoe, didn't have a chance. Bled out like a stuck pig."

"How long has he been dead?"

"The coroner will confirm it, but I'm taking a stab at three hours."

She chuckled at Brandon's word choice turning her head sideways to examine the victim's face. For the second time, her eyes widened. "I know him. He's ... he's my groping Russian in the Cossack hat."

"When did you start going with a Red? I thought you said you didn't sign anything."

"I didn't, but he's that mugg who met with my bad hat on Monday night. The one I pick-pocketed that snapshot from."

"Pick-pocketed?"

A smirk preceded her lie, "Found sticking out ... of his pocket. I ... borrowed it."

"Well, now Mr. Volkov is your very *dead* Russian. So you can't return it."

"Any sign of the murder weapon?"

"Nothing yet, but it's early."

Elizabeth glanced over her shoulder at the other victim. "What's his story?"

"C'mon. I'll introduce you to Private Andy Chisholm from Topeka. Like I said, poor slob, dying in a striptease joint. He was probably girding his loins for deployment to Korea before a small caliber bullet to his head ended his happy visit to the Big Apple."

"Well, at least, his loins died having a good time before going off to war."

Brandon snorted. "Yeah." He tapped a uniformed cop on his back. "Step aside, rookie; let the lady through."

The crowd separated and Elizabeth approached the blood-splattered table. Bright flashes popped, lighting the scene as the police photographer's camera snapped images of the dead body.

Elizabeth abruptly stopped inches from the table.

Shell-shocked, a gag heaved her upper body. Her hand flew to her mouth.

"Eli?"

She knew the dead man sporting an Army crew cut, his blood-stained head drooped over one shoulder. Wide-open, lifeless-glazed eyes stared right at her.

Oh God! The sight made her knees go weak and she grabbed Brandon's arm. Her personal cold case had frozen over permanently with a bullet through the victim's temple.

It was George Wickham—dead as a doornail.

••

Ten

"hat's wrong, Eli? What is it?" Brandon asked.

"I ..." Her hand remained fixed over her lips to keep from tossing her cookies. "I know him, and he's no soldier. He's my case ... my personal case."

Her body trembled, and Brandon wrapped his arm around her waist to keep her from falling at his feet. All these months of investigation and then finally—a lead closer to Mary. And now nothing—nothing but a cold corpse. A literal dead end.

"The cold case?" Brandon asked.

"Yeah. Please, Chris, I ... I gotta get away from here."

He held onto her, supporting her, leading her through the crowded room, and then veering off down a long hallway.

By the time they reached a small, secluded room at the end of the hall, gone was the jovial flatfoot she adored. In his place was the hard-boiled homicide detective she respected. He pointed to a chair at the desk, commanding a little more brusquely than she expected, "Park it."

Turning to the glass water cooler in the corner of the room, he filled a paper cup then placed it in her shaking hand. "Drink, catch your breath, and then start flappin' your lips about that dead body out there."

Her head spun from the shock, attempting to fully fathom what she had just seen. Her mind repeated the evident truth again and again: *Wickham* is dead ... Wickham *is dead.*

The expression on Brandon's face softened as he rolled the wooden chair from around the desk, seating himself beside her. He always was a sap when it came to her. His puppy dog eyes emitted genuine sympathy, the tone in his voice almost fatherly. "I want to hear it all, Eli. This ain't no ordinary murder. This has Commie written in bright red all over it— in a strip club suspected of aiding un-American activities. A nightclub, I might add, you visited four days ago, peepin' on the very man now lying dead out there with a hole in his head. No doubt there are a couple of witnesses that would testify to your visit. Soon the Feds are going to be crawling all over this place, and I might not be able to keep your name out of it. That shot was made with a .41 caliber derringer."

"What? You think I had something to do with it?"

"Let me see Sally."

Now her heart rate was going a mile a minute. "Turn your head," she said, hiking her skirt upward. She removed the pistol from its holster at her garter then placed it into his outstretched palm.

Brandon examined the barrel, followed by a sniff.

"I assure you I haven't fired it. But keep this up ..." she said.

"I'm just checkin'. You know how tenacious those G-men are."

She nodded when he handed it back to her.

"What's your grifter's name?"

"George Wickham. He served in the Navy during the war, but went AWOL in '44."

"And how do you know him?"

Raising the cup to her lips, she couldn't help but look away and fix her eyes on the risqué pin-up calendar on the wall. *Damn.* Only Oscar knew the story—the whole story. The part about her, too.

"Eli?"

"After he came to Jackson Heights spouting a sob story a couple of years ago, my father gave him work in his garage. He repaid the kindness by stealing money from him, then tampered with the books to make it look like an accounting error."

Pausing, she swallowed hard; her free hand gripped the edge of the desktop. "Two months after he had his way with a friend of mine, she disappeared. I believe he may have kidnapped her, or maybe murdered her. After the police investigation declared her a runaway, I opened Bennet Private Investigations to find her. That was eighteen months ago. Wickham had been off the radar for about nine or ten months—until the other day." *With my youngest sister.*

For the first time in a long time, tears welled in her eyes. "And now he's dead, and I may never uncover Mary's true fate. I've failed her and her parents."

Brandon leaned forward, lifting her hand from the wood surface, wrapping her fingers in a gentle squeeze. "Aw shucks. Don't cry, sister. I hate when dames get the weeps. Why did you never tell me about this? I could have helped you find him on my dime."

She sniffled then withdrew her fingers from his grasp. "Personal reasons."

"Ah, I see. So apart from your old man's dough and this friend of yours, you had a personal ax to grind, too. Are you a woman scorned?"

"No comment."

"Is there anyone else you know who might want to see the mugg dead?"

"Honestly, there's probably a whole lot of people who want to see Slick Wick floating in the East River. My first assumption would be the Soviets that he was deal-making with on Monday night. Maybe those two out there had an argument, maybe the deal went south."

"Maybe. Or maybe that moneybag Darcy is the one who did Wickham in. Is he connected to him?"

Her head snapped up. "Darcy? Why do you ask?"

"So he does know the deceased?"

Her back straightened. Although she may have considered the same deduction, she donned her best poker face suddenly feeling the compulsion to lie on Darcy's behalf, even to Brandon. "Like I implied earlier, Chris, I met Darcy for personal reasons. I don't think he knows Wickham. He's just a suit—a high roller whose name was given to me by my sister's hoity-toity husband attempting to play matchmaker." She snorted. "As if we could ever ..."

"Then how do you explain the snapshot of his sister if he's not known to the deceased or his dead Russian *business* associate?" He raised an eyebrow. "Maybe your suit did them both in. He is a Commie-hater after all."

Her eyes met his as she attempted to stifle any and all emotion he might make out. "No. I don't think that lollipop did anyone in. It's just a wacky coincidence about the snapshot, but I'll let him know anyway. It's irrelevant now that both criminals are dead."

"I'd love to say I entirely buy your story, so, for now, I'll take your word. Never known you to kiss and tell, but you're on the up and up and I can take that to the bank. Look, I'm sorry the stiff is your man, but if you ask me, you can move on now. Some things and some people are meant to remain a mystery. Maybe your friend did run away. Hell, if I lived in Jackson Heights I would have beat a path out of there, too. Sorry, kid."

"No offense taken. I couldn't wait to leave, so maybe she couldn't either." She *loved Jackson Heights!* "Look, Chris ... will you keep me in the loop if you have any suspects? I need closure on this. Complete closure." *And God I hope it wasn't Darcy who pulled the trigger.*

"We're on the same side of the street now, working this case together, doll. What I know, you'll know and that's my promise. But you're gonna have to keep clear of the crime scene. Can't have your fingerprints anywhere near that Wickham fellow. It's bad enough you were in one of these booths the other night."

"Yeah. My thought, too, but had I not been, then I never would have known about this Georgiana Darcy."

He stood, removed the cup from her hand then placed it on the desk beside them. "C'mon. I need you to interview those shake dancers. As much as I'd like to go back into the dressing room, I don't think I'd make it out of there without needing a cold shower and a cigarette. *Capisce?*"

"Sure." She kissed his cheek. "Thanks. Thanks for everything."

Taking a deep breath, she adjusted her hat then raised her chin. "You know, if I didn't feel so terrible that Mary's disappearance will likely never be solved, I might rejoice that George Wickham is dead. He was a cruel son of a gun and if someone else hadn't pulled the trigger, I might have let Sally do the job."

"Now, Eli, you keep that between you, me, and these walls. As far as I'm concerned this conversation never happened."

••

An overwhelming scent of cheap perfume wafted through the back-stage hallway leading to the dancers' dressing room. Elizabeth could hear chatter from behind a door; its plaque read "Kittens" in pink sequins. This interrogation was new territory for her and she wanted to conduct a proper one that would make Brandon proud, yet, at the same time she wanted to fit in so that the girls wouldn't clam up the minute she asked the first question. She removed her raincoat and hat, laying them upon an old secretary desk where the stage crew telephone sat. On the wall above, little slips of paper inscribed with telephone numbers were taped up alongside snapshots of the girls performing. After the interviews, she'd come back to examine them more closely, making sure to jot down every name and number.

Smoothing her knit dress, she readied to enter the kitten lair, possibly to be eaten alive. These ladies of the stage were no high-class burlesque dancers who ran with the likes of Gypsy Rose Lee and the Anatomic Bomb Lili St. Cyr. The Kit Kat Klub represented the brash world of striptease, which Charlotte had explained. Sure, she could talk the talk and had the figure to pull off a proficient performance herself, but, in her heart, the refined Elizabeth Bennet still ran the show, even if her own actions the night before wouldn't have passed any morality board's stamp of approval.

She opened the door into the dimly-lit world of feminine mystique—an erotic dreamscape for man or femme. Although all the women were covered—some already dressed in their everyday apparel set to beat it out of there, far away from the sordid goings on in the lounge—the hanging brassieres and dangling stockings were enough to set any hot-blooded man whacky. It was a good call on Brandon's part, to avoid these women like the obsessed pussy-loving lion he prided about himself.

Two costume racks lined the center of the narrow dressing room and on each flanking wall were small vanities with wood-framed mirrors, each illuminated by a single protruding bulb. Barely giving the performers room to navigate, props of all kinds hung from coat racks and hooks between the mirrors. Even a caged parrot sat on a shelf in the corner of the dressing area. She didn't want to think what the bird was used for. Feathered fans and boas seemed to be everywhere; shedding remnants of down floated in the suffocating air, surrounding the women like falling snowflakes.

Several bump-n-grind girls glanced up from their conversations of murder speculation when she entered the room, but largely she went ignored until clearing her throat.

"Yeah? What do you want?" said a dancer she recognized from the other night.

"You're Miss Angela the A-bomb, aren't you? I saw your impressive performance on Monday night."

Immediately, the blonde woman's demeanor changed. "You liked it? Really?"

"I did!"

"What did you think of the music? Some of the girls laughed at my selection." Her eyes bore over to her neighbor. Obviously, there was tension between them. "I simply had to have it. It's from that strip movie last year. You know ... the one with Mickey Rooney. The music was absolutely lulu and I just couldn't resist the title of the movie!"

"I enjoyed *The Strip*, too. It was clever how they used the nightclub to hide from a murder investigation. Your selection of "A Kiss to Build a Dream On" was perfect!" She lied about enjoying the B-movie, but life seemed to imitate art these days and the stripper gave her the perfect segue. "Speaking of murder ... did you know either of the victims, Angela?"

"Who's askin'?"

Elizabeth held her hand out for a shake as all the women in the room suddenly clammed up, curious or hiding something. "My name is Eli Bennet. I'm a private eye, who ... unfortunately ..." she looked over her shoulder to the ajar door before whispering, "had intimate *knowledge* of that soldier boy with a bullet to his head." She hoped that would make them feel comfortable with her questions. Of course, she didn't add "intimate knowledge two years ago, that I have regretted every day since."

"Yeah? You went with Slick Wick? Ain't this a small world," another dancer said.

Elizabeth looked at the photographs tacked to the mirror beside her. She thought this afternoon couldn't have gotten much worse by what she saw. The woman didn't need to reply; the confirmation was two feet away in a snapshot he'd probably given to every girl in every port. George Wickham's Navy portrait. No wonder he spent so much time here. Now there was another woman he had put his degenerate hands on.

"The girl ... whose vanity this is ... is she here?"

The second woman sauntered over to the closed powder room door, her costume barely containing her backside. She pounded her fist against the wood. "Hey, Dixie! Someone's askin' about your dead boyfriend."

The door flew open and for the third time that afternoon, Elizabeth's mouth went slack, her eyes widening.

Her wayward sister, Lydia, lacquered in layers of cosmetics, stood at the threshold, wearing a g-string and blue garters, flaunting fishnet stockings. Blue-fringed tassel pasties stuck to her bared breasts. A stunning, vibrant sapphire necklace hugged her collar bone.

"Lydia!" She blurted, and her sister laughed, sauntering toward her with a swivel to her hips and an air of arrogant superiority.

"Well, if it ain't Miss High and Mighty. What brings you to Stripper's Row? Lookin' to make a switch from the ladies department at Macy's? I heard Club Samoa is hiring a few girls."

The seventeen-year-old parked herself on the cushioned stool at her vanity and began to remove the blue feather headdress from her short blonde locks. Elizabeth thought her heart would stop at the reality that this was where her sister had been spending her days and nights. No wonder their parents didn't concern themselves. Lydia was most likely bankrolling their booze—keeping them well-stocked, drunk, and blind to her comings and goings.

Some women in the dressing room waited and watched for the heated exchange to mushroom between the two, others slipped out, obviously knowing what would spew from the uninhibited, smart-mouthed girl.

Elizabeth tugged a kimono off the clothing rack and flung it at Lydia. "Cover yourself up!" she demanded.

"What's the matter? Do mine look better than yours? I always knew you were a jealous dame, Lizzy. First fighting with Jane over George, only to find out that I'm the one he wanted all along." Her fingers toyed with the necklace. "I'm the one wearing the sapphires, and what did you get for giving it up in the backseat of Pop's Chrysler?"

Furious, she couldn't suppress her retort, hands flexing beside her, fisting and releasing. "Lydia, you were the last chippie of a long, meaningless line that he used and abused. You were nothing to that smooth talker either, and don't fool yourself into believing otherwise. He was, at the very least, a grifter but most likely a kidnapper and murderer. Be thankful you didn't end up dead like Mary King."

"He didn't kill Mary. Anyway ... It doesn't matter now."

"It will *always* matter. As our friend, her disappearance will always matter."

"Who are you kidding? You just feel guilty because you were mad at her for going off with George after he dumped you!"

Elizabeth took a much-needed breath trying to calm herself before indulging the impulse to slap her sister. Her eyes settled on the image of Wickham in his uniform. "I'm curious, sister dear, now that *he's* dead, I don't see *you* crying. Why is that?"

Coldly, her sister snapped the photograph from the edge of the mirror and tore it into little pieces. "Yesterday's news. Why are you here, Lizzy?"

How could she answer honestly? The girl would clam up for sure, and there was more to Lydia's flippancy over his death than met the eye.

"I'm here to take you home, *Dixie*."

She grabbed her sister's earlobe, pinching it hard between her fingertips, and yanking her up from the seat. Her voice was cold and steely. "Get dressed before I call Pop to come and scrape your nude backside off the floor. Do *not* monkey around with me. I am not above smacking you like you well deserve."

Lydia blanched at the words "call Pop." Their drunken parents still provided every reason for her to be fearful if they were faced with the immorality of their daughters. Not even their mother would look the other way should she discover that her youngest (second most-loved daughter) was a stripper—and floozy. The girl promptly shoved her arms into the robe then jutted her chin.

Elizabeth laughed sardonically. "Yeah. I thought you'd react that way. What did you tell them you were doing every day?"

Looking away, Lydia replied. "They think I'm a hat check girl at the Latin Quarter. I bring them a bottle of hooch from the bar after each shift and they don't say a thing."

A groan escaped Elizabeth's throat when Lydia removed the fringed tassel nipple covers. She cringed at the sight of her young sister's pebbled peaks looking raw and dark from the necessary accessory. "Look at what you're doing to yourself."

"Mind your business."

"You are my business. I want an honest answer, Lydia. What's all this talk about Cuba when you were up at El Barrio?"

"What? Are you spying on me? You think you're the law or a private eye or something?"

As expected, Lydia turned her back to Elizabeth. Stripping out of her "costume," she dropped the robe from her shoulders. "That's none of your beeswax anyway."

"Do you know who Georgiana Darcy is?"

Lydia spun around to face her sister, naked as a jay bird with only the necklace sparkling against her alabaster skin. The hand petulantly installed upon her hip matched the tone of her voice when she barked. "I don't know anyone by that name. Now, beat it while I change my clothes. Otherwise, I'm not going anywhere with you!"

••

ELEVEN

Turnabout was fair play at one o'clock in the morning when Elizabeth stood at the door of the Darcy's sixth-floor suite at the Dakota Apartments. Thank goodness for her private eye badge and a brilliant smile—alright—she'd used some other skills—like a little flirting to gain access, but she considered this visit necessary.

She was bone tired from the revelations at the Kit Kat and the stress of sneaking Lydia out of the club unseen by the police. A combustive cab ride with her petulant sister did not help matters. And neither did her arrival at her parents' home in Jackson Heights; none other than Miss Pregnant Priss Jane was also on the scene.

The only thing she desired was a hot bath. But her day wasn't done. She'd force a second wind and summon the indomitable night owl PI persona. She must. She owed it to Darcy to warn him that his sister's name came up in her investigation and deliver the news that Wickham was dead. Oh, yeah, then there was that little detail of trying to ascertain the beefcake's whereabouts during today's lunch rush at the Kit Kat.

Before ringing the buzzer, she smoothed a lipstick over her lips. Cherry red was blotted with a pop before the makeup tube slid into her coat pocket and her index finger depressed the button. She wondered if a butler would answer. Would Darcy be angry for her intrusion at this hour? Most likely. And, being a private man, he would probably not appreciate her not-so-subtle questioning of Charlie in order to acquire his address. What was a girl to do? The City Directory yielded nothing.

She unbuttoned her coat and waited, anxiously staring at the wood door, palms sweating. She wanted to see him—desperately. And not just because of the case, but because of how they'd left things between them—the things he had said, alluded to, the way he made her feel both inside and out. All of it left her unhinged, and when faced with two bloody corpses, her sister's defiance, and her drunken parents, her mind repeatedly gravitated to Darcy and how she desired to forget it all in his strong arms.

When the door opened, he stood on the opposite side, looking a bedraggled mess. His dark hair was unkempt, exaggerating the frown lines of his brow, which softened slightly as their eyes met. He wore a white tank T-shirt that exposed his hard body, toned shoulders and chest—and an incredibly sexy eagle tattoo across his left bicep. In appreciation, she drank in every taut muscle and sinew from his head to bare feet planted on the cold-looking marble flooring. The man was gorgeous even in disarray.

"Oh, it's you," he said with a measure of, what struck her as, wounded disdain.

"Yes. It's me."

"Are you here to return that hat on your head?"

"No. It's mine now." Grinning mischievously, she touched the brim.

He opened the door wider, and she brushed past him into the foyer that seemed too large for an apartment in Gotham. In fact, the foyer alone was the size of her entire apartment. It was a showplace: opulent, but frigid and lifeless.

"I'm sorry to show up at this hour, but I needed to discuss something important with you."

"I thought I made myself clear last night, there's nothing to discuss."

His tone made her fidget; her hands wrung together anxiously. "I know what you said, but today at the ... I ... um ... listen, can I have a drink? Something stronger than soda water," she blurted. Hesitant to begin with the news, she was unable to pronounce the words: *Someone murdered George Wickham. Was it you?*

Darcy ran a hand through his hair. "I thought you didn't drink?"

"I don't, but tonight I need one and I'm outta smokes, too."

"I didn't know the Dakota had been turned into a liquor store."

He stepped into the center of the foyer, turned from her, leaving her standing alone with only the view of his disappearing back—and exquisite backside.

"Aren't you going to take my coat and hat?" she asked.

"The butler is off for the night. Hang it yourself or leave."

"Are you deliberately being a sourpuss?" she called after him.

"Yes," reverberated back into the stark entry way.

Sighing, she considered that maybe this wasn't such a good idea after all, but she hurried after him nonetheless. Black heels clicked on the marble as they followed his wake leading her to an elegantly appointed drawing room. Darkened but for a low fire glowing in the grate and a dismal green banker's lamp, there was eeriness to the room; the furnishings and a tapestry on the wall were barely illuminated. Heavy draperies covered floor-to-ceiling windows. As evident by the half-empty decanter and a partially filled snifter on the coffee table, Darcy had been drinking. Only the amber liquor glowed brightly from the scant firelight.

"I'm sorry I woke you," she said, her gaze fixing on his severe mien, unable to tear her eyes from him and his powerful energy.

"You didn't wake me. I couldn't sleep."

"Are you alone? I mean ... is your sister at home?"

"No, she's traveling. I expect her back tomorrow."

He poured her a glass of whatever it was that he had been drinking, then walked around the sofa to hand her the crystal snifter, waiting for her to finish removing her outerwear. "I didn't expect to see you again," he said flatly, scrutinizing her every movement.

His gaze burned her flesh as she removed the hat, placing it on the hunt table beside the door.

"I hadn't intended on coming here, but the events of the day, the things I saw ..."

He looked so endearing the way he listened to her, giving her all his attention but clearly struggling with his justified anger from the night before. She walked to his outstretched arm and finally took the glass. "We didn't leave things in a good way last night and I want to apologize."

His eyes narrowed, his stare now chastising her with unspoken words but she pressed on.

"I'm sorry I led you on, and I regret that you left my apartment believing my intentions ... my actions last night... were different from what they really were."

She took a deep drink of the brandy, reveling in the warmth of the fine liquor as it slid down her throat, hoping it would calm her nerves. Giving voice to her emotions—especially to a man, particularly this man—was new, but, like the liquor, it was necessary. Putting aside gross affluence, involvement with Wickham, and political aspirations, Darcy was everything she wanted in a man. She sensed from the very beginning that like the demure Elizabeth Bennet hiding beneath her bold life as a private eye, Darcy's own persona was merely a construct. Below his reserved exterior hid a man craving passion and excitement.

"And what was your purpose?" he asked moving closer to her, examining her face. "What were your true intentions when you let me touch you like that? Kiss you like that?"

She looked away, unable to meet his heated gaze. "I had only one purpose."

"Yes?"

Overcoming the growing knot in her throat, she swallowed hard. "The dream of making the impossible, possible. A wishful thought that despite both of us having our reservations, something could still develop between us, something more than falling into bed."

She looked up and even in the dim light she could see his eyes grow dark with desire written in his expression. His lips parted slightly when he took another step to her. Her breath caught, her confidence teetering.

"I'm afraid that if I kiss you, Elizabeth, you'll bite me," his voice was husky, the scent of sweet liquor tickling her senses.

"I won't hurt you. I promise. I want ..." she panted; her breath was ragged with anticipation. "I want ..."

"Tell me." He removed the glass from her hand then placed it beside the hat, his eyes never leaving hers as he willed her to say what respectable women never did.

"Why are you really here, Elizabeth? What do you want tonight?"

She wanted to be honest and free—to give in to her desires and emotions. "I wanted to be with you tonight. I ... I want to continue what we started last night."

Darcy wrapped his arm around her waist, pulling her against his firm chest. "Is that the liquor talking?"

"No. I have a clear head. I know exactly what I'm saying and what I want and from whom. And I know exactly why I want it from you. Now tell *me*—what is it that *you* want? In spite of your doubts, why did you come to me last night?"

His fingers wove through her long waves as his face lowered to hers. There was a spellbinding thrill to his touch, his lips inches from hers as he whispered. "You were wrong. It wasn't because I thought you cheap and that I could charm you into bed so easily. It was because never in my life have I felt the way I do when you walk into a room. My world lights up from your mere presence. The golden sparks in your eyes ignite my soul. Your laughter caresses my heart. What I want is to have … tonight … and every night with you because there is something between us that I cannot deny. I want to hear my name from your lips as I hold you in my arms."

"A poet *and* a charmer—and I believe both of them are accurate portrayals of your true nature. You, Darcy, are no smooth operator by design, but a very successful one nonetheless. Now, shut your yap, and kiss me."

His lips met hers tenderly, slowly building in intensity as he savored every intoxicating movement her mouth made in tandem with his. Elizabeth was born to be kissed by him alone, and he groaned when he pulled her even closer to his body, wrapping his arms around her. Their tongues met, and her small purr of delight reverberated against his chest. She tasted like a sweet elixir, and he was drunker than before her arrival, his head reeling from the feel of her hands traveling up his shoulders, brushing into his hair. Her tongue gliding against his drove him nuts, but when her calf wrapped around his, sliding downward, he lost reason.

He didn't want this kiss to end, wanting to take her right there beside the fire on the bear skin rug. Already, his body was responding ardently, his arousal growing as hot and ready as it had been in her office.

She surprised him when her fingers thread through his as their lips separated. Elizabeth was wasting no time, leading him to the fireplace, her thoughts mirroring his.

"Here. I want you here," her breathy voice panted before her mouth met his again, gently tugging on his bottom lip.

He groaned and unzipped her dress in a slow peel. The careful descent of the metal was sheer torture for he wanted nothing more than to tear the clothing from her.

Navy fabric slid down her long legs, pooling at high heels, and he stepped back, admiring her shapely form in the firelight. Yeah, she was a vixen. Her voluptuous bosom spilled from a black strapless brassiere and a garter girdle accentuated her narrow waist, both made him absolutely nuts. An ivory handled ladies pistol hid tucked in a black leather strap holster at the top of jet stockings. Femme fatale—just as he first imagined.

The pistol holster, too, dropped to her feet.

"Do you like what you see, Darcy?"

"I do. You're stunning."

Her lips twisted at his appreciation as she stepped over the discarded dress and sashayed toward him, her hand rising, then smoothing around his tattoo. "I like this," she cooed depositing a languid kiss to his bicep. "It's exciting."

"It was foolhardy."

"I don't think so. It's sexy. You're sexy," she said sliding her hands under his T-shirt, lifting it slowly over his chest and head until it dropped to the floor.

She was taking control tonight, just as he had taken control the night before, making her quiver in his arms. Yeah. She would make *him* quiver.

Elizabeth kissed his chest, trailing nips and pecks to his shoulder, and he breathed in her scent; her hair smelled like fresh summer rain. His eager hands slid down the satin confines of her bottom.

"Will you undress for me, Elizabeth? I'm afraid, I may rush things. I don't think I can get you out of your undergarment without tearing it off." He literally heard the ferocity of his heartbeat when she chuckled, and he felt as he had when a horny teenager.

"There's no need for me to undress."

"I assure you, there is."

Then she did it. What he had dreamt of every night since seeing her at the Kit Kat: she unzipped his trousers, dropping them and his boxers to his feet. She kissed him again, evading his full staff throbbing with anticipation only inches away from her hand. His burning tip brushed against the satin at her hip.

She stepped back from him and he felt bereft.

Just as he had done, she admired him, her index finger tapping those beckoning siren lips. Her eyes scanned up and down settling on his manhood.

"Do you like what *you* see, Elizabeth?"

"Very much. I think you'll do just fine."

He stepped from the fabric and reached for her, pulling her into his bare body. "I thought you don't go to bed with just any man?" he couldn't help teasing, reciprocating her playfulness.

Finally. Her hand surrounded his shaft, stroking him with a lethal grip.

"You, obviously, aren't just any man." She smiled then kissed his chin, followed by an impertinent push, signaling him to sit on the sofa. The vixen placed her hands on her hips and moved to stand between his legs.

Sprawled and ready for domination, his eyes met hers. There was fire there, burning in those liquid amber sparks. His arousal twitched for her to see, to tease her, to arouse her for what was to come; he wanted to give everything to her, love her, and hear her moan his name.

"Will you undress now?" he asked.

With a reach behind her back the black bra fell to the floor.

Now he was dying. The woman was an ignited fuse and he had a stick of dynamite about to blow.

"Why are you smirking?" she asked stepping toward him, first placing one knee beside his hip and then the other. Kneeling over his straining erection, her dark waves cascaded around them, her plump lips looking ready to devour him. He immediately reacted to the tantalizing sight of her magnificent breasts dangling over him and cupped them with both hands, squeezing and pinching those berried nipples that he couldn't wait to taste. "I'm smirking ..." he said.

His thumbs brushed over her hardened peaks and she moaned, throwing back her head in exaltation.

"I'm smirking because after I get you out of that contraption, I'm going to love you like you've never been loved before."

She kissed him hungrily.

The girdle was crotchless. The surprise sensation of her slick heat engulfing his erection was the most erotic, sublime feeling he ever had. Both cried out when flesh joined flesh, when heat penetrated heat, when her wetness consumed him. She purred, "Yes," as though she had waited a lifetime to go to bed with him.

Elizabeth moved upon his lap with controlled passion, but her lips raged against his. She was hungry and unfettered; her hands gripped his shoulders coaxing each rise and fall.

He cupped her face, their lips parted, eyes locked as he thrust upward into her. He loved watching her unbridled release. The passionate flush to her cheeks increased with each breathy pant emitted, orchestrated by every ferric thrust. *He* was doing this to her. She leaned back with hands threading through her hair when she arched, rocking her hips against him wildly, the heels of her shoes stabbing at his legs delivering the best kind of pain.

Craving her nipple between his lips, he slightly rose and pulled one into his mouth—nibbling it with love bites, toying with it as she rode him without inhibition, crying out in the firelight.

She was ready and so was he, but it was too soon. He wanted all of her: heart and soul. He wanted to savor every erotic movement, every wet motion, needing to peel back her many layers until she was as bare as he felt—until she was his.

Grabbing her waist, he pulled them both to the floor, lying on her, crushing her body below his.

Slowly, he ground his hips into her. "I want you out of this girdle, vixen," he groaned, needing to feel her soft flesh below him.

"Are you ... taking control now?" she panted, reaching around her bottom to unzip the girdle.

"It's not about control. It's about freedom, yours and mine."

"I do feel ... liberated."

He slid from her and rose to his knees, removed her high heels then peeled the form-fitting undergarment still attached to her stockings from her body, thrilling at the soft silken feel of her shapely legs as the nylon slowly came off. She laid there before him, her flushed skin tickled by the licking flames in the grate, her dark tresses spread out on the white fur. His breath caught at the image she presented and the naked desire in her eyes. She wanted *him* when she could have anyone with a mere come hither glance.

Elizabeth couldn't stop the giggle that escaped, seeing Darcy kneeling over her with that sappy look upon his face, his massive erection poised for absolute, welcomed destruction of her impenetrable walls. The man was not only physical perfection but had succeeded in capturing her heart on every level.

"What are you thinking?" she asked.

"You know what I'm thinking."

He lay beside her, resting on his elbow as he gazed down at her. One hand trailed a sensual path down between her breasts to her abdomen as he spoke with such tender regard. "Of all the fellas, why me, Elizabeth?"

"Because we're the same. There's balance in us when we're together. I feel safe and understood in your arms. I trust you 100%. From that first moment when you walked into the Kit Kat, I knew you were the guy for me."

"Could there be a future between us? A real future?"

With teasing boldness, she took his meandering fingers and placed them on her sex. She spread her legs when they ran through her pubis. "I'll let you know, Darcy."

As arousing as his fingertips felt exploring her folds, it made her writhe for more, her legs suddenly restless, aching to wrap around his waist. She arched, meeting each titillating stroke. His lips wordlessly made love, moving against hers with so much emotion that she had no reservations about what they did.

"Please, Darcy. I need you in me. Give it all to me and don't hold back."

"Oh, I won't hold back. I've waited a lifetime for you," he assured rolling onto her, hands gripping her hips.

He filled her deeply with a slow entrance, the base of his shaft rubbing against her pearl. She'd never felt that before, never experienced sex without barriers of fabric or insecurity, without the influence of alcohol. Their nude bodies glided upon one another, perspiring and clinging with each powerful plunge he made.

She gripped his bicep as he thrust deeper, pounding flesh in passionate slaps against her sex. Her walls clenched around him, quivering each time his manhood touched something deep inside. That, too, was new. *Oh God! Is this what an intercourse-induced orgasm feels like?* It was only the buildup to his growing intensity, both their need to explode rapidly increasing. Her heart thundered and breath labored as her purrs grew to mews of rapture.

Darcy cried out, "Say it, Elizabeth. Say my name!"

"Yes! Darcy Yes! Oh God! Fitzwilliam!"

Her reality spun then everything flashed white. Their bodies shuddered as Darcy groaned in absolute pleasure before collapsing onto her.

Their chests rose and fell against the other with the same ferocity. He kissed her shoulder then neck, until finally his lips found hers, panting.

"Stay the night," he whispered and she couldn't help teasing him, feeling euphoric.

"Do you have silk bed sheets?"

He grinned. "Yes. And a hot bubble bath to soothe you."

"Will you join me?"

"That's my plan."

Yeah. Darcy was a real gentleman and she kissed his smiling lips, letting him know she thought so.

••

TWELVE

In Darcy's opulent, art deco master bathroom, Elizabeth leaned against his chest in the marble tub. His legs surrounded her body like a warm, strong cocoon. They'd had sex twice, unable to keep their hands or bodies from exploring new heights of rapture and expressive passion. There was no doubt he had succeeded in engaging her heart. She felt delightfully content—scratch that—positively lulu in spite of the disturbing topic of conversation looming in her conscience. Although the water had cooled tepid, she had no desire to leave the tub, no desire to discuss the things she knew she should.

"You're not such a sourpuss, after all," she joked.

He nibbled her ear from behind in retort, then whispered. "And you're not as tough a private eye as you try to convey."

"You're right. I'm a sap at heart, a real pushover when it comes down to romance."

His hand caressed down her arm, until his fingers found hers. He raised them to his lips, depositing a kiss before speaking. "I'm sorry for last night, my wrongful assumptions and accusations."

"I would have thought the same. You're forgiven."

She took a deep drag of her cigarette followed by a thoughtful exhale of release. "Darcy, have you had many lovers?"

"I've had my share, but not for some time."

"Martha Roarke?"

"And how do you know about Martha?"

"It was in the gossip column in *Variety*—so I'm told."

"So you did a little snooping around on me, did you?" He tickled her and she giggled, squirming against him as the water splashed and sloshed around them.

"Just ... a little."

"Most gossip rags implied that she was my lover, and God knows she tried, but I never slept with her. I'm very selective with whom I share my bed. I wasn't always that way ... but I was young."

She laughed. "Glad I made the grade."

"And then some." He kissed her wet head. "You shouldn't ask such questions."

"Why not? I want to know everything about you. I'm not upset that you had other lovers before me. I assume a dreamboat like you has had very many."

"I wouldn't say very many. How about you? While I don't think you had many, I know I wasn't your first."

"No. You weren't." Here was her opportunity, but did she have the nerve to take it? Her free hand rubbed his knee below the water and she took a deep breath. "There was one other. A real smooth operator—a swindler—who came to our neighborhood in Queens in 1950. Everyone in town loved him—maybe I thought I did too. He talked a good talk, leading me on with sweet nothings before taking my virginity following a local dance at the American Legion Post. I was drunk, and apart from his touch feeling so cold and empty, I don't remember much of it. For that, I'm thankful. Suffice it to say, your touch and experiencing the throes of passion with you are entirely different. To him, I was just one of a long line of girls in town, another was my best friend, the last and final was my youngest sister, Lydia, which I discovered this afternoon.

He's the reason Jane and I don't talk, and she is one of the reasons I was so susceptible to his attention."

"I'm so sorry, baby. What happened to the rat bastard?"

"He was murdered at the Kit Kat Klub this afternoon, a bullet to his temple, just below a jagged scar."

She paused, hoping he would ask something, even flinch, but he did neither, so she continued.

"After I met with Detective Brandon from homicide, I could only think of one place I wanted to be—and that was here, in your arms. I needed to tell you, but we obviously both had more pressing needs tonight."

Again, she waited for anything he was willing to give up. His only response was to kiss her head for a second time. Silence fell heavily, and she flicked her cigarette into the crystal ashtray on the small table beside them before taking another drag. Questions swirled in her mind: Had Darcy killed Wickham? Did he know whom she referred to? Had he suspected it was the bad hat of her inquiry? Surely the mention of that striptease club was a tip off, yet Darcy didn't take the bait.

"C'mon, let's get out. The water has cooled," he finally said, clutching her waist to help her rise from the bubbly water.

Nude, she unabashedly stood over his submerged body and searched his face. "Aren't you going to ask who he was?"

"I don't need to, Elizabeth. Don't insult my intelligence. I can put two and two together."

"He's dead, Darcy. The man of our mutual acquaintance is dead. Acknowledge that."

He rose from the water, rivulets rolling down his muscular physique, remnant bubbles clinging to his chest and pubic hair.

"I heard you," he replied tonelessly, his face now set in impenetrable stone as he removed a towel from the rail warmer, dried her shoulders and bosom, then wrapped it around her.

Chilled, she was thankful for the bathroom appliance; the warm towel felt as soothing as lying against Darcy in the bathtub.

She watched as he dried his back, the muscles in his arms flexing with the movement of the towel as it went from side to side. He wrapped it around his waist creating, yet another, sexy sight for her eyes.

They stepped from the bathtub onto the cold white tile and he removed the cigarette from her fingers, taking a drag before snuffing it into the ashtray.

"Don't be sore at me for telling you. You asked about my experience, and just as you were honest, I wanted to be as well," she said.

"I'm not mad. I *hate* him for hurting you, for using you. It guts me to know that animal took something so precious just for his twisted pleasure. That his filth, his hands violated your person, your heart, whether by your consent or drunken manipulation. It makes me sick." He paused furrowing his brow until his lips finally quirked into a tender, wistful smile.

The feel of his hand smoothing her cheek bowled her over and she was surprised to see this intense, brooding man moved to such sentiment by his softened expression.

She reached for his tattoo, sliding her fingers on the wet skin over the eagle. "You knew him from the war, didn't you?"

The telephone down the hall rang, but they both ignored it. His indigo eyes fixed on hers as he considered her question.

"Fitzwilliam ... tell me how you know him."

"You're right. I knew George Wickham in the Navy."

He turned, leaving her in the bathroom to watch his retreating back, but that didn't stop her from following him to the dresser where he decanted the booze, promptly filling two rocks glasses. She switched on the lamp and came up behind him. Trying to soothe the confession from him, she wrapped her arms around his waist, resting her head against his back. He tensed when cheek met chilled flesh, his agony apparent.

"Before I tell you, I need to know what tonight meant to you. You thought me a sourpuss, a man concealing the truth, maybe even a skirt chaser, but what do you feel for me now, Elizabeth?"

Tender pecks against his cool skin gave her vital seconds to choose her words carefully. She wasn't quite ready for that admission. "I have the same question for you. It's not your character I am struggling to sketch but your real intentions. You mentioned a future together. Is that true?"

Darcy abruptly turned to face her. "Dammit, woman. For a private eye, you are certainly blind. Can you not see that I'm in love with you?"

Wacky flips again. Her heart skipped at his passionate declaration. "Well for a man about to run for congress, you're not so smart either. Can you not see that tonight was more than a roll in the hay? I'm in love with you, too, you dimwit."

He chuckled, wrapping his arms around her waist, drawing her to him. "We are quite a pair."

"Yes, we are." Her lips met his in a sweet kiss of reassurance. No. She would never divulge the contents of his confession, even if he had killed Wickham, *especially* if he had killed that scoundrel.

She smoothed over the tattoo again. "You have my word that whatever you tell I'll keep buttoned."

Threading his fingers with hers, he led her to the armchair beside the bed, unknotted her towel, and then held open his dressing gown to her. He kissed her before returning for his brandy.

"Yes. I knew Wickham," he stated, before taking a swig. "He was my C.O., and under his command, I did things that still haunt me."

"It was war, Fitzwilliam. Every soldier did things that went against their fiber. You were all just boys back then, doing as you were told."

Abruptly he turned. "No Elizabeth, that's not what I'm talking about. Yes. I was a boy, an impressionable one hell bent on defying my father and still grieving over the unexpected, tragic death of my mother. I looked up to Wickham and his unchecked behavior, following his poor example as I tasted liberty from *all* this." He swept his hand across the room then began to pace before her.

She held her breath, afraid to move, afraid to distract him.

"I'm tormented by one particular memory from November of 1943 in Nouméa, a naval port in New Caledonia in the South Pacific. A fight broke out over a card game with a Marine. We had all been drinking, but the mugg was a card sharp, cheated at winning my entire bankroll. I punched the lights out of him with one angry swing, but as he fell, his head hit the edge of the bar."

He stopped, ran his hand through his hair then sighed deeply. "Wickham confirmed that his neck snapped on impact."

She gasped.

"Yes. I had killed a man and Wickham and I fled the scene to avoid arrest and an eventual firing squad. Later that night, he went back to the bar to confirm, make sure the situation was calm, maybe pay off a few local witnesses, if necessary. The next day, our ship left for the Solomon Islands."

"Maybe you didn't—"

"I did! I killed a man, and I was at El Barrio because Wickham was trying to blackmail me in the hopes of ruining my political career, my sister's future! Later, I followed him everywhere just to be sure that he stayed clear of her. I tailed him to the Kit Kat—the night you saw me there—attempting to build a strong case to present to the military for his court-martial."

"Because he was AWOL."

"Yes. I hoped to uncover further evidence of his criminal activities."

He stopped pacing then turned to her. "Why were *you* following him?"

She exhaled. "I think he kidnapped and murdered my best friend."

"I hate to say it, but you're probably right."

"But now I'll never know."

Darcy walked to her then knelt on the floor at her feet, resting his head on her legs. Wanting to weep for him, she ran her fingers through his damp hair to comfort him. "I'll never tell a soul what you shared, but given what we know of the man, you must consider that he most likely lied to you—like he lied to everyone about everything."

"I wish it were true. God, I wish it were true."

"Fitzwilliam?"

He looked up, a tell-tale glassiness to his eyes stabbed at her heart.

"Did you kill Wickham?" she asked, terrified of his answer.

"Do ... do you think I did?"

"I don't know, but the police asked ... I lied that you knew him." Her own eyes flooded with tears. "But if you did kill him, I'm glad you did it. I may never find Mary, and I may never get back that girl I once was, but I'm glad he got waxed, glad that he won't hurt or use another girl."

She slid off the edge of the chair onto Darcy's lap, holding onto him tightly. Her palms cupped his flushed cheeks as she whispered, "Tell me."

"No. I didn't kill him, but I wanted to. If he went near my sister, then I would have."

"Where *is* Georgiana?"

He furrowed his brow. "How do you know her name?"

"Detective Brandon told me. Where is she, Darcy." *Please don't say Cuba.*

"She's vacationing with friends in Havana. Why?"

"Oh no!"

"What's the matter, Elizabeth?"

She rose from his still-toweled lap, leaving him on the floor. "Where's your telephone?"

"What is it?" Terror ran through him like lightning, his body suddenly coursing with fright. He rose from the floor then stormed to her, demanding, "Tell me!"

"Your phone, Darcy! Where is it?"

"It's in the study, down the hall. Who do you need to call at this hour?" Gripping fingers clasped her shoulders and he shook her. "I want an answer. Now! What is this about?"

Anguished words blurted from her. "That night at the Kit Kat, I witnessed an exchange between Wickham and a Soviet."

"I remember. I saw it, too."

"I pick-pocketed what Wickham gave the Ruskie."

"I saw that as well."

"I only found out this afternoon that it was a photograph of Georgiana along with a slip of paper that read the Hotel Nacional de Cuba in Havana."

Darcy dropped his arms from her and stepped back, his heart almost stopping; a cold perspiration overcame his bare flesh.

"Is that where she's staying?" Elizabeth asked, alarm evident in her voice.

Panicked, he barked at her, causing her to step back. "Yes! Why didn't you tell me when you first arrived?"

"Because you didn't give me a chance! How was I to know she was in Cuba? As of ten minutes ago, I considered you a suspect in Wickham's murder!"

He stormed to his rocks glass, downing the remaining liquid before angrily smashing the glass against the wall.

"Darcy, I understand your fear ... your anger with me for not telling you immediately, but you have to admit, you hardly gave me a chance."

Scowling, he turned to face her, examining her earnest expression. Any reflex thought he had, any suspicions he considered about her using him for information about Wickham dissipated as quickly as they surfaced. He trusted her and she had trusted him—giving herself to him —exposing her heart. She was right. The power of his emotions and her allure had prompted his almost immediate response to her declaration of wanting to be with him. Hanging his head, he quietly said, "I'm sorry, Elizabeth."

The telephone rang again, and Darcy bolted past her through the doorway. His bare feet ran over the cold marble toward the study, hoping against hope that Georgiana was telephoning.

He picked up the receiver.

"Darcy," was all he could manage, his throat constricting in agony.

"Mr. Fitzwilliam Darcy?" the Russian man on the other end of the line asked.

"Yes."

"I have something precious of yours."

Darcy stiffened ramrod, his voice lowering as it did with Wickham at El Barrio. "I'm listening."

"She is beautiful girl. You would not want harm to her, no?"

He gripped the edge of the desk. "If you hurt her ..."

"Not if you cooperate."

Elizabeth came to him, soothing her hand along his back, but it did nothing to calm the anguish. The darkness of the room and the unfolding conversation felt suffocating. Ominous. He turned to face her, their eyes gazing deep into each other.

"Where is she? I want to talk with my sister!"

"She is safe ... for now."

"What is it you want? I'll pay you anything. Anything!"

"Yes. You will, and you will start by announcing run for government seat."

"What?"

"That is correct. Then there is matter of money, which you will deliver to my associate at Kit Kat Klub. One hundred thousand American dollars. He will give instructions for remainder of trust fund."

"What trust fund?"

"Do not lie. Twenty million dollars."

"I'm not sure I can access what you need."

"I will not warn a second time."

He ran his hand through his hair, his face contorting. "Fine and ... and how will I know your comrade at the Kit Kat Klub?"

Elizabeth shook her head, motioning with a slicing finger across her neck but he concentrated on the telephone call, his heart hammering, perspiration beading upon his brow.

"He will know you. Tomorrow, noon. Be alone, no *politsiya*." The thug hung up and Darcy stood immobile, unable to move or think. Helpless.

"What did they say?" Elizabeth asked.

"They have Georgiana. They want one hundred thousand and her trust fund. I'm to meet their comrade at the Kit Kat, tomorrow."

"The Soviet. He's dead, too. I guess word hasn't traveled to Cuba yet, but there were two victims at the club. One was Wickham, the other ... our Russian from Monday night."

She switched the desk lamp on, examining Darcy's face set like stone. Wiping his brow, she said, "Let me call Detective Brandon; he's a friend. He can help us, maybe get information from the Central Investigation Bureau at the NYPD. They have a Red squad."

"No police. I can't run the risk of those Commies hurting Georgiana or the police discovering my past."

"Your past died with Wickham."

"How do I know that Wickham didn't sell that out too? No, Elizabeth. I'll do as they ask. Georgiana's life is at stake!"

"How can you do as they want? The man you're supposed to meet with has been murdered, and his killer is still on the lam."

He took her hand in his, reduced to nothing and needing her more than he cared to admit—even to himself. This doll had done the unthinkable, broken him. "I don't know where to find her, but I'm going to Havana. Come with me," he said.

She nodded, then kissed his lips sweetly. "We'll find her, together."

They turned from the desk and Elizabeth glanced up at the portrait above the fireplace. She suddenly halted.

"That's my mother," he said forlornly, ashamed that he had failed to protect Georgiana.

"Those sapphires ... are they Georgiana's now?"

"Yeah."

"Well someone else is wearing them."

"How can that be? She took them to Havana with her."

"Yes, and George Wickham brought them back. We need to get to Jackson Heights immediately."

••

THIRTEEN

The sleek contours inside and out of Darcy's Coupe de Ville were as sexy as he was, particularly when that brooding expression was back in place. Strangely, Elizabeth found his hard-boiled look extremely attractive. Seated beside him on the front seat, she attempted to control the inappropriately timed wanderings of her mind and suppress the visceral reaction of her body recalling his touch only an hour before. She glanced over at him behind the wheel; those same strong hands gripping the leather had clutched her backside when she sat upon him, rocking toward orgasm. She couldn't help the slight sigh that escaped her lips. Their intimacies were just as she had always dreamed her lover would perform, but with Darcy, it was so much more. Not only was he tender and attentive to her needs inside the bedroom, but outside, he listened and joked and was a surprising conversationalist. This man was everything she hoped for and she was in love.

Freezing rain turned the Queensboro Bridge icy and the drive into Queens tense. Few cars were on the Bridge as they entered; lone sets of headlights blurred in the teaming pelts at the beginning of the East River. On the opposite side of the bridge, the vibrant red neon Silvercup Bread sign signaled the gateway to Queens from Manhattan. In the silence of the vehicle, the repetitive thump of the wiper blades sounded like the beat of a funeral drum against the glass.

Her mind wandered in the silence, morosely settling on the disturbing thought that her friend Mary never had the experience of real love. It saddened her that Mary's death could never be solved, and she looked over to Darcy for comfort. He raised a cigarette to his lips, waves of gray smoke floated around his lips like a menacing fog. He was just as troubled as she. They were two sides of the same coin.

Elizabeth rubbed her hands together since the Cadillac's heater did nothing to warm the chill brought on by so much more than the winter weather. She furrowed her brow, watching the passing waterscape as Darcy drove with focused control over the vehicle and metal structure. She knew his thoughts were worrisome especially when he stamped out the cigarette then reached for her hand, grasping it in his. A quick glance in her direction revealed a gentle smile of admiration.

"My fedora looks good on you," he stated.

She touched the brim with her free hand and beamed mischievously, feeling so self-satisfied at having stolen the hat without a modicum of guilt. "Yes. It sure does. Thanks."

Silence again. Long seconds passed until he squeezed her fingers. "They want me to run for Congress."

"That's what you want right?"

"Yes, but I think they have plans. My outspoken support of the House Un-American Activities Committee obviously hurts the Soviets hiding in plain sight on American soil. Perhaps they believe that Georgiana's kidnapping could turn me."

"It wouldn't be the first time a government official was strong-armed."

He squeezed her hand tighter, swearing in anguish. "Damn! Sorry. I shouldn't curse so in your company."

"I've heard worse; I've said worse. This is a 'damn' moment."

"Tell me everything is going to be alright," he pleaded.

His vulnerability surprised her. This strong, powerful man, whom she had no doubt would care for her in all manner, needed *her* reassurance. Her heart swelled. Apart from her clients, no one needed her—except, of course, Kitty, but she only wanted her money.

"It will be. Lydia will give up the sapphires and any information she has. With any luck, my parents are sleeping it off after tying one on. If Pop wakes, he's a fearsome sight when he's lit up. Faced with the information of my sister's new career, I don't think she'll be such a smart mouth."

She observed his jaw muscles flex and release before he swallowed. "He was drunk at Charlie and Jane's wedding."

"He always is, as well as my mother. They drink the profits from the garage. Not even my sister Mary's prayers in the nunnery will sober them up."

"Right. I remember her at the wedding, too. Charlie's sister Caroline laughed at her all night."

"Of course, she did. That dame is a lush, too."

"And a thorn in my side."

"Ah, understandably so. You're one of New York's most eligible bachelors."

"Where'd you hear that?"

"A friend of mine."

"Hmm. So about your parents ... is that why you didn't attend the wedding?"

She glanced out the window, eyes settling on the inactive trolley track beside them. "One of the reasons."

It seemed a natural topic of conversation to get his mind off the matters at hand. She didn't mind. Darcy had previously demonstrated that he was a compassionate man; his concern for her was evident in slight, but meaningful, actions. It was only logical that he'd focus on her. That is if she could continue to keep his mind occupied. They had driven in silence for too long and, no doubt, his mind was over working.

"And the reason you left home?" he interrupted her musing.

"In part. Jackson Heights was a dead end for a girl like me. We briefly talked about this at the Copa, but what I didn't tell you was that after the war, I had *convinced* myself that I wasn't the marrying type. It was just as well. I had no desire to be that type of homemaker Jane became. I wanted more for myself than what society dictated following the war. It altered so much, yet everything went back to the way things were with a focus on family. Before 1945, I had once wanted marriage and a passel of children, but ..." she shrugged. "Things changed."

"What changed?"

"My sweetheart came home married to another woman."

"Ah, I see. So you *don't* want marriage now?"

"Now? I didn't say that. It depends on which fella is asking," she flippantly joked as the Cadillac officially entered Queens—the "other side" of the East River.

He smiled softly, his thumb brushing the pad of her hand. "And what about Bennet Private Investigations?"

"I opened up because of my best friend's disappearance. Given my love of crime fiction, I thought it could be a swell profession for me as I continued to look for her. Everyone said she had run away, but I know Mary, and she would never have left Jackson Heights."

"So you love being a gumshoe?"

She couldn't help beaming with pride. "I do! Bet you wouldn't expect a girl like me to be a crack shot, either, but I am—thanks to Brandon."

Darcy finally chuckled and that made her feel so much better.

"*And* you have a good head for figures," he said followed by a wink.

"Yeah, that, too. I'm not loaded, but I do alright."

"I'll help you invest what you have; don't worry about that. I was, actually ... um, toying with you when I said I couldn't help you."

"Yeah. I knew it."

"This Brandon gee, he hasn't ... you know ... tried anything?"

"Chris? He talks a good talk, always flirts, but he's a good egg just like you. He'd never try anything." She examined his profile; his expression looked relieved by her admission. "But Darcy ... I was meant to be your girl all along."

"Yeah. You were, baby."

He squeezed her hand, tugging on her arm to slide her body beside him on the seat. His beefy physique was warm against hers, and he slipped his hand under her coat, placing it upon her knee, his thumb caressing the nylon stocking in slow circles. "I'm sorry I barked at you earlier. My temper rises too quickly."

"I understand, Darcy. In my line of work, I see all kinds of reactions to bad news. Yours was no different. I'm used to being in the firing line."

"I'm glad you were there when I got the phone call. Thank you for calming me down," he said, his voice humbled.

"Sure. I know you're a softie at heart."

"I am in love with you, Elizabeth. I didn't lie about that."

"I know that, too."

"Is that crazy? I mean ... so soon to feel like I do?"

"Then we're both crazy. I never bought into that whole whacky love at first sight mumbo jumbo, but it wouldn't be the first time I was proven wrong." She pointed to the traffic light up ahead. "Make a left on 89th Street."

They turned down another residential city street lined with closed up shops and markets.

She was surprised when Darcy blurted. "You *will* marry me, right?"

Stunned, she nervously laughed. "Is that a rhetorical question?"

"No. It's a bona fide offer. When Georgiana is safe and we get back from Cuba with all this behind us, I don't ever want to part from you, again."

"The wife of a politician? I'm not so sure. I'll have to think about that."

"What's to think about?"

"A lot. What happened to your reservations? I'm a career girl with boozehound parents. Definitely not the type you'd take home to meet your debutante sister, Darcy."

"You're wrong about that. You've got more class than most of those society dames, and you could still be a career girl. We'll take out an ad in the society pages: Mrs. Elizabeth Darcy, private investigator. I'll move you out of that dump in Hell's Kitchen and set you up in a luxury midtown location. You can take your pick, have any office suite you want in any building."

"You didn't even see my office in the light of day. How would you know it's a dump?"

"I notice everything. And that neighborhood is unsafe for you. You can work days and spend your nights with me. We'll take baths and lay beside the fire, go dancing 'til dawn."

The more he went on with cold puffs of breath exiting his mouth in enthusiasm, the quicker panic rose in her. It *was* all too fast, too soon. Declarations of love didn't have to mean shacking up immediately did it? Whatever happened to dating first?

"Whoa there, you big lug. Let's take one step at a time. First we'll get Lydia to flap her lips, then we'll fly to Cuba to get your sister. The rest we'll work out one step at a time."

The vehicle stopped at a red light and he glanced over at her, furrowing his brow, frown set upon that gorgeous puss. She could tell that he didn't accept that answer. A man like him—a moneybags who owned people in addition to half of Gotham—was used to getting what he wanted, when he wanted it.

"And another thing, Darcy. That's not the romantic type of proposal girls dream of. So you better come up with something better than 'it's a bona fide offer' if you expect a trip down the aisle with *this* girl." She grinned so as not to upset him and he grunted in reply, returning to driving. "Turn left at the next light. The house is the second one on the right. Oh, and I want a ring, too."

He felt an embarrassed burn to his cheeks, feeling like a buffoon. She was right; Elizabeth deserved more romance than *a bona fide offer*, and she deserved his mother's seven-carat diamond ring.

The pleasant tree-lined street of brick row homes was beginning to ice over as the temperature dropped with the falling rain. Stark branches bent from the accumulated ice, glistening in the dim light of the occasional street lamp. He would have thought it magical if he allowed the reflection on their beauty. The very fact that he was on this street, at this hour, kept his mind occupied with dread and fury, not to mention great disappointment in his sister's deception. If only he had listened to his gut when she lied to him before leaving on holiday. If only he had told both her and the military all about George Wickham. Regrettably, he had tried to cover his own hide and protect her genteel sensibilities. And for what? What a mess.

The one positive thing he tried to focus on was the fact that Elizabeth had declared her heart to him. She had been as surprised as he by that half-assed proposal, but truly, he couldn't imagine a life without her now the he found her.

He parked at the curb in front a house that looked like every other, only the Bennet home had a blue star flag hanging on the small glass panes of the front door. "You don't have any brothers, right?"

"No. Why?"

"That flag is from the last war."

"Oh. My mother must have hung that for Slick Wick since she believes he's in Korea, *serving his country*."

He cut the engine and shook his head, thinking his ears played a trick on him. "You're pulling my leg, aren't you?

She didn't answer, just fixed her hat and opened the door. "C'mon. I'll tell you about his relationship with my parents on the drive home. It's complicated."

"It always was with Slick Wick," he said morosely, coming around the front of the car to Elizabeth.

In silence, he held her small waist from behind, steadying her in those heels she wore as they gingerly traversed the icy walkway toward the front door. Above them, the oak tree crackled in the breeze under the weight of the ice. Through the front window, he could make out the snow on the television, still on long after viewing hours had ended. It illuminated the room like a beacon on the darkened street.

As she put the key into the wood door, she turned and whispered. "You stay in the parlor. I'll go up, and let's hope to God she's there since the Kit Kat has closed."

The house smelled like vodka, cigarettes, and musty curtains: his stomach roiled at the noxious scent. He walked past the coats hooked on the rack and caught the odor of moth balls and a greasy spoon diner. Already, he hated that Elizabeth grew up in this house. However, in spite of the odor, he could see in the television-induced lighting that the homemaker kept a tidy place. Porcelain figurines lined a shelf at the end of the staircase. A newer looking telephone bench was positioned in the hallway, which led to a swinging door that probably opened to the kitchen at the far end. It was a typical home for lower-class Americans, but truth be told, the first time he'd ever stepped foot in one.

Elizabeth pointed to the parlor to their left, and he took her gloved hand in his, pulling her close to him before she ascended the staircase.

Shadow and light played across her strong cheekbones and painted full lips. He kissed her in a tender lip-lock, conveying the appreciation in his heart.

"Stay here." She cautioned again, then caressed his temple, her gentle smile attempting to calm the storm brewing inside him. It worked. This surprising woman knew all the right triggers in him.

The wooden step creaked with her first step up, and those red, kissable lips of hers spread into a grimace.

Yes. It was best if he waited downstairs. No doubt, all hell was about to break loose, but he had confidence that his girl, the crack shot lady dick would ask all the right questions of her sister.

••

Elizabeth quietly opened the door to the room that was once hers, Mary, and Jane's bedroom. Lydia and Kitty's smaller bedroom had been turned into a sewing room by their mother. Not that she sewed much anymore, but during the war, they had all become proficient with a needle and thread. That whole "make do and mend" credo was almost the death of Jane who loved her fashion—vain creature that she is.

Heavy perfume lingered in the air, and the diffused glow of the streetlamp coming through the window curtain provided the only light in the room. Lydia's room was a mess: clothes lay scattered on every available surface; make-up and perfume bottles fought for space on the vanity; and lingerie was draped over the back of the chair. Yet, in many ways, her sister was still a child—magazine photographs of the dreamy, pretty-boy Tab Hunter and covers of *Movie Life* were tacked to the yellow flowered wallpapered walls.

As quickly as the tender feelings for her sister arose, they vanished when her gaze settled on the dresser. *Foolish girl.* Beside a torn up Navy photograph (yet another one) of George Wickham, was a brand new, white Philco radio and what appeared to be a ritzy rhinestone necklace. She shuddered. Was it really fake ice? Maybe it wasn't. Maybe that, too, was Georgiana's jewelry.

A swipe of her gloved hand across the dresser grabbed the necklace then pocketed it, just in case. She tip-toed to her sister's sleeping form then sat on the edge of the bed, her hand pushing at Lydia's hip to wake her. "Lydia, wake up."

The next nudge wasn't so gentle.

"What?" Lydia snapped awake, her mascara-covered lashes clumped together.

"We have to talk."

Lydia pulled the covers over her head, rolling to face the wall. "Telephone me tomorrow. Now get out."

Elizabeth snapped the covers from her sister, pulling them back, exposing her to the chill in the room. "Get up. You and I have something to discuss before the law arrives. Detective Christopher Brandon's going to be here any minute to take you down to police headquarters and book you as a conspirator in the kidnapping of Georgiana Darcy—unless you start flapping your lips."

Yeah. That got her sister's attention, obvious by the way she sat ramrod in bed, pulling her knees to her chest.

"Where are the sapphires George gave you?"

Lydia looked away.

"The ones you wore this afternoon. They're antique, and her brother—the very powerful and influential Fitzwilliam Darcy—is going to press charges against you for theft. Looks like your rap sheet is growing by the minute, sister—unless you're honest with me and turn over the stolen goods."

"They're ... they're in my jewelry box on the vanity. Get what you came for and scram!"

Partial success she thought. She was pleased with the results, but too tired to go on like this all night. She decided to cut to the chase and scare her self-absorbed, petulant sister with a little personal harm.

"Tell me about Cuba."

An obvious snap of her head, wide eyes, and stammer of words alerted Elizabeth that Lydia knew quite a lot about the island and was shocked that her "shop girl" sister was asking ... well, she was surprised that Lizzy was asking *anything* about it.

"I ... I don't know what you're talking about."

"Oh yeah? Wait until I tell that Communist owner down at the seedy strip dive you work at that he has a minor performing as a bump-n-grind girl, and then I'll tell Pop that you've been shaking your bosom all over Strippers Row, not to mention that you probably had a hand in Slick Wick stealing all that dough from the garage. I don't think that pretty face of yours will look so good with a hand print or two on it. So you better start singing."

"You wouldn't dare tell."

Elizabeth raised an eyebrow. Her sister was all figure eights; her polished fingernails tapped the outside of her shin where it clasped her legs. She had a panicked look in her dark eyes, made darker by the pitch of the room.

Elizabeth gripped Lydia's arm, applying more pressure than she normally would have, but a girl's life was at stake—not to mention, she had reached her threshold for the day.

"Tell me about Cuba or I'll give Brandon the go ahead to send you up the river. You're in real trouble. If Miss Darcy is already dead then you can be tried as an accomplice to murder."

"Murder? George never said anything about murdering that girl! I knew he'd hang a red light on me with those jewels! He only said that flossy dame would be held for ransom. He got some of the money, I got the necklace, and the plan was to leave for Rio ... that is, until he changed his mind on me, that no good, rat fink!"

"Where is she, Lydia?"

"I don't know." Her eyes darted around her room. "Keep your voice down. All I know is that she was staying at some ritzy hotel in Havana."

"Do you know who George was going to meet there? Who his contacts were besides the Russian stiff at the Kit Kat this afternoon?"

Elizabeth looked at her watch. "Brandon is probably turning onto 89th Street now, ready to slap the cuffs on you and haul you down to juvie detention. With nowhere to hide, you won't like being in the slammer when the H-bomb goes off over New York."

Lydia recoiled, her eyes widening. "If I tell you, that's all you want, right? That's the only information the coppers think I know?"

"Why? What else are you hiding?"

"Nothing. Nothing at all."

"Do you know who killed George or the Russian?"

"Why the hell would I know that?"

She didn't believe her, but she'd take what she could get. "Because you seem to know more than you're letting on and unless you tell me what you know about Miss Darcy, I'll be telling that to Detective Brandon when he shows up."

"Fine, I'll tell you but you have to swear not to tell Pops about my working as a bump-n-grind girl. It's the only job I could get, and George had friends. I needed to make a lot of dough in a very short time. It was only supposed to be a short gig."

Elizabeth perched a hand on her hip and narrowed her eyes. "Start spillin'."

"George met with some Cuban government man and his stooge at the Tropicana Club in Havana. They were going to take the girl and hold her for some sort of political scheme. The Reds wanted the brother to declare himself a Commie-lover after he got into Congress, challenge that McCarthy in public debate now that he's running that anti-Commie committee. They wanted him to hide money for them, too."

Lydia's ramble sobered Elizabeth. It was just as Darcy figured: a political shakedown. Damn. She hated politics. And it surprised her that Lydia knew a thing or two about what was going on in the world around her. Did she read the newspapers?

"Are you sure about this? You didn't misunderstand George, did you? When he's drunk he slurs his words."

"Yeah. You would know about that, wouldn't you?"

"I'd slap you if I didn't think it would make noise."

"Whatta you want to know all this for anyways? It's none of your high falutin' business. You ain't the law. You're just a measly shop girl."

"My business is none of *your* concern. But it became my business when Slick Wick hurt another girl. And—not that you seem too concerned about this—you narrowly escaped his evil clutches."

She stood gazing down at her sister who surprisingly had tears welling in her eyes.

Lydia looked away when their eyes met. "Yeah. I got away, and had some sparkly jewels to send me off in style, but now you got the necklace and that mugg is dead, and I ain't sayin' no prayer for his miserable soul. He got what was coming."

"What did he do to you to make you so suddenly cold over his corpse, Lydia? A week ago, you were hanging all over him at El Barrio."

"That ain't any of your beeswax. Now get lost!"

"One last question. Do you remember the name of the government official in Havana?"

"I don't know, Lizzy! Something complicated. Fuego. We made a joke because he had five names. I think Pedro was his first name."

Elizabeth stepped to the vanity and lifted the cover of the jewelry box, revealing the gorgeous sapphire necklace memorialized in the portrait of Mrs. Darcy. As she removed them, she glanced over her shoulder to see that Lydia's eyes were pinned upon the dresser. "Don't bother looking for them. I took the diamonds. They're hers, too, aren't they?"

Her sister sighed. "Yeah. You'll tell that flatfoot that I cooperated, and tell Mr. Darcy I returned the jewels, right? Promise me."

"You have my word." Elizabeth's heart broke, hearing the desperation in Lydia's voice. She wanted to help, wanted to be there when no one else was.

"Lydia, listen, if you need my help, you just have to ask. I'm not as 'high and mighty' as you think. I'm your sister, and I love you, and I've walked your walk of disappointed hopes, even making changes in my life that made me a laughing stock. Trust me when I tell you that I understand your misery and anger over George Wickham."

Illuminated by the street light coming through the window, a tear trickled down Lydia's cheek and she angrily swiped at it. "You don't know anything."

She, too, wanted to cry. "Maybe not, but I am here for you. I'm here to help you keep your nose clean and get on with your life."

"Forget it! I don't need you. I don't need anybody. I just need to get out of Queens."

Elizabeth turned, leaving Lydia in the darkness, alone with whatever pain she was experiencing. She said what she needed to say, and got the information she sought in the process, and felt terrible about it all. What a day.

••

"Talk to me, baby," Darcy said with his right arm wrapped around Elizabeth's shoulders as she rested her head on his bicep. He pulled her closer to him on the front car seat, encouraging her to stay near to his warm body.

Although the roads had become more treacherous during their short visit to Jackson Heights, half his focus remained attuned to her frown, her sigh, her silence. He wanted to support her after what she'd just been through with her sister. After only fifteen minutes in conversation with Lydia, his girl had quietly descended the steps, jewels in hand. Although dark, he could see that the ever-present flame in her eyes had diminished, her expression saddened. This was the soft side of Elizabeth hidden below all that bravado and moxie. The girl deep down, the wounded sensitive one who valued family, even if they didn't value her, had come to the surface.

He hugged her tighter and she reached up, removing the fedora she wore so she could bury her head in his neck. She deposited a kiss above the collar of his coat.

"What happened up there?" he asked.

"She's climbing the walls about something, and I don't know how to help her."

"Were you ever close?"

"Never. Lydia has always been the spoiled handful, but I love her. She's my sister." She paused before speculating, the tone in her voice filled with worry. "She's hiding something about Wickham."

He was sure that his kiss to her forehead did nothing but hoped she'd find some comfort in his support. Both their sisters were in trouble and it had to do with one man. The guilt he felt was immeasurable. Whatever Elizabeth needed, if it was in his power, he would give it to her. Right now, it was his love and attention.

"Do you think she knows more about Georgiana then she led on?"

"I don't think her troubles relate to Georgiana, but more about her. My sister has a one-track mind: Lydia. No. This is about the bad hat who promised her the world. One minute she was hot for him, and now she's dancing on his not-so-cold grave. She tore his photograph into little pieces."

"She's young, right? Not yet eighteen?"

"Yeah, and he fed her the malarkey that they'd skip town when he got back from Cuba, but she said he changed his mind."

"Of course he did. Slick Wick was never going to settle down with a ball and chain."

"Hey!"

"You know what I mean. He never was the family type. Grew up in an orphanage and he's been on the lam for so long, I don't think he'd even know how to care for a woman, get an honest paying job, and raise a family."

"Hmm ... family. Lydia may be many things, but I don't believe she would have left without thinking that life was going to be wine and roses outside of Jackson Heights. She's not me, not cut out to be a career girl, and stripping was only temporary. I was surprised when she said the jewels were going to help her leave anyway."

They entered the bridge, heading back to Manhattan. "Your place or mine?" he asked.

She paused.

"Mine."

He could tell her mind was working out what he suspected already.

"Say, you don't think ... nah. Lydia would have said something," she said, the light bulb diminishing as quickly as it illuminated.

Thank God *he* didn't say what his speculation was, but the sharp lady dick would figure it out. Seventeen. Needed the jewels to get out of town quickly. And hated the very man who had put her in this position. He could do the math: one plus one equaled three. Perhaps Elizabeth's intimacy with the situation made her blind to the possibilities.

"Is there anything I can do to help?"

"Nothing. Until I know what troubles her. I just wish Jane would be a little more helpful when it comes to my parents and Lydia. After she got married, she turned her nose up to us all—more than she ever did. And when she does show up, like earlier this afternoon, she's too busy telling me that I'm irresponsible."

"I'm sorry. I wish I knew what to say about her. What happened between the two of you to cause such a rift?"

She sighed. "I have lived in her exalted shadow my entire life. Never the pretty one, never the intelligent one, never the one men wanted. It was always about her and I was made to feel insignificant. Janie's looks and pleasing smiles got her everything she wanted—including Charlie."

"And where did Wickham fit into this scenario." He pulled her closer, as if it were possible.

"Jane wanted him when she saw that he was paying me more attention, not that she would have gone all the way with him, but it was the victory she sought. We fought and she said cruel things that I don't care to repeat. As I reflect on that now, I think how Wickham must have enjoyed that catfight for his affections. The rest you know. In many ways, Jane did emerge the victor. I got dumped, he moved onto Mary, and then Charlie rolled into town with that happy grin of his. The rest is history."

It near gutted him to hear her dejection. In a swift move he turned the steering wheel, bringing the car to a stop at a street corner. After sliding the car into parking gear, he turned in the seat and cupped her soft cheeks in his hands.

"You are beautiful and brilliant and significant—not just in my life, but in your clients' lives, too. In Lydia's life and your parents'. Never forget that, baby. I love you and Jane has nothing over you."

He kissed her tenderly, giving her all that was in his heart. A bona fide, forever commitment.

"Elizabeth, whatever Lydia needs, you know you can come to me. My connections and resources—my money and my heart are at your disposal."

She lifted her head and kissed his cheek. "Thank you. You're one in a million, Fitzwilliam."

"So are you, sweetheart."

••

Fourteen

When Elizabeth had telephoned Oscar before leaving Hell's Kitchen for the airport, he gave her a little tip: Havana operated on "Cuban Time." In other words—as slow as molasses in January. And now Elizabeth was seeing it in action (so to speak). The glacial speed of the hotel clerk opposite them in the luxury Hotel Nacional de Cuba triggered Darcy's sourpuss expression, accompanied by the drumming of his fingers against the reception desk. But she waited patiently. Darcy was in control here and her private eye moxie would have to take a back seat to his all-business, unyielding persona.

Not that he understood the local denizens and culture. This was Oscar's world. Half-Cuban and half-Italian, her stoolie friend knew a lot about the tropical locale. He was a real sweetheart, and laughed when she told him that he was right: Darcy the suit was brooding, smoldering, and she was his property now. Well, as much as she would allow any man to own her. But he did own her heart and that was saying something. Oscar had been silent when she told him that the man in question was currently lying in her bed and they were headed to Havana on the luxurious DC-6 airplane— followed by a swell time in the sun, drinking pink daiquiris, and making whoopie under the full moon.

That was a lie of course. There would be no fun, just danger, and in order to make a few Commie hoods bend to her will, she'd have to call upon all those skills she had honed over these last few months. This was the big time—not a two-bit case of a cheating husband. A girl's life was at stake and, by God, Georgiana Darcy would not become another Mary King. Not on her watch.

Annoyed by the lack of attention, Darcy cleared his throat. "Can you tell me if a Miss Georgiana Darcy has checked out?" he asked the pretty hotel clerk. Of course, he knew she hadn't, but they needed to get into her room, collect her belongings if they were still there, look for evidence, something ... anything.

The young woman on the other side of the counter seemed to have one speed: reverse. She smiled then slowly reached for the wooden file box of registrations, careful not to mess her red-tipped manicure as she flipped through index cards.

Elizabeth watched as her man impatiently tapped his fingers on the counter; his jaw flexed as though he was carefully considering his next words. Where did he think he was?—A boardroom?

The long morning of air travel certainly did not bring out the best in her man. With each passing mile over the Atlantic Ocean, Darcy had become more anxious, more taciturn, his mug set like cold marble. Of course, she had been no help on the flight south. The tough gumshoe had abandoned her the minute they boarded the airplane. It was the first time she had ever been on one and suffered from her own fears: falling from the sky and Lydia's plight.

With the exception of exotic potted palm trees, colorful flowers, and luxury furnishings, the lobby was empty. The shutter slats were partially closed to shield the interior from the harsh tropical sun. She stood beside Darcy below large ceiling fans, which barely alleviated them in their winter apparel. The blades turned with a slow tick like the ominous sound of a grandfather clock counting down to the hour of death. He glanced down at her, their eyes locking against the background of gentle strains of Cuban rumba coming from the radio in the office behind the desk.

Elizabeth glanced at her watch. One-thirty in the afternoon—siesta time. Oscar told her about that, too.

Finally, the clerk removed the reservation, holding it up with a smile. "No, *Señor. Señorita* Darcy is scheduled to depart this afternoon. Her passport has not yet been claimed."

"Has Miss Katherine "Kiki" Kavandish checked out yet?" he asked, the tone in his voice grave.

Again, the woman ticked through the hundreds of index cards, one by one, carefully reading each one to herself, and, again, Darcy gazed down at Elizabeth, furrowing his brow. She imagined that she could hear the rush of blood in his temple in stressful anticipation of her reply. If the answer came back "no" then it was apparent that his sister hadn't traveled with friends as she had promised—only George Wickham.

"*Lo siento.* I am sorry. There is no one registered at the Hotel Nacional by that name, *Señor.*"

"Hmm. I'm Miss Darcy's brother, and I would like a key to her room." He tightened his fist.

His voice was now stern, brooking no opposition, expecting immediate submission to his demand, but Elizabeth knew it would get him nowhere. He wasn't in Gotham and his name had no bearing down here in Havana. No doubt, the young clerk was accustomed to the demands of Hollywood starlets, Mafioso, and dignitaries, but she was unaware who Mr. Fitzwilliam Darcy was, and the power he yielded inside the Big Apple.

"But that is not allowed, *Señor. Señorita* Darcy may be indisposed."

Thankful for that foreign language correspondence course she took and all the time she spent at El Barrio within Oscar's circle of friends, Elizabeth spoke in Spanish as she reached her ungloved right hand across the counter to grasp the young lady's free one. Some woman-to-woman talk was needed.

"We need your assistance, Miss. We believe that—my sister-in-law—Miss Darcy may be in a compromising position with someone who sets to take advantage of her. Her loving brother is understandably very concerned, as I am sure any respectable girl's brother would be. We left New York City first thing this morning in the hopes of keeping her from making a terrible mistake." She squeezed the clerk's hand. "*Por Favor, Señorita.* She could be in danger."

She could feel Darcy's astonished stare burning down upon the top of her pillbox hat.

The clerk nodded, releasing Elizabeth's hand, then turned to the open cubby holes behind her, removing a key from one of the boxes.

"Room number 204."

"Thank you. Thank you so much," Elizabeth said in English, subtly elbowing Darcy.

"Yes. Thank you, Miss ..."

"Rivera."

"We appreciate your assistance, Miss Rivera. Will you see that the bellman brings our bags up to my sister's room?"

"*Sí, Señor.*"

Another not-so-subtle elbow met his ribs, and Darcy knit his brow, gazing down at Elizabeth. A raise of her eyebrows and a quick cock to her head in Miss Rivera's direction made him begrudgingly dig into his breast pocket, withdrawing a billfold. He removed a fifty-dollar bill and handed it to the clerk; her eyes fixed on the American greenbacks, not Pesos.

"That's better," Elizabeth said, feeling self-satisfied. Apparently, moneybags was a tightwad. Surely he must have learned by now that good dough yields faster, better results than any stakeout could.

Probably not. He was as straight-laced as they came, even if his punch—and thrust—were killer.

Miss Rivera grinned holding out a wooden box partially covered by colorful labels and stamped, *Hecho en Cubana*. "*Señor* Darcy, please enjoy premier Cabañas cigars—a gift from management."

"Thank you. I will."

"Oh, and Miss Rivera," Elizabeth said before leaving the desk. "Can you tell me where I can find *Señor* Enrique Guzman?"

According to Oscar, everyone in Havana knew Tricky Ricky, and he knew everyone and everything that happened on the island. Of course he did—he and her stoolie East Harlem friend were half-brothers. Further, Ricky hated Communists as well as Batista's new regime. Oh ... and lest she forget that last bit that Oscar informed her: Tricky Ricky appreciated fine cigars and shapely gams. Two things she happened to possess.

The clerk smiled, her eyes lighting with delight. "Yes, I know police captain." She moved closer, bridging the separation between them over the counter, ignoring the towering presence of Darcy, who was keenly listening with fascination to the bi-lingual conversation. "I can take message to him for you?" she asked.

Oscar's half-brother is the police captain. Boy, he is connected. No wonder Señor Guzman knows everyone in Havana.

"You are a darling! That would be swell! Tell him Oscar sent Eli Bennet ... um ... Darcy. I'd like to meet him at the Tropicana tonight. Ten o'clock by the bar."

"Oh, the Tropicana! You will have wonderful time, in style. The cabaret! Paradise under the stars is *muy romantica*. Carmen Miranda, Brazilian Bombshell is performing."

"Unfortunately, we're here because of Miss Darcy, but I do love to cha-cha, as does my ... um ... husband."

Elizabeth glanced up at him and delighted in how his lips twitched into a playful smirk. Apparently, he liked the part where she said Eli Bennet *Darcy* and cha-cha. *That* didn't need to be translated.

Arm-in-arm they walked to the elevator, visibly parked at the second floor. Darcy leaned down, whispering into her ear, his breath tickling her. "You're one killer dame, *Eli*. You surprise me at every turn."

"I know. Don't you forget what a catch I am when one of those high society dames comes knocking on your door, wanting their high-roller financier, talk-of-the-town bachelor back. Your acumen with digits should be restricted to *my* bedroom only."

"*Our* bedroom. You're not going to lose me, Elizabeth. I have no reservations. My offer remains. I only await your reply."

"Hmm ... Well, until that time, you'll just have to settle for the hotel registry joining us as husband and wife."

Her smile met his when they stopped at the gated entrance to the lift, and her breath hitched at his softened expression. Yes. She would accept—of course she would. If—and only if—he got down on his knee with a big piece of ice for her finger and some sappy poetic sentiment to declare himself. A girl—even a Big Apple gumshoe—had standards.

"You didn't mention your nickname or that you spoke the language," he said, taking her hand in his.

"A private eye can't divulge all her secrets in the first 24 hours. Can she?"

Humored eyes bore into hers. "Secrets?"

"Just a few, but don't worry, Darcy, they don't involve taking you to the cleaners. I'm not playing with your heart, either. I'm as wacky over you as you are of me, and *that* you can take to the bank."

Soft lips kissed when she stood on tiptoes before the elevator operator slid back the gate.

••

The possible scene of the crime. In Elizabeth's opinion, Georgiana's dimly lit luxury suite appeared as eerie as any in her crime fiction whodunit novels. Narrow slits of light escaped through the closed shutters, casting shadows in a room where darkness held its ransom. She near expected the kidnapper or Mike Hammer to appear from the adjoining door, revolver cocked and ready to fire. The image of the rumpled bed made her flesh goose pimple and she thought of the "*Silencio, No Moleste*" sign hanging on the outside of the door.

Apart from the bed, to the naked eye, nothing seemed out of place. Everything appeared just as a brother would hope to find it—with the exception of the sheer black negligee draped over the vanity chair. Darcy's fingers touched the flimsy, lace-edged fabric, promptly dropping it with disgust, his expression more dour than she had ever seen. She could feel the pain and worry shrouding him.

"I know how it appears, Darcy, but that may not be the case at all. In my line of work, it's only circumstantial."

"It *is* how it appears. I have no doubt. I saw that look in her eyes when she spoke about him. You get that look."

"That means nothing. I had that look, and so did you, *before* you took me to bed. But had you continued to brood much longer, we might never have fallen into each other's arms. A look and a see-thru negligee don't mean she *actually* slept with the man any more than a sloppy proposal without a ring means that we're engaged to be married."

Yeah. She couldn't help to still rib him for that ridiculous proposal in the Cadillac.

"Besides, why is it okay that you're sleeping with *me*, yet you're appalled to think that your unmarried sister could be *dishonored* by any man?"

He grunted in reply and turned from her, throwing open the shutters, flooding the room with bright Caribbean sun.

"Darcy?"

"Because she's my sister, that's why," was his only reply before disappearing into the powder room. She heard him move bottles and then open Georgiana's cosmetic case, shuffling through the contents.

Anger-laced words called out to her, "She must have purchased those diamonds downstairs at their jewelry shop, the wrapping is in the wastebasket," but she ignored him and continued with her own investigation. She wanted to tell him to give his sister the benefit of the doubt about her behavior, but understood Slick Wick's charm acutely. He had a way of convincing people—especially women—to do his bidding. Lydia was an ideal example. Besides, Darcy was a hard-headed man, not easily convinced of anything outside of his own opinion, but he was learning. Just as she was in how to soothe his hot-temper. She thanked the Lord that he was putty in her hands. That, she proudly acknowledged, was the power of a femme fatale's man-baiting skill.

She bent to examine the hardwood flooring now illuminated by the southern exposure of sunrays.

Large footprints had left a subtle trail of white substance leading to and from the door to the foot of the bed. Squatting, she licked her index finger then dabbed at the evidence, followed by its raise to her nose. A slight sweet scent tinged the granular matter and she licked her finger so sure of the familiar substance. "Sugar," she confirmed aloud, standing.

"What?" Darcy asked, peeking his head out of the bathroom.

"There is sugar on the floor. It's possible that the kidnapper works at a sugar mill."

He stepped into the suite, wiping his hands on a towel. "Havana is known for sugar production."

"My friend's brother will help us tonight."

"Your friend Oscar?"

"Yeah. He gave me a contact of someone well connected down here. Like you, he hates the Commies, but he's not a Batista lover either."

"He's a revolutionary? A member of the *Partido Ortodoxo?*"

She glanced at him sideways, raising her eyebrows then shrugged. "Beats me. Lately murders, kidnappings, and cheating husbands are up my alley. But politics, Cuban politics? No thanks."

He walked to her, tossing the towel onto the armchair beside the desk. "I may not dabble in politics either."

"You don't mean that. You'd make a good congressman."

"I do mean it. I'll give it serious reconsideration after we bring Georgiana home. I cannot—I will not—put either of you in further danger because of my outspoken beliefs. Not only that, but I'm afraid that my entrance into that profession runs the chance of you dying of boredom while I spend months at a time in Washington. I can be passionate about my country and help others without becoming a politician."

"Me bored? Impossible. Well, maybe at the Dakota I would be. I like Hell's Kitchen. It has real energy."

"You would get bored uptown. My mother did, and she ended up taking the easy way out of an unhappy, lonely marriage to a politician who loved his mistresses as much as the graft. Father's ideology extended only as far as his greased palm by his special interests. He failed miserably as a husband and a Senator, doing only damage instead of good."

"But that's not you. You're an honorable man. I'm sure of it. Your time in the Navy helped you become the man I've fallen in love with. I don't see you as being greedy; I see you as a man who can help people."

He walked to the window and reached his arm out for her to join him in the view of the sea. There was more—something else he'd put a blanket on, something that obviously tormented him. An occurrence that may have shaped the man he became, definitely one that sent him to the Pacific in anger at his father.

Darcy took her hand in his, fingers entwining as his thumb brushed back and forth on her skin.

"Thank you, but you hardly know me, Elizabeth," he said morosely, his voice barely a humble whisper.

"I do know you, Darcy. I know people, and just like I knew that you didn't kill Wickham when Detective Brandon asked about your connection to him ..."

His head snapped up, a frown upon his face, now recalling that she had mentioned the inquiry last night.

"... I know you'd never become that type of political stooge. You're a grouch sometimes, but top notch in my book."

"Do the police suspect me of the murder?"

"Nah. I made sure Chris wouldn't consider you a suspect." *Even though he considered me one.*

"Thank you." He sighed in obvious relief. "Elizabeth ... I may be angry with Georgiana for her dangerous actions and hurt by her deception, but I understand her. In my fear of people taking advantage of her naiveté, I sheltered her. She was as bored as my mother, begging for fun and that is why I allowed her this holiday. My sister's wealth makes her highly sought-after by chiselers just like Wickham."

Elizabeth squeezed his hand, feeling the guilt rolling from his body.

"You weren't to blame for this—neither your political beliefs or your relationship with Georgiana. You were doing what you thought best, just as I try to do where it concerns Lydia.

He ran his fingers through his hair then narrowed his eyes as he concentrated on what to say before spilling his guts. "I don't know if I did the right thing by letting her experience the thrill of independence and freedom; look where it got her—where it got me in '43. But if I hadn't let her go ... I just ... I just had this fear that she'd become my mother all over again."

He turned to gaze out the window. "I lied when I said that my mother had been ill. The only sickness she suffered from was dejection and isolation. She took sleeping pills. She killed herself."

Her posture sobered, his confession knocking her for a loop; here she thought she'd had a bad lot. This poor man carried *heavy* burdens that could break any other gee: Nouméa, Wickham, and his mother. Now his sister's kidnapping. No wonder he was so severe.

How had she been able to crack his façade, peel back his layers so easily? What could she say? Nothing. She just wrapped her arms around him and held him tightly.

••

FIFTEEN

The Tropicana was no juke joint, and the cabaret was no Kit Kat Klub. Scantily clad showgirls shook and danced below fabulous feathered headdresses and provocative costumes in class and style. And in Elizabeth's opinion, the show taking place on stage was more titillating than those bump-n-grind girls who wore less and danced more sensationally hoping for other outcomes. Under the open-air nightclub's "Arches of Glass" canopy, she sat beside Darcy at the bar waiting for the bartender to signal them of Tricky Ricky's arrival.

The club was an intoxicating combination of glamour, music, and sex. The crowd was filled with an excitement that Elizabeth had never witnessed or felt before. In between shows, the dance floor burned with energy. Cuba was magical; its people warm and friendly; the tropical breeze under the full moon and brilliant stars above made it all the more incredible. What made it *paradise* was being on the arm of the most dashing man of her acquaintance. In spite of the nerves Elizabeth was experiencing, her heart did a little cha-cha-ing as she admired Darcy in the white dinner jacket. Her lips twitched into a tender smile at the image he presented, and she tried to focus on her man.

She thought that she couldn't get any more nervous than when she had shown up at the Dakota needing Darcy—all of Darcy—but she was wrong. Gazing down at her drink, she stirred the liquid with the pink swizzle stick, her thoughts drifting. Tonight she was a wreck. Any number of things could go wrong: they could be killed, Georgiana might already be dead, or at the very least ruined. Then there was that pervading thought that Brandon could easily put aside their friendship and hang Wickham's murder on Darcy—even her—she did, in fact, have motive—and a derringer. And lastly what role did Lydia play in all of this?

Darcy cleared his throat, snapping her from the negative train her mind was rolling on. Playing off her anxiety, she forced herself to focus on pleasant thoughts and gazed up at him again, gaining her strength, her calm in the storm. Surprisingly, in spite of the danger ahead, her man seemed relaxed.

She gazed at him as he lit two cigarettes, one for each of them. Unable to suppress the smile that crossed her face, she wondered if the cause of his relaxation was their spontaneous coupling in the bathroom after she had bathed in preparation for the evening. After a kiss that had burst her heart, he bent her over the sink, giving her every incredible inch of himself as their gaze held steadfast in the mirror before them. Or perhaps it was the oral sex that followed that calmed him further. She could still feel the swollen rim of his manhood below her lips. The recollection of him tilting his head back and moaning in ecstasy was now making her fidget on the bar stool. This high class, yet, at times, uninhibited man was teaching her things she had never imagined.

Without thought she licked her ruby lips when she reached for the cigarette, her fingers brushing his.

"You're flushed," he said, concerned by her silence. "Are you nervous?"

"A little but that's not the cause. I was ... um ... just thinking."

"About?"

She took a deep drag. God, she needed that. Already he was getting her heated and they weren't even on the dance floor.

"Earlier."

"Ah. I'm so sorry if I embarrassed you." He blushed and honest-to-goodness blush. "It's just that I—

"Oh no, Darcy, you didn't. It's the opposite. I'm not embarrassed." She interrupted, then inched closer to him, whispering. "I want more."

A little chuckle escaped his lips and her heart delighted. The less danger he felt tonight the better it would be when she had to butter up the police captain or that government thug, Pedro García López y Fernández Fuego.

"I'd like more, too." He cocked an eyebrow as he raised the rim of his rocks glass to his lips.

"Was that something you learned in the Pacific?"

He leaned toward her then deposited a tiny kiss to her lips. "No. That was something I experienced for the first time with Elizabeth Bennet."

"Really?"

"Yes, really. I'm not the tomcat you believe me to be, and even when I was, I was green."

Now she was beaming inside and out.

"You look gorgeous tonight, baby," he complimented, smoothing his free hand over her cheek. "If we get through this, I'll buy you anything your heart desires. Dior suits you."

She ran her black, elbow length gloves down the snug fitting bodice of the evening dress, feeling every bit the glamorous Hollywood starlet. "Thank you. You were very generous to take me shopping in the Prado. The dress is the most elegant thing I have ever owned, but I can hardly breathe. If we *do* get through this, I'm staying in your bed *without* clothes for repeat performances of earlier."

"That's fine with me."

The bartender came toward them with a cocktail shaker in hand; his mixing movements matched the Latin rhythm, causing his ruffled shirt sleeves to sway. A simple chin lift toward the approaching diminutive man wearing a uniform indicated that Tricky Ricky had arrived for their meeting. *Thank you, Miss Rivera!*

"Here's our man," she whispered. "Now, Darcy, listen. I'd prefer it if you didn't speak. Let me do all the talking."

"What? That's not—"

"Don't argue with me," she interrupted, loving how his jaw dropped in astonishment. "Trust me. I know how to get results, and your irascible self is only good at deal making in the boardroom, offending people, or getting me into bed. So whatever you plan on saying ... keep your trap shut. You're in my world now."

He snapped his mouth closed at her command.

Yeah. Cream puff. "That's more like it."

He sat back on the stool and took a drink, and she could see how he attempted to control his laughter at her ballsy attitude.

"And another thing, try to smile like you're having fun."

He gave her a false, yet absolutely stunning grin and she smiled back before leaning against the bar. She struck a pose, one that was sure to get the police captain's attention given the black strapless evening dress she had specifically chosen to do the most damage—or good—depending on one's perspective. Crossed legs, showed sufficient flesh, and she dropped a bared shoulder. Trying to ignore Darcy's stare, a seductive lift of the cigarette to her lips accompanied a sideways, half-hooded gaze in her contact's direction.

Their eyes met and Oscar's brother's lips quirked in a familiar fashion. The two were near spitting images of each other, with the exception of Ricky's mustache and salt and pepper hair.

"*Señora* Bennet y Darcy, I presume?" he asked.

"Captain Guzman," she purred.

"*Sí.*"

He took her free hand and kissed her fingers. "I am enchanted to make your acquaintance. You are as lovely as my brother explained."

"Oscar speaks highly of you as well." She laughed lightly, "I assume your brother also explained that I am not *Señora* Bennet y Darcy, just *Señorita* Bennet."

"He did mention that."

"Well Captain, I do believe you're more handsome than my dear friend."

A humored snort left his lips as he continued to hold her hand. "I never hear from him unless he needs particular assistance with something." His eyes scanned her figure, his expression becoming just what she had hoped for. He smiled then released his gentle grip on her fingers. "How may I assist, you, *Señorita*."

Darcy placed his glass on the bar with a thud, abruptly standing. He gazed down at her and cleared his throat, obviously choosing to ignore her earlier caution.

Petulant, headstrong, jealous man! "Captain Guzman, please allow me to introduce my *client*, Mr. Fitzwilliam Darcy."

The men shook hands like two posturing bulls, finally exchanging cordial greetings.

"*Señorita* Bennet would you care to dance?"

She looked up at Darcy, her eyes sternly boring into his before turning to the police captain. Deliberately, she spoke in Spanish. "I would be delighted." Her smug smile spoke volumes to Mr. Jealousy while enamoring the police captain whose connections could help them find Georgiana.

After crushing her cigarette in the decorative ashtray, she took Tricky Ricky's hand and together they navigated the crush of dancers. The man smelled of sweet tobacco and aftershave. Slender, his bicep below her hand was firm to the touch, but even with his hat on, she was at least two inches taller than he was. He was as charming as Oscar, his accented words as smooth and seductive. They swayed to the lively beat of "El Negro Zumbon."

"You are a lovely dancer."

"Thank you. It's one of many skills a woman in my profession must possess."

"Ah ... Oscar mentioned some of your other skills, as well."

"He's very generous with his compliments, if not a little one-track minded at times, but he's harmless and good for a girl's ego."

"He is in love with you."

Well, that knocked her for a loop but she laughed. "No. I don't think so."

"Perhaps not, but I have been told to help you in any manner, no questions asked. He is a good man, in spite of his suspect activities in New York."

"So I can trust you?"

"*Sí.* What is the purpose of your visit in Havana?"

He pulled her closer to him, but she wasn't afraid. "Mr. Darcy and I are looking for a young woman, taken against her will from the Hotel Nacional by whatever Communist organization is operating in Cuba."

"*Partido Comunista Cubano,* perhaps *Socialista Popular.*"

"An informant back in New York tells me that a Cuban government official is working in conjunction with them."

"There are many Communist collaborators who have been rewarded positions in Batista's Consultative Council." He sighed. "A love-hate relationship, but one I believe will come to an end very soon."

"I'm not familiar with Cuban politics, Captain."

"It is complicated, corrupt, and money is king. But that does not answer why they would kidnap an *Americana.* Batista walks a fine line with your President Truman as well as with the *Americano* Mafioso. He would not allow such action."

"You see Mr. Darcy over there looking like a sourpuss as he watches us?"

"Now *he* is a man in love."

She glanced back over to the man in question; the corner of his lips twitched into a semi-smile, and she chortled. "Yes, he is in love, but he's also a would-be politician, a *wealthy* candidate. Of course, it doesn't help that he's an outspoken detractor of the Red menace. His every word is recorded by the press and gossip columnists, and his kidnapped, socialite sister is heiress to a fortune. Simply put: he's being blackmailed."

Guzman turned her under his arm, his eyes pinned to her swaying hips. Entering his dance frame he said, "Fuego may be the person you seek, but you will need evidence."

She threw her head back and laughed. "Tell me something I don't already know, *Ricky*."

"He spends much time at the old Central Hershey sugar plantation now that it has been sold to the Cuban Atlantic Sugar Company." He raised an eyebrow.

Sugar! That was just what she needed to hear, but his next words further itched her trigger finger. Maybe Sally would get to see some action tonight.

"Fuego will be here this evening. Would you like for me to introduce you? He has a weakness for *mujeres Americanas*."

"Why, Captain Guzman, that sounds positively divine!"

His smile turned grave. "But I cannot assist you further than the introduction in this matter, *Señorita*. He is powerful man, very close to Batista himself. I put my family in jeopardy if I am discovered, but this I do for Oscar, and, of course, you."

"I understand, and we thank you for whatever assistance you can lend us."

"Trust no one, *Señorita*. Apart from what little help I can provide, you and Mr. Darcy are alone in your endeavor."

••

Darcy had stolen a dance. It was about damn time that Elizabeth relinquished her hold on the police captain. He tried not to be angry— or jealous—but she made it so hard. His girl did whatever the hell she wanted in this game of cat and mouse.

"You're frowning," she said, gripping his bicep as they danced to "Guantanamera."

His hand delighted in the feel of her hip encased in luxury fabric that clung to her like a second skin. "Finally," he said.

"Finally?"

"I can hold you in my arms. I missed you."

"I'm sorry, darling, but you know how it is."

"I wish you would allow me to be a man here, Elizabeth. I'm reduced to sitting at the bar drowning in my cups like some boob while my woman charms other men. You're emasculating me, making me look like a spineless lollipop."

"Emasculating you? I don't think so. You know my methods are much more effective than yours here. We're a team, so be thankful that I'm no shrinking violet. Your time will come, but just not yet. Besides, I've seen your legs, Darcy, and as sexy as they are ... I don't think Captain Guzman would like to imagine them wrapped around his waist."

"And I don't quite like that he's imagining *yours* doing the same. I'd like it more if you left your 'methods' in our bedroom."

He knew he was in trouble when she suddenly stopped dancing, huffed, and immediately installed her hand on her hip. Her eyes flashed and the corner of her painted lips raised in an expression he had yet to witness. She was madder than a hellcat. Of course she was. That was probably the stupidest thing he'd ever said to a woman.

Outstretching his arm to her, he tripped on his apology. "I'm sorry. I ... I didn't mean that."

Elizabeth turned on her heel, leaving him to stand alone in the crush of dancers. The burn of embarrassment coupled with her sashay in Tricky Ricky's direction made his blood boil especially since the police captain wasn't the only admirer watching his girl: the man he assumed to be Fuego leered at Elizabeth, making Darcy's flesh crawl. That provocative sway of her hips cast a spell upon all three men—a hypnotist's swinging pendulum, left to right to left then right.

He departed the dance floor, eyes fixed on the introduction taking place. The smarmy government official appeared to be a wealthy version of Slick Wick: dripping with hubris and deception right down to his calculated grooming and false grin. Fuego scanned Elizabeth up and down in appreciation. Of course he would. She was an alluring woman. Hadn't he done the same time and again? But he wanted to possess her heart and soul, and this man, like all the others, wanted only her body and those succulent lips on them.

Darcy clenched his fist, hating that she was in harm's way due to him and him alone. To make matters worse, they had parted angrily. *She knows what she is doing. The dagger and Sally are on her legs where I secured them and she has me as her bodyguard. This is for Georgiana!*

The police captain took his leave with a wink and a kiss to her gloved hand then walked to the end of the long bar where he stood. Unseen by Fuego, Guzman spoke low, placing into Darcy's jacket pocket a pair of handcuffs. "Be careful, my friend. I will contact you tomorrow."

"Hopefully, we'll be gone by then, Captain. Thank you for your help."

"So long, *Señor* Darcy. The planes back to Miami do not leave until late morning, but there is ferry to Stock Island. I am sure *Americano* dollars will pay for an unexpected, late-night transport." They shook hands, a crisp wad of dough sandwiched between their two palms. The Captain smiled, then nodded, his expression concerned. "Good luck."

Taking a seat at the bar, Darcy observed the interaction between Fuego and Eli, just as he had in the Kit Kat. His gumshoe girl was good at getting men to warm up to her immediately, and by all appearance, Fuego had fallen into her spell as soon as they moved to a table on the outside perimeter of the club. Straining to watch how she was going to subtly pump him for information, Darcy was tempted to move nearer, but didn't want to blow this opportunity to get close to the man who most likely was behind Georgiana's kidnapping. Instead, he observed everything through the slow, floating smoke from his cigarette, never breaking his stare upon them.

The once intoxicating music was soon an annoying background distraction; the cigarette a necessary usage of his hand; the smoke a shadow of concealment.

Elizabeth threw back her head in laughter. Fuego placed his hand over hers on the table. Darcy shifted uneasily, and his heart rate picked up speed.

"So tell me, *Señor* Fuego what do you do for fun in Havana?" Elizabeth purred, chatting him up.

He laughed. "I am busy man but not too busy to enjoy my thoroughbreds."

"Ah, so you own race horses?"

"Among other things. Horses are one of my many mistresses. Perhaps you would care to join me at Oriental Park tomorrow? My filly *Heliodoro* races and it would give me great honor to have you as my special guest, *Señorita* Bennet."

"Perhaps. Father owns several horses, so I desire other recreation. Boating, sunbathing, and several activities *inside*."

She sipped the cocktail he had insisted on, careful not to lose her focus from the rum, needing to convince him that she, like Georgiana, was a wealthy socialite.

"Do you not care for El Presidente drink?" he asked, followed by a light to his already half-smoked cigar, drawing in the flame and air as he puffed. The pungent smoke rose between them and she tried not to crinkle her nose as she did when Darcy smoked one earlier.

"It's a very nice drink. Sweet. I like sweet things, which seems appropriate since I am visiting the sugar cane capital of the world."

"*Sí*. Sugar is another passion of mine, having purchased *Centrales* Air-Shee *azucarera*." He puffed his chest, boasting the distorted truth, but confirming what Tricky Ricky had disclosed.

She reached over, touching the black linen square peeking from the jacket's pocket and he smiled wryly in response, clearly falling for her manner of "interrogation."

"You purchased Hershey chocolate? You're a sugar baron! I would love to see the village! It sounds positively divine."

"It is not possible. Although the orphanage remains, and the electric railroad runs, the mill is off limits. The Air-Shee Hotel needs restoration. That, too, you cannot visit. It is currently occupied by Soviet friends of the Consultative Council and, of course, the Cuban Atlantic Sugar Company."

"My, my you're a busy man and with such powerful—admirable—friends. How do you find the time between your horses, sugar mill, and your impressive position in President Batista's council?" Her shoe slid against his shin under the table.

Fuego moved his hand holding the cigar away from their faces and leaned closer to her, his pupils dilating when his eyes immediately zoned in on her pointed bosom and pronounced cleavage. "I enjoy many things, particularly those inside activities with a beautiful woman. I have many friends, some powerful, others not, but I have eager ones who oversee the old sugar worker village. It is not far, only thirty miles from Havana in Santa Cruz del Norte, but I travel there only when necessary. I choose to spend my time in more pleasant ways."

He looked away, suddenly appearing distracted by his thoughts and the direction the conversation had taken. "Lately, I have spent too much time in Santa Cruz, but some business cannot be avoided. I am a very important man. No. I wish not to take you there, *Señorita*. You will come to the racetrack with me—or we will find other things to occupy us—inside the Hotel Nacional."

Darcy witnessed the man wiggle his bushy eyebrows and he tightened his grip around the rocks glass.

Not giving Elizabeth time to respond, Fuego asked, "Now, tell me, what is your family business in New York City?"

"Oh *Señor* Fuego, Father doesn't have a profession, just more money and power than God himself." She leaned closer, whispering, "He applies his wealth to his political interests."

The man raised an eyebrow.

"Let's just say that our Senator McCarthy would love to get his hands on him."

"Is that so? Your father has leanings toward the Soviet cause?"

She ran her finger down the lapel of his dinner jacket. "We both do."

Yes. Darcy's girl was very good. Based on Fuego's body language following her physical attention, she was playing him perfectly: earning his trust and making him desire her more than he desired anything in his life. He knew that feeling well.

Elizabeth smoothed her finger over the bottom of her lip then smiled coyly. "Please excuse me, Pedro, I must powder my nose." Tapping his sneering lips, she added, "Don't go far; I'll be right back."

He caught her hand in his, promptly kissing her knuckles, eyes fixed to hers. "Of course, my little kitten. Do not keep me waiting too long."

••

She hoped to God Darcy was following her through the tables toward the direction of the powder room. Her heart thundered and she felt like she was going to shoot her cookies. Up until this moment, she had felt proud of her methods. Playing the role of femme fatale to gather information was what she did best, but this was no two-bit case. She was scared and sick to her stomach and, in some strange way, felt as though she was betraying Darcy. The smiles and flirts she gave away should be only for the man who owned them all—owned her heart. No wonder he had felt so dejected earlier; his obvious jealousy was behind his earlier comment.

Stepping out into the open air, she hurriedly walked from the nightclub's canopy and patrons, heels sinking into the sandy soil until she stood within the shadow of a majestic palm. In the dark, with only a few strands of party lights swaying feet from her in the breeze, she took a deep breath, calming herself. A tender smile formed when she realized the scent of Darcy's woodsy aftershave mixed with the tropical sea air filled her lungs.

His arm encircled her waist from behind and he pulled her against his firm body, his mouth depositing tender pecks on that sensitive place at her nape. He kissed her there and her flesh goose pimpled in delight.

"I'm sorry, baby."

"Me, too." She tilted her head, giving him greater access, unable to keep from purring when his cool lips met her heated flesh.

"Do you forgive me for being such a buffoon?"

She leaned her head back against his shoulder and looked up into his eyes. "I forgive you for being a *jealous* buffoon."

"Do you blame me? You drive me wacky."

"I think ... I think I know where your sister is."

Ignoring her, he kissed her poised lips, pouted upward near his mouth. It was a slow, tender caress, their tongues barely meeting each others; his lips did all the silent talking. They molded against hers, asking for forgiveness, giving acceptance until separating.

His hand slid down along the tight confines of her dress. "Mmmm. Darcy ..."

"I love you, Elizabeth, all of you: your mind and body, your heart and soul. Marry me."

"Knee ... mmm ... ring ... then you'll get my answer."

"You're gonna beat that horse dead," he whispered.

"Yes, I am. Kiss me, darling."

He turned her in his arms, his hands sliding down her waist, stopping on the curve of her hips. That kisser of his lowered to hers in an attack that traveled directly to her womanhood. She felt the pulse there and it matched the flutter in her belly. Her lover had lips hotter than an atomic blast as they consumed her with raw energy.

Two steps, that's all he took, until her back leaned against the towering palm tree. Concealed in the shadow, Darcy's lips traveled down her neck, giving her love bites to each curve. She purred, needing to moan when his kisses left their invisible burn on the tops of her spilling bosom.

He was making her spin again, drunk on the power of his emotion with each suckle and bite. One hand clutched the back of his head, her fingers raking through his waves. Then the urge came ... that undeniable need to feel him inside her ... that quiver in her sex ... the wetness ... legs that felt like rippling water.

Her hand slid between their bodies, needing to feel the strength of his love. Raging, he needed what she did; his lips reconnected with hers and she was sure she would die from rapture in his arms.

Her legs trembled as he continued his erotic assault of teasing and petting. "Mrs. Darcy?" he suggestively commanded, his lips hovering over hers. "Please."

"May ... maybe," she replied dreamily. "You're very convincing."

"I was a student of law ... remember?"

She heard laughter in the distance, the sound of samba and crickets filled the night air. The palm tree swayed in the breeze, adding to her raspy pants that joined the chorus.

Firm yet gentle fingers cupped her face; he kissed her deeply, nearly stopping her heart. That boyish grin afterward, told her so much. Her intense man needed to know that she was his and his alone forevermore, no matter how she acted with others in this dangerous gambit.

"I promise, you'll get a ring baby, the biggest in the Big Apple, and I'll get on my knee with a poetic proposal that the romantic in you deserves."

"Yeah?" she asked grinning ear to ear.

"Yeah. Now give me Sally."

"What?"

Holding out his open palm, he requested the pistol with a raised eyebrow. This time, she held her defiant tongue, hiked her skirt, then withdrew the stocking gun from its holster.

"Do you even know how to shoot it?" she asked teasingly.

"You forget, I was in the war, sweetheart. I may not have your particular skill set but I do have others. I think I can handle this lady peashooter with proficiency."

He slid Sally into his inside breast pocket, then leaned forward, whispering his game plan into her ear. Grasping her hand he said like a tough gumshoe, "C'mon, doll, let's get the heck out of here and get Georgiana."

••

Sixteen

"Oh, Pedro! You are so witty," Elizabeth flirted as she and her catch walked arm-in-arm to the waiting government car at the entrance of the Tropicana. She tried to control her anxiety and wanted to turn yellow at that moment. Without Sally she felt naked, but she knew Darcy had her back. This was his plan, and he'd never let her get into too compromising a position.

The official-looking driver held the passenger door open, and she sat at the edge of the vehicle's backseat, deliberately allowing her skirt to hike, giving Fuego a glimpse of what he hoped to get his hands on later. His eyes raked over her long legs as they slid along the seat making room for him.

He settled beside her, placing his hand on her kneecap, the signet ring on his pinky reviling her.

Once the driver installed himself behind the steering wheel, readying for departure, Darcy abruptly opened the back passenger door and took a seat beside Fuego—Sally jutting into his ribs.

"Don't move, don't fight, or I'll shoot," his deep voice warned, brooking no opposition.

Fuego wanted to struggle; she could feel his body tensing against hers, his face contorting. The driver looked in the rearview mirror; light from the headlights behind them illuminated his eyes in the reflection.

"It is only a guest needing a ride, Juan. No worry. You may drive."

"*Sí*, Mr. Fuego. Where will I be taking you tonight?"

Darcy stuck the pistol in deeper, but Elizabeth spoke quickly. "The Central Hershey Hotel, and no monkey business."

Fuego chuckled. "Ahh ... you must be *Señor* Darcy."

The car departed; Juan said nothing, but his eyes flicked back and forth between the road and the rearview mirror. More than likely he was just another government employee doing a job, but Elizabeth kept a close watch on his actions, ready to withdraw her dagger if need be.

"And who are you, *Señorita*? You played your part very well. I am not usually so easily fooled."

She smirked, her gaze pinning to those milky-gray eyes of his and she couldn't help quoting Philip Marlowe from *Farewell My Lovely*. " 'Your problem', *Señor* Fuego, 'is that you like smooth, shiny girls, hard-boiled and loaded with sin'. Let me introduce myself. I'm Mrs. Darcy." Her eyes met her lover's over the diminutive man's head. She loved how those sexy lips of his twitched in the darkness.

"Wickham said you would come, but I did not think you would. You surprise me," he said looking to his left, straight at Darcy.

"You have someone very dear to me. Why would I not come get my sister back?"

Elizabeth assumed that Fuego's squirm was due to Darcy putting pressure on the gun.

"My comrades assured me that you would capitulate to the ransom demand. You should have done as instructed. But now you will die.

"Not likely. Both Wickham and your Soviet man at the Kit Kat Klub are already dead, and you most likely will end up with the same fate."

He shrugged a shoulder. "I am not surprised by Wickham's demise. Those were my instructions, but I do not think you will have the same successful results, *Señor*."

"You had your man at the Kit Kat Klub kill Wickham?" Elizabeth asked, doubting that was how it happened. A derringer was a dame's number one choice of weapon for waxing a man.

"*Sí*, of course. Why would I pay such a ridiculous amount of money to such a ridiculous man when I just as easily could have kidnapped your sister on American soil at no expense?"

"Then why the ruse in luring her to Cuba?" Darcy asked.

"No ruse. My Soviet comrades insisted on it. Would not your McCarthy be vindicated by the press when an heiress—sister of an outspoken detractor—is kidnapped by *the Red menace*? Then our plan for you would not be so."

Darcy sniggered. "Perhaps it's more a test of your loyalty."

"Perhaps so."

"Is she alive? Is Miss Darcy safe?" Elizabeth asked.

"For now." Again, he shrugged, his action almost acting as a nervous tick. "You will watch her die when we arrive. It will take more than that child's pistol in my ribs to stop my friends."

Darcy withdrew the handcuffs from his dinner jacket pocket then tossed them to Elizabeth. "Cuff his wrists, baby."

"My, my Mr. Darcy, you're getting good at this PI stuff. I might have to consider offering you a *permanent* position. Steer you away from all this political mumbo jumbo." She looked down at the man between them. "We see where that career goal got you."

Fuego's glance switched from left to right at the playful banter.

"Permanent position? Is that your answer or are you toying with me, *Mrs.* Darcy?"

"Baby, that's a bona fide offer."

"I'll need more of a reply than it's 'a bona fide offer'. Oh, and I'd like a ring, too," he added.

"How about I ring you on the horn? Will that suffice?"

"No. I want a shiny gold one and some nice pillow talk afterward."

He smiled an impish grin and she rolled her eyes followed by a chuckle.

"Enough of this!" Fuego demanded causing Darcy to move the pistol's barrel to the man's temple.

"Do not *ever* interrupt my wife and me from a little lovemaking. You got that, pal? This might be a child's pistol, but its bullet will fly through your brain lickety-split. So shut your trap."

Fuego's gaze switched to Elizabeth when she lit a cigarette. The flickering flame from the lighter illuminating her puckered red lips lured him into silent submission.

She blew the smoke into his face in one long, thin stream, and then shot him a look, eyebrow raised with an expression that said "do as you're told."

The thirty-minute drive to the former Hershey village continued in near silence. Even in the darkness of the car, Elizabeth could see in the rearview mirror that the driver looked shifty-eyed. More than once she had to scrape her nails across his nape to remind him that a woman's talons could be lethal should a man make even one wrong move. She knew he packed a rod by the way his fingers itched, tapping upon the steering wheel wanting to reach for it and shoot them both.

"Darling, if you reach for that gun in your breast pocket, both you and Fuego don't stand a chance of seeing your families again," she threatened in Spanish from behind his ear.

At that hour the only road to Hershey, flanked by dark seas of sugar cane plantations, was void of other cars. Empty husks rose from the earth like ominous-looking scarecrows. A moonless darkness shrouded the vehicle as they traveled farther from the nightlife of Havana. The two narrow beams of light from the headlights joined as one leading the way to who knows what at the horizon before them. Ahead, a monolithic structure, blacker than the backdrop of midnight, rose from a field; its silent smokestacks welcomed them.

This was it. They had arrived at the edge of town.

Her heart thundered, but she'd never let on.

She and Darcy's eyes pinned to each other. His lips drew into that unyielding thin line of determination. He was no lollipop—never was and never could be. In that moment, she fully recognized his complexity. He'd given her many glimpses into his soul, but now, as the shadow played across his cheekbones, she saw that when faced with his loved ones in danger, Darcy was a man who had in him the power to kill and annihilate his enemy. No wonder he lived in torment, in fear of those base instincts every human possessed and the past actions he took under their possession. Darcy contained a raging beast inside: the person Wickham had nurtured to the surface, provoked, and encouraged. Cross him, and he was a fierce man to reckon with. Love him, and he was the cream puff he was meant to be. That look in his eyes told her that tonight she would witness that angry seaman in the Pacific.

She mouthed the words, "I love you."

His lips twitched into a half-smile, a slight nod to his head, but that was all he managed before trampling on his soft side as quickly as she had enticed it to the surface. "Stop the car here," he commanded.

"But hotel is just up ahead," the driver said, stopping the car not far from a street lamp.

"Yeah. As are your gang of heavies." Elizabeth opened the car door, one long gam exiting first then the next.

She wanted to laugh at how the driver glanced out the open window, watching her withdraw the dagger from her garter. The male species all had that same look—like they were going to eat her alive for Sunday dinner. If not for the fact that most of them were two-bit hoods and cheaters, it would have been gratifying.

"Outta the car, *Señor* ... *por favor*, and toss me the keys then walk slowly to me. No funny business. You hear?" she commanded with an alluring smile and the presentation of Lady Cat, the *cajone*-slicing, razor-sharp knife—a gift from her friend at El Barrio. "Don't let these high heels fool you. In my hand, Lady Cat is very talented at cutting men down to size."

He did as she bid. The keys flew toward her, promptly caught in her outstretched hand. The surprised look upon his face made her laugh aloud, especially when she tucked them in her cleavage.

Cat was positioned to do the most harm—at his private parts—just like Oscar had taught her, as Elizabeth patted him down with one hand. She immediately went for the gun holstered below his jacket.

Noting the Soviet star embossed on the grip of the gun, she complimented with a smile, "Nice heater," keeping the barrel pointed at his chest. "What is this—a Russian Tokarev?"

"You are good, *Señorita*."

She smirked, feeling like the tough Detective Brandon. "So I've been told, but you'll never find out. I belong to him." She lifted her chin in Darcy's direction, attempting a little levity before all hell broke loose.

"Move. Over there—to the trunk. One false move and I'll plug you full of holes."

With a tight grasp upon the back of Fuego's dinner jacket, Darcy pulled him from the car, pushing him in the direction of the trunk.

Neither Cuban made a move to break free or go for the guns when Elizabeth tossed the keys to Darcy, then handed him the second gun, cocked and at the ready.

She had work to do.

All three men stood agape, mesmerized by her legs when she kicked off her shoes, hiked her black evening dress, then placed one foot on the bumper of the car. She unhooked a stocking from the garter, followed by a teasing roll of nylon down her leg. Her eyes never left Darcy's until she repeated her seduction on the other leg.

A glance over her shoulder with flowing tresses tickling her knee and a wink to Darcy jolted him from his stare.

"Show's over. Both of you in the trunk. Now!" he said, pocketing the small pistol and pressing the Tokarev into Fuego's back. "If you're lucky, we'll let the police know where to find you. For your sake, you better hope no harm has come to my sister."

They climbed in and Darcy shackled them together using the handcuffs.

The stockings? They made excellent gags wrapped around their heads. Yeah. That was her idea. She wasn't such a green private eye, after all.

Darcy closed the truck on the pleading eyes and grunts of protestation from the two thugs within and he turned to face her, a furrow to his brow. "Are you ready, Elizabeth?"

Stepping to him, she smiled wistfully, feeling suddenly nervous. All this moxie and false bravado was beating her down. She was only a gumshoe, not the law, and certainly not a true femme fatale motivated by evil intent, for goodness sake. "Hold me, just for a moment."

Strong arms wrapped around her, and she felt as though she was becoming one with him, melting into his being through his dinner jacket. The ferocity of his heartbeat against her ear confirmed that he felt the same way as she did—apprehensive before the adrenaline kicked in.

"Don't worry, baby. We'll get through this," he assured.

She gazed up into his handsome face. "I know. Now give me one last kiss before—"

His kisser crashed against hers, scalding with intensity. A clinging hand swept through the side of her hair, his tongue plundering hers before their mouths parted.

He left her breathless, causing her to lose her footing in his arms but, as expected, she remained firmly encased in her lover's embrace. Her fella wasn't going to let a damn thing happen to her.

··

The streets of Hershey town were desolate. A lone lamplight shined at the end of the main thoroughfare leading toward the stone hotel within sight on the opposite side of the street. Looking like Hollywood glamour or having just come from a society ball, they walked arm in arm—in the shadow—careful to keep the element of surprise on their side. Not even their footfalls could be heard on the dirt pathway. No doubt, the place was loaded with Fuego's gunsels.

In the distance a train passed. Powering over the track, its wheels and whistle disturbed the silence. As they hurried by the candy store display windows, Darcy noted the remnant Hershey advertisements as though some surreal enticement—a sweet experience in a town loaded with Commie thugs, unscrupulous government officials, and a kidnapped socialite. Ah, the irony. His own persona was an artifice, too. Debonair financier of the best society, he controlled men and their fortunes—but deep down he thrived on this sort of excitement. He had killed a man in cold blood—he knew what his base self could do if he let him loose again. Only docile, innocent Georgiana and loving, astute Elizabeth—from real society—helped him to hold onto the soft side of his nature.

His girl bent at the edge of the tree-lined street, lifting her tightly encased derrière up for admiration. He knew it wasn't her intent to tease him, but he admired it just the same. What he didn't expect was her rising with a handful of dirt, nor for her to smear it on her cheek.

"What are you doing?" he whispered.

She reached into his jacket pocket with her clean hand withdrawing Sally, promptly installing her back where she belonged, and then removed her lipstick from the small purse she carried.

"Elizabeth?"

"You'll see."

A slow glide of ruby refreshed her plump lips—then pop. God, he loved that sexy sound. It made him smile in spite of the situation they found themselves in.

"I guarantee you, Darcy, I can discombobulate them all without a single gunshot."

"I have no doubt, but that's not something I would like to put to the test."

She rolled her eyes. "Just follow my lead. I'll go first. You look to see if there is a back door. This is where we part."

A quick kiss to his cheek, and she was gone before he could object—crossing the deserted street with an air of confidence and that hypnotizing sway to her chassis. Left, boom—right, boom. Her sensual come-hither sashay was lethal in its own right.

He did as she bid, but against his will. She was, again, going off half-cocked, doing what she damn-well pleased. Shaking his head in wonderment with a humored smile, he realized that was exactly what he found most attractive about Elizabeth: her free spirit, her need for liberty in all forms, and the strength of her resolve rising at every challenge. This Bennet sister could never be domesticated like Jane. She needed both sides of life, and only then she'd find harmony and true happiness. Yeah. He'd give that to her every damn day of his life, and never, ever allow her to become a house frau unless that was what she truly wanted.

Before turning the corner toward the back of the two-story hotel, he watched how her sway turned into a slight run in high heels until she stood at the hotel entrance. Out of breath, she gazed up at the iron-trimmed balcony, one hand on her heaving bosom, the other grasping a porch pillar. "Help me," she cried in Spanish.

Crocodile tears. Every dame used them and every guy fell for them—every damn time. Elizabeth could probably pull them off without even a second guess from the poor unsuspecting slob who got caught in her honey trap.

She moved out of Darcy's sight, and a man wearing a white guayabera with a holster installed around his shoulder exited the darkened hotel onto the porch. Elizabeth fell into his outstretched arms, her lips trembling, her act as good as Joan Crawford in *The Damned Don't Cry*.

His girl was fantastic at playing the damsel in distress.

"*Señor*, help me, please!" she wailed, wet tears sliding down her cheeks.

"What is it, *Señorita*?"

"He hit me! I cannot go back, please ... please protect me." She gazed into his concerned face and gave her very best doe eyes.

"*Sí, sí*. Come inside."

••

SEVENTEEN

A lone banker's lamp illuminated the reception desk of the former Hershey hotel lobby. Even in the shallow green light, Elizabeth could tell that it was once an opulent accommodation, but not any longer. Remnants of a card game, liquor bottles, and empty glasses covered a round table beside a long-empty decorative fountain in the center of the hall. She could hear a ceiling fan ticking overhead. The large lobby smelled sweet and pungent—the odor of sugar and cigars.

"Sit, *Señorita*," the tall gunsel directed, pointing to a section of tropical furnishings beside the closed shuttered windows. "You are shaken, but safe now. No harm will come to you here."

She sat, tear-filled eyes fixed on his every move as he walked to the table then filled a glass with rum. "Thank you! I cannot go back. I don't know what to do," she sobbed continuing to speak in the native tongue when he handed it to her. A pouting mouth and weepy expression sealed the deal; she had his sympathy.

Another light flickered on at the top of the staircase leading to the second floor and a burly man (with a thick head of dark curls that any girl would envy) descended. He scratched his chest then rubbed the fog from his eyes. That was a good sign. He wouldn't be on his game at this hour. It was obvious that hood number one had been sentry for the night.

"What goes on here?"

The two men spoke in low tones, buying her some time. Her heart thundered as she raised the glass to her lips but did not drink. Thankful for the dim lighting she was sure they didn't notice her eyes scanning the tables and desk for weapons, sizing up the obstacles between her and the staircase where Georgiana was most likely held. There were six glasses on the table—six heavies to dispose of. Her claim of not using gunfire dissipated when she considered the odds and the position she had put herself in. She would have to let Sally do the talking.

The second Cuban looked in her direction, his hungry gaze traveling over her bare legs before he approached. Clearly he was in charge, and not at all sympathetic to her plight. Her hand trembled when she placed the glass down on the coffee table—real trembles, not like her tears. "Please, sir, my husband ... he ... he ..." she wailed, even spouting some religious phrases for help when he sat beside her.

If she didn't know what to expect, it would have repulsed her when his fat fingers caressed her knee.

"Do not cry so. You are safe now. But there is price that comes for protection."

"I will pay anything! I have money ... other things."

"*Sí.*"

The other hood sat opposite them, watching in some sick voyeur position with his hand on his pistol. It was as though she was the headliner at the Kit Kat and his heater needed to fire. That was fine by her—he had his back to Darcy when he snuck through the lobby from the back of the hotel. She was able to hold their attention as her man quietly ascended the steps in the shadow. The brim of his hat and the barrel of the Russian pistol shined, picking up a sliver of light. Once he was out of sight, she inwardly sighed in relief, especially since the old decrepit stairs hadn't creaked, but she had cried all the same. Soppy, wet, loud tears—probably brought on by fear more than her Oscar Award acting.

"Your tears mar your beauty. Your man was fool to hurt you."

He kissed her hand, then her neck.

As Oscar would say, "It's now or never, toots." As Brandon would say, "Make it count, doll." She didn't want to think what Darcy would say.

Her free hand quickly slid under her dress and withdrew Sally who asked no questions when she fired straight into the trigger hand of the Cuban seated opposite them, followed by a quick shot into the hip of the groping scum beside her. He abruptly released her body and she promptly grabbed the glass, smashing it into his head with all she had before standing, adrenaline humming like the engine of Darcy's Cadillac.

Out of breath and wild-eyed, she gazed down at her groaning would-be violators. "You boys fell for the oldest trick in the book," she said, removing the holstered pistol from the first thug. "Another Tokarev. Your Commie friends are good to you."

He made a move for her, even though limited by the hole in his hand, but she was faster and cocked the Tokarev and popped one into his knee. The red flame muzzle flash was so powerful it lit the darkened room; the recoil from the gun nearly knocked her backward as the gunshot reverberated in the sparsely furnished hall.

"¡*Dios Mío*!" he cried, his bloody hand cradling his leg blown open by the powerful Russian slug, but that didn't stop her from pushing at his shoulder sending him back against the chair. Deft fingers unhooked his belt buckle and a bat of her amber eyes met his silent stare of hopeful wonderment even in his debilitated condition.

"Where's Miss Darcy?" she purred.

He said nothing, just groaned in pain—or pleasure—she couldn't be sure. With a tug, she slid the leather from his waist then patted his head. "If you know what is good for you, you'll stay here, *Señor.*"

His comrade wasn't going anywhere either. It seemed the rum had gone straight to his head. He was knocked out cold and losing blood fast. Damn she was good. Oscar would be so proud.

One flight up, she heard a loud noise and thud.

After those three shots and that crash, all hell was about to break loose.

••

Darcy stood before a hotel room door with a knocked out Soviet at his feet. His Southpaw "torpedo" was his best and most lethal punch, but the thug wasn't dead—just lying there with a broken nose and probably a concussion. Trying to tether the beast within him, he'd use the gun only if necessary.

Resisting the urge to call out for his sister, he pursed his lips, unsure of how many others, besides this one at his feet, would come running following the three gunshots below. The two thugs downstairs had obviously met their demise by Sally after Elizabeth cast her spell over them in the eerie green lobby. That thought made him sick, recalling that Cuban's paws on his woman, but he couldn't think on that right now. But she was a dishy, one-woman wrecking crew; she'd be fine. He willed himself to focus on his breathing and calming his powerful heartbeat pounded in his ears like a conga drum.

The landing of the staircase creaked and he spun around, fist and pistol ready to fire. It was Elizabeth with a twinkle in her eye, a Russian pistol in her hand, a black evening dress skimming her body, and a leather strap draped around her neck. His brilliant, adventuress, sex pot was illuminated by the staircase overhead fixture. It was the most alluring sight he'd ever seen.

"Are they dead?" he whispered before licking his thumb, followed by a brush to her cheek to wipe the dirt, feeling an enormous sense of relief that she was safe.

"No, just out of commission." She looked down. "Him?"

"No, but he'll be out for some time."

"There are at least three more," she said, her hand wrapping around the doorknob at their left. "I'm surprised they didn't come running after those shots, but there are four spent rum bottles down there. Their boozing may be our advantage." She opened the door slightly.

"Where are you going?"

She winked and stepped into the room.

Shaking his head at her moxie, he entered the one to his left, the light from the hall barely breaching the space, but he could see it was empty, and moved to the next. Silently, stealthily making his way along the hallway the luminosity behind him diminished, the corridor growing darker with each step.

Rushed footsteps tapped the wood floor behind him. He spun around again, this time swinging, but Elizabeth ducked away in the nick of time.

A strong expulsion of breath and a furrowed brow of admonishment met her grin. "Don't do that! I almost killed you!" Darcy scolded in barely a breath. "Where's the strap?"

"We're down to two thugs now. I tied him to the bedpost. Sleeping off the booze, he thought I was some sort of pie-eyed sex dream."

Truly, he wanted to laugh, but just couldn't bring himself to do so. Elizabeth was calmer than he but supposed she was used to this sort of dangerous affair. Never before had he met a woman who wasn't squeamish at the sight of blood and a little foul play.

Elizabeth held the bottom of his dinner jacket, allowing him to lead the way toward the end of the hallway, stepping together in quiet unison until they stopped. He chanced a glance around the corner.

Playing sentry outside Georgiana's obvious prison sat their fifth obstacle. Awake with muscular legs spread apart, the Commie's, at least, six-foot-three frame was dressed in black. He lit a cigar; puffs of smoke wafted around his face.

Either this was gonna be easy or hard and Darcy wasn't about to let Elizabeth have her way again. The man before them was a stone-cold killer. Even in the dark, he could see the manner in which the thug held himself, the way he lit his smoke. He'd see through Elizabeth's honey trap in an instant and snap her neck with one hand. Sally wouldn't even make a dent in him. These Commies, hell bent on their cause, had no conscience. All they saw was red: in anger, ideology, or blood.

Darcy straightened to his full height, throwing back his shoulders. "Stay here, Elizabeth, and do not defy me on this." He smashed his lips against her kisser before he turned the corner.

All she heard was a single gunshot that shook the entire floor.

Her breath caught in fear.

A second later, she felt a strong arm come from behind, nearly choking her when it brought a cool, sharp blade to her neck. The scent of familiar cologne filled her lungs when she gasped. Fuego.

"Do not move, *Señorita*. Do not cry out or I will slice," his foul breath commanded as he slapped the free end of the handcuffs around her wrist. He hiked her dress, removing Sally and Lady Cat, but not before dragging his fingers over her inner thigh.

"You pig!" she spat and he laughed, throwing the dagger and derringer on the floor.

Dragging her backward, toward the staircase, she felt his jagged blade nick her skin, their hands connected by the metal restraints gripped her waist like a vice. She was helpless to fight.

••

Darcy stepped over the dead Soviet, ignoring the pooling blood at his head. He kicked open the locked door, flipped up the light switch, and his heart broke at the sight before him: Georgiana, white evening dress torn, mouth gagged, and hands bound to the brass bed by rope.

He ran to her then sat on the bed beside her, fighting the urge to cry. The anger he had felt toward her dissipated in a flash. "Thank God! Are you hurt, Georgiana?" he asked untying the gag, cradling her head and kissing her dirty forehead.

"Fitzwilliam! Oh God!" she cried, tears streaming down her cheeks as he undid the bindings to her hands. "I thought they were going to kill me!"

"You're safe. Are you hurt?"

"No."

"They didn't?"

"No. They didn't."

Feeling her tremble and afraid that she'd go into shock, he held her tightly. "I'm taking you home, but first you need to be strong so we can get out of here quickly. Can you walk?"

She nodded.

Gingerly he placed her hand in his and led her to the door. "Don't look down, Sister. Just follow me, stay behind me."

"I will. I'm so sorry, Fitzwilliam."

"I know. Me, too. We'll discuss that when we get back to New York. I'm just happy you're alive."

They turned the corner of the hallway and Darcy stopped cold. Elizabeth was gone, her pistol and dagger staring up at him from the floor.

He heard heavy steps take command of the staircase and his head snapped up, bracing himself for another of Fuego's gunnies. It was the driver of the sedan, illuminated by the stairwell light. Their eyes met over the dark chasm between them.

With his right hand, Darcy guided his sister to stay where she was then took two steps to the center of the hall, visible and ready for the battering ram with cut wrists charging toward them. Apparently, he hadn't shackled him to Fuego tight enough.

Standing his ground, he waited. Seconds seemed to drag, the thug's form growing darker as he ran from the light. Darcy tightened his fists, his feet firmly planted, his lips drawn.

It was over before it began. A single punch to the driver's jaw sent his head and body flying backward. The man was out cold before he was able to throw a single punch.

This was different from Nouméa. This was life or death and he had no regret.

Taking Georgiana's hand in his once again, he said, "We need to find Elizabeth."

"Who's Elizabeth?"

"The woman you can thank for finding you," was all he could bring himself to say, his mind focused on her whereabouts. He was near panicked at the thought that she was in danger but couldn't let it show to his sister, already figure eights and for good reason.

Again, Darcy stopped dead when they arrived at the top of the steps. His heart stopped along with his body. Across the wide expanse of the lobby, with the fountain separating them, Elizabeth struggled in Fuego's arms, attempting to get free yet bound to him by the handcuffs, a blade rested along that slender throat of hers. He'd kissed that spot a hundred times. Her eyes glistened in the dim light. With the hotel door opened, she was back dropped by the black stillness of the street behind them.

Fury rushed like a bleeding river in his veins and he saw red; the beast was unleashed. He dropped his sister's hand, then descended the steps, expression frozen.

"Let her go, Fuego," he bellowed.

"It is fruitless, *Señor* Darcy. I have sent for my men. They are coming, and will love to taste your wife and sister when they arrive. We will watch, and then you will die."

"It ain't gonna happen. Not like that, anyway. We're gonna walk out of here. Me, my sister, and Mrs. Darcy."

Fuego laughed, a maniacal sound that filled the lobby.

Darcy removed the pistol from his pocket, raising it, adrenaline electrifying him. "Drop the knife."

"I do not think so."

The small man's grip around her was surprisingly strong as Elizabeth fought him, his feet managing to circumvent each calculated stomp of her heels.

Thirty feet away. You can make this precise shot to his head. But doubt crept in. *What if you miss? What if you hit the woman you love?* In only mere seconds perspiration had formed on his forehead as he held the gun steady, aimed at Fuego's head. He took a few steps closer.

"Take the shot, Darcy," his brave girl shouted, but the now visible fear in her eyes told him something else.

A trickle of sweat rolled down his temple.

The second hand of time spent in indecision continued in the stand-off: tick ... tock ... tick.

Bang!

Georgiana's scream pierced the air.

Fuego fell dead.

Elizabeth fell with him.

Darcy hadn't fired, but when they dropped to the floor, he could see Captain Guzman standing on the porch behind them, gun smoking, and a quirk to his lips.

Relief flooded Darcy's entire being, feeling as though he'd collapse in a heap beside his girl.

Both men rushed to Elizabeth, but it was Darcy who lifted her from the floor into his arms, as Guzman unlocked her from Fuego's death grip.

"It's about damn time, Ricky!" she chastised, throwing both arms around Darcy, clinging to him.

The captain laughed. "How did you know?"

"Call it a dame's intuition. I didn't think you'd really leave us in the lurch. Besides, if there's one thing my friend Detective Brandon of the NYPD taught me is that no flatfoot ever gives his handcuffs away without a guarantee that he'll be getting them back."

Darcy hugged her tightly, then set her from him for examination. "Are you okay, sweetheart? Let me look at you. You're hurt."

"It's just a scratch, Darcy. I'll survive. I'm not such a lollipop."

In spite of the wistful smile she offered, he looked straight into her eyes, reading her and saw it there hidden below all that fearless attitude—she was terrified and holding back a flood of tears.

He felt her legs going weak and pulled her back into his embrace, kissing her head. "C'mon baby, let's go home."

"I ... I heard Georgiana scream. Is she okay?"

"Yeah. Physically, she's okay, emotionally and mentally, I don't know. She's frightened, as expected.

Gazing down at her, his voice softened as he brushed back the hair from her forehead. His heart swelled with absolute pride. "We did it, Elizabeth. You were fabulous. My God, we're a great team."

"We are, Mr. Darcy. We saved the damsel in distress and killed the bad guys, and I might even come through this with a proposal and a diamond ring."

She was still beating a dead horse even in her trauma. His lips met hers and he closed his eyes at the sublime feeling just before Georgiana descended the steps, wide-eyed and silent until she croaked.

"Fitzwilliam?"

She ran into his outstretched arm. Yeah. They were gonna be fine. Both his girls had come through this.

"We must go ... now," Guzman said. "I have car waiting and have arranged for ferry. You will be safe in Florida in only a few hours."

They ran from the hotel where a brand new convertible waited for them in the darkened street.

"It is my brother-in-law's," he said with a proud smile. "Very fast— *Americano* Buick Riviera Super Eight."

"I'll make sure you get one, too, Captain."

"And Oscar, or I will never hear the end of it on his next visit to Havana."

"Sure, I owe you both for saving our hides."

••

EIGHTEEN

The Kit Kat Klub's doors re-opened for business only two days after the scandalous double-murder, even though the investi- gation was still in full force. Having taken in the first bump-n-grind show as the clean-up crew finished mopping the club up of blood and brains, Brandon's day had been off to a promising start. The sex onstage was followed up by a cigarette and a lucky break when one of the boys found a murder weapon beneath a booth's seat cushion. They dusted the knife that sliced the Ruskie's neck for fingerprints, and now all he needed to do was to impatiently wait to see if the murderer was a repeat offender.

His mood grew darker, and his morning worsened as the newshawks had a field day and the mayor demanded answers. Even CIB had stayed clear of this case so that their on-going intelligence gathering into Soviet activities wasn't compromised. To make matters worse, he just heard from the top brass that the Feds would be making an appearance after lunch. It was about damn time they decided to show up—most likely a deliberate stall, waiting for him to do all the work and process the crime scene. He had indigestion already. He'd just pulled his second white night and was cranky, but rationalized that all of it was to be expected in the life of a homicide detective. At least it was in his life.

He leaned against the wall in the hallway outside the Kitten dressing room, needing to occupy his fingers to keep from turning the doorknob and barging in. With the strike of a match he lit the first cigarette from his third pack of Lucky Strikes smoked today. Yeah. The last 35 hours had been hell, but at least they were giving him free smokes.

This job at this sleazy striptease place required patience; he'd wait until someone exited the room. He wasn't going anywhere until he asked a few more questions. Eli had been thorough, but she'd beat a path out of there sooner than expected. And this was one lead he wasn't going to overlook: rumor had it that one of the strippers was dating the poor dead slob with a bullet through his brain, a fact his new "partner" had failed to uncover. Maybe his gorgeous lady dick friend wasn't going to play on his side of the street due to her connection to the deceased. It was just as well because with the Feds arriving, he didn't want her anywhere near this case. He'd have to wait and see if the nickel dropped because she had a case of the nerves when she skipped out on the investigation. He long knew murderers often smelled like roses, and maybe this homicide wasn't so black and white. There was still the issue of the missing derringer, a dame's number one choice of weapon when waxing a man.

Cackling laughter came from behind the dressing room door, and he took another calming drag of his cigarette, moving to the opposite wall. His eyes settled on the stagehand desk and the two dozen or so photographs tacked on the wall above the telephone.

Honky Tonk music filled the hallway as Miss April Showers did her little cowgirl number on the stage, its entrance just a few feet from him. He tried not to focus on that saddle she used as a prop, instead attempted to examine the photographs with a clear head, but it didn't work. Angela the A-bomb looked almost as good in a snapshot as she did on stage, but no one would hear that come from his lips. His dirty old man thoughts about the club's performers remained locked in his mind. That autographed publicity shot showed Miss A-bomb's claim to fame in all their glory. She had the largest bombs he'd ever laid his peepers on, even from three-feet away. He stepped toward the collage of images and withdrew the detective pad from his inside suit pocket. His pencil worked furiously jotting all the telephone numbers displayed between erotic images. Most of the women were nearly nude, all of them pin-up calendar worthy. Holy Toledo, he was going nuts and needed a cold shower. This case was going to be the death of him, but he'd never squawk. It was the most action he'd seen in months.

He took a deep drag of his cigarette, eyes zeroing in on an image of an ample-bosomed, blonde broad sitting on the lap of the late Mr. George Wickham. He was obviously a regular and that rumor was now confirmed. The corpse looked different below that beard and black hair, but that was him alright—the scar was a dead giveaway. His cold, lifeless eyes, like a doll's glass eyes, told him that he was a bad seed.

The dressing room door opened and he abruptly turned, glancing over his shoulder, able to catch a glimpse of curves, flesh, and feathers. A petite, Oriental dame wearing a pink negligee exited, smiling demurely at him. She was a real dish with hair as black as his mood. He'd have to get a load of her performance.

"Say, Miss. Can you tell me who the dancer is in this snapshot?"

She spoke in an accented, sing-song voice that nearly undid him. "Her name Dixie."

"Is she here today?"

"No. She telephone sick. No perform tonight."

"Do you know where I can find her?"

"Don't know; ask Dimitri. He know everything."

Dimitri. The uncooperative owner of the Kit Kat Klub. The stonewalling, investigation-obstructing, most likely card-carrying Commie was due for a real New York-style, third-degree grilling, and he was in just the mood to do it.

The delicate China doll giggled and walked away from him with a sway to her chassis that dropped his jaw.

"Thanks, sweetheart. Say ... what are you doing when you get off work?"

"Not you, round-eye," was her reply.

••

Dimitri was as tight lipped as the mouth on a smelly flounder out of Sheepshead Bay, and that was about as big a compliment as Brandon could bestow when the mugg produced the name and address of that chippie sitting on Wickham's lap. It all became clear as to why Eli skipped out on the investigation: Her sister Lydia was the stiff's girl.

He furrowed his brow, thinking what a mess Eli was in, but his cop gut told him that there was more to this bubble-gum story than met the eye. Eli wasn't answering the horn and he had a bad, bad feeling about "Dixie." The young girl was trouble with a capital *Y*-in-hell was she working at a place like the Kit Kat?—and where in hell was she tonight?

After having shown up at the Bennet family row home in Jackson Heights three hours ago, he understood why Eli couldn't wait to beat a path out of that part of Queens. As a Brooklyn boy, that Borough never had any appeal. The broads, with the exception of his young friend, were about as exciting to him as a whorehouse filled with Venus and mercury.

It became clear after only five minutes in the parlor with the television on full blast that mom and pop Bennet cared more about the questions on "What's My Line," then the ones that a homicide detective was asking about their seventeen-year-old daughter. Nope. He couldn't pump one iota of information from the low-class, lush parents. They were about as cooperative as Dimitri had been, and taking a flutter at explaining that Lydia's boyfriend, Wickham, had been waxed in a strip club turned out to be a feat, too. The poor slobs thought the dead grifter was fighting Chinks over in Korea. The screwball mother wanted to hang a Gold Star flag on the door! The father, wearing greasy coveralls, "invited" him to leave with a Louisville Slugger in his hand. Obviously, unfazed by the shiny gold NYPD shield pinned to his overcoat.

If it wasn't for Eli, he'd have hauled Thomas Bennet's pie-eyed ass down to the precinct.

Could this day get any worse? He'd driven all over the city, following the trail of every damned lead he'd gotten and now he stood at the door of Wickham's rundown tenement in a South Bronx slum.

On this cold winter night, the building was lousy with bad hats hiding in the shadow of stairwells. He heard low, plotting voices, but he was a crack shot, his .38 caliber at the ready. The noxious smell of urine and fried chicken permeated the hallway where a bare light bulb overhead flickered. It buzzed and flickered off and on. Someone turned their television on and Ed Sullivan's distinct voice caused raucous audience laughter.

There for a second look around, just in case he missed something the first time, Brandon was about to open Slick Wick's door when he heard a bang come from inside. As far as he knew, the mugg was still dead, still lying in the morgue. Right now, he was the one holding the only key.

Slowly, he cracked open the door. The place was dark, and he heard the noise again. Stepping in, he unholstered his pistol, keeping it close to his chest.

Even in the pitch he could see a mess. Who knows, maybe the victim was a slob, maybe he was robbed. Or maybe ...

Quietly, he made his way toward the noise emanating from the only other room. The racket grew, a few swear words made by a woman mumbled and he wondered if it was Eli. His heart hammered; his thoughts prayed not.

He peered his head around the door frame.

It was "Dixie" and he sighed in relief, watching as she turned drawers over, emptying them onto the floor. A nervous wreck—the dame was looking for something.

Brandon cocked his pistol then flipped the light on. "Park the body, Miss Bennet. No false moves."

The girl halted with a wild look in her eyes and a brown paper bag in hand. "How ... how do you know my name?"

He walked to her, pistol still drawn. "I'm a homicide detective; that's how I know, and I have a feeling you know who killed Slick Wick." His free hand removed the bag from her and he glanced in—it was filled with cash.

"Take a seat, Lydia. You and me are gonna have a little chat."

"No. I ain't talkin'."

"Then we'll take a ride down to the precinct so I can put you on ice. How does that sound?"

"Are you that detective Brandon whose been looking for me?"

"In the flesh, sweetheart."

She petulantly plopped down onto the edge of the bed.

"Yeah. I thought you'd see it my way."

"Well, I won't talk without my sister Elizabeth present."

"And why is that?"

"Cause I know who killed that Commie at the Kit Kat and she promised to help me."

"And do you know who killed the mugg whose apartment you're ransacking?"

Lydia folded her arms across her chest. "Nope."

Brandon raised an eyebrow and peered into the paper bag, again. "There's gotta be at least three *G*s in here. Where'd a shmoe like Wickham get this kind of dough?"

"Like I said, I'm not spillin' anything until my sister gets here."

Then the waterworks came. Big, fat tears that didn't fool him for a minute.

••

NINETEEN

Happy and relieved to be back in the Big Apple, Darcy and Elizabeth had allowed exhaustion to overcome them. The dramatic rescue of Georgiana, followed by a half-day of travel, had done them in and they fell into bed—after a much-needed, damn-good cry of relief, on her part. Keeping it bottled up took its toll on her during the flight home and she broke like a dam the minute Darcy's bedroom door closed, falling into his arms and sobbing like a baby.

Six hours after their return to the Dakota, she rolled to her side in Darcy's massive bachelor bed, luxuriating in the sensation of the silk sheets below her nudeness. In the dark, she reached out, expecting to feel the warm, bare skin of her lover beside her, but was, instead, greeted by empty bed linen. Her hand smoothed over the coolness of his vacant side, and she felt bereft. His snores had become welcome company, his cuddles even more so, acting as soothing balms to the weary, lonely soul she had been before falling into his arms three nights ago. Since then, it had been quite a whirlwind romance with unexpected, deeper feelings and declarations more than the "I'm in love with yous" claimed before departure to Cuba.

A razor-thin light escaped from the bottom of the dressing room door that led to the bedroom. She heard a noise from within. "Darcy?"

No answer came and worriedly, she sat up, switching on the light. The clock read one in the morning.

Her hand slid under his pillow, withdrawing Sally, newly loaded with fresh bullets, after having spent the ones taken to Havana.

A half-filled glass of scotch sat beside Darcy's money clip and wristwatch on his highboy dresser. He was drinking tonight. Something was wrong. Maybe he was still wound up, still worried over her. She frowned.

"Darcy? Are you in there?"

"Just a minute!" he barked, his voice clearly agitated.

"Are you okay? You're frightening me and going to wake Georgiana."

He slid back the door and stood in the threshold wearing his dressing gown, his broad chest exposed by the haphazard sash tied around his waist. A hand flew to his unkempt hair, attempting to smooth the dark waves that mussed while he had slept. Her guy looked so damned adorable when he righted the robe and attempted a smile.

"Darling, what is it?" she asked moving to the edge of the bed, clutching the sheet to cover her bosom. "Why are you awake and drinking? Can't you sleep?"

"I ... no, I couldn't."

She made to get up, but he stopped her. "No! Stay right there. You look so beautiful." He took a deep breath, his expression softening as he drank her in.

She, too, felt the same consuming emotion when their eyes locked on each other, expressing silent words of admiration and love just as they had in the car on the way to rescue Georgiana.

"Thursday is Thanksgiving," he said, which seemed an odd topic of conversation given what they had just come through and what they were feeling at that moment—particularly since they were both nearly nude.

"Yes. It is."

"I'm thankful."

"Me, too."

Darcy walked to her, his lips drawing into a faint smile and her heart did a little dance. She wondered if he was going to do what she hoped he would do. The man needed to make a respectable woman out of her soon, knowing that she wouldn't be anyone's floozy, not even his.

Sitting beside Elizabeth, he ran his fingers through the luxurious waves that fell in an adorable mess around her shoulders. He was spellbound by the golden sparks twinkling in her amber eyes. Her pupils dilated. They hadn't been intimate in over 24 hours and it was obviously killing her as much as it was him. They were good together, and not just in the bedroom.

He bent, brushing the hair away from her neck, then kissed the minor cut, still upset by how close he came to losing her.

"Baby," he said followed by a hard swallow of something the size of a baseball stuck in his throat, which he couldn't get out. He started again, unable to temper the ferocity of his heartbeat. "Baby, my words can't do justice to the intensity of emotion that I feel. Your love ... well ... it saved me."

She bit her lip. He'd never seen her do that before.

Of all the things he'd done in life, this one had to be the hardest. His palms sweat. Loving Elizabeth was easy, telling her that he loved her more than life itself—not so much. This near-perfect dame and all her moxie was in his blood. He slid off the bed to his knee and took her delicate hand in his.

"I ... I know I promised poetic verses, but we don't need them. Our love is the sonnet, strong enough without another's words to nourish it. I'm humbled that you love all of me—the good and the bad."

He looked away, then back, regrouping, swallowing again at the sight of her eyes filling with tears. "We found each other in the shadows, and you brought me and my lonely existence into the light. In just three short days, we have been through so much together, and I wish to never part from you. Elizabeth Bennet, marry me, and I'll truly be the happiest man alive."

He felt like a total sap—a real cream puff—with that proposal but it was the God's honest truth—all of it—and his doll deserved that and more.

A tear rolled down her ivory skin and he reached up, brushing it away. Her bottom lip quivered, and his thumb brushed that, too, before he deposited a gentle kiss. Her soft, unpainted lips felt like heaven on earth below his.

She bent forward, holding his head to her, unwilling to end their lip lock until he finally pulled back, needing to finish what he started.

"And ... and um ... there's this."

Her eyes widened when he removed the blue velvet ring box from his pocket. Then her jaw slacked when he opened the cover. Yeah, he expected that.

"It was my mother's, and I'd be honored if you'd accept it ... and my hand."

"Ho ... ly ... Toledo, Darcy!"

"Do you like it?"

"What are you kidding? What girl wouldn't? That's the biggest piece of ice I've ever seen."

She laughed reaching her hand out, but he couldn't help joking with her, pulling back the box from her grasp. "Not so fast," he said with a raised eyebrow. "I believe you have something for *me.*"

That saucy smile of hers undid him.

"As if I'd have to say the words that you already know, you big lug. It's not like you don't know how I feel about you. I absolutely, positively adore you. Of course I'll marry you, Darcy!"

Elizabeth dropped the silk wrapped around her chest and slid from the bed onto his lap, planting a huge one right on his kisser. The woman was buck naked with tears of happiness streaming down her gorgeous face. She playfully wiggled her eyebrows and damn if that alone didn't get his johnson up. He snapped the ring box closed then tossed it aside as soon as she dropped the dressing gown from his shoulders.

Those sexy gams wrapped around his waist and between scorching kisses to her neck he murmured. "We'll ... announce our engagement ... at Charlie and Jane's on Thanksgiving."

She chuckled and he knew why. "I think that's a wonderful idea. I can't wait to see Jane's face."

Her supple skin below his caressing palm sent a frisson up his arm. Yeah. This was gonna be one hell of a marriage. He'd never get enough of his alluring private dick wife. And yes, she had spades over her sister.

••

The following morning brought rain and that sure as heck confused Elizabeth because as far as she knew—Wickham was still dead. The gloomy weather was supposed to have stopped.

Although there was mist and heavy fog shrouding the Big Apple, and the Dakota apartment felt cold and dreary, Elizabeth was able to examine the suite of rooms for the first time. With the heavy draperies pulled back, she admired the art deco opulence. It's clean, geometric lines and frosted glass fixtures were striking in spite of being a little dated. They were holdovers from Anne Darcy, his mother, but she understood why the residence had never been updated. Her man loved the bittersweet memory of his mother and change had been difficult.

The arrival of a Mrs. Reynolds on the scene at the crack of dawn had surprised Elizabeth, not expecting "domestic help" and it really knocked her for a loop when a cook arrived, followed by a butler an hour later. This army of intruders would be something she'd have to grow accustomed to after she became the lady of the house. She'd have to consider that. Maybe she could remain in Hell's Kitchen, but that would mean she'd be far from the suit and that was an unthinkable option—since the man owned her heart. All three servants had cheery dispositions and did not question her presence at the breakfast table but, no doubt, they were confused. Respectable women, even those from real society, did not stay overnight at a bachelor's apartment, especially with his sister present.

Breakfast was a strained affair to say the least. Between spoonfuls of poached egg from the sterling cup, Darcy's sour puss vacillated at moments from hints of happiness to clear anger every time he glanced in the direction of his sister's pretty blonde head and delicate features. Elizabeth could understand his disappointment even though he felt immeasurable guilt and understood acutely Georgiana's desire for freedom. The fact remained that she was a grown woman who had acted foolishly—but then, so had he during the war.

None worse for the wear, apart from sheer mortification and shame (for the most part), Georgiana remained silent. Darcy would never ask the intimate details between her and Slick Wick, and she didn't offer. Maybe she would open up about it after the wedding. Now *that* issue also caused confusion at the breakfast table. As far as Georgiana had expected, Elizabeth was to return home following their arrival back in the city. Her presence was met with a furrowed brow, much like Mrs. Reynolds'.

Elizabeth could plainly see the questions swirling in the young woman's mind every time her eyes settled upon her mother's diamond twinkling on someone else's ring finger. But nothing was offered as explanation, and it made both women uncomfortable exchanging slight smiles between mouthfuls and much needed coffee. Even her own pleading expression, raised eyebrows, and head quirks to Darcy went unaddressed by him as he continued to eat in stoic silence. He was barely civil and unwilling to announce their engagement to his sister; she near expected him to open a newspaper and ignore them both. The man at the table was entirely different than the one who got down on one knee with a proposal worthy of Charlotte Brontë, then thrilled her in his arms right afterward as though straight out of a lurid dime store novel. This morning he had been ripped from an Edgar Allen Poe novel. Dark and brooding. No smolder this morning.

"What will you do today, Georgiana?" he coldly asked.

"What would you like for me to do, Brother?"

"It obviously doesn't matter what I would like. You'll ignore my suggestion."

"If only it was just a suggestion, and not a command."

"Perhaps you would like to go with me to purchase a wedding dress?" Elizabeth blurted.

"You're getting married? To Fitzwilliam? When?"

"Do you have an issue with that?" Darcy asked, clearly attempting to pick a fight.

Georgiana blanched at the tone in his voice.

A loud clank from Elizabeth's tea cup into the saucer startled the siblings to attention. "Stop it, Darcy! You're acting like a petulant child. Your sister has been through a traumatic event at the hands of a vile man who sold her a bill of goods. A little compassion is what is warranted this morning, not this foolish condemnation and guilt laying. So what if she lied? Be happy she's alive and remember why she wasn't honest with you in the first place."

His face turned dark, his eyes boring into hers. Those lips. That tightening kisser.

Suddenly, he pushed the chair back, stood, and scowled. He didn't even grunt as was his usual fashion when she called him on the carpet. A toss of his napkin onto the table preceded his abrupt departure from the room.

Elizabeth sighed deeply. *Damn!* She had crossed the line. "I shouldn't have said that. I should go after him."

"Please wait ... Thank you for coming to my defense, but it was unnecessary. He's right and I'm ashamed. I foolishly put myself in that position. Fitzwilliam had warned me away from George Wickham and I chose to ignore him. Warned me about Cuba and the danger there." She looked away, fisting the napkin in her grasp, obviously shamed. "I learned a hard lesson, and I'm thankful I'm alive. I wish ... I wish ..."

Another sigh. "Oh Georgiana. You can't be angry at yourself for being a sappy romantic." She blotted her lips on the napkin then rose from the table. "Follow me. We need to have a conversation about the man you went to Havana with. You may have made an unwise decision but he was a charming con man who knew how to manipulate women."

"You knew him?" She, too, rose, eyes searching Elizabeth's.

"I did. It's because of him that I met your brother—but now I'm the happiest girl in the world, and your sensitive brother has shown me how a man ought to act when in true love."

"*How* did you know George?"

They hooked arms and walked toward Georgiana's bedroom. "It's a long story, and it ain't pretty, but maybe when you hear it, it will help you to forgive yourself—and to wise up. You're not the only girl who believed the first man to come along with sweet nothings."

"He said he loved me, Elizabeth, and I hate that I was so insecure, so naïve, to have believed him."

"I understand that ... he said the same to me. Unfortunately, as we both learned, his reasons were less than honorable. Lessons like these come hard, but give us greater clarity for the future. Help us to see when the right man comes along."

The telephone rang and they heard Darcy's resonant voice in the study as they passed the open door. A moment later, he stood at the threshold to the hallway, calling after them.

"Elizabeth! ... that was your friend Detective Brandon ... We have to leave; Lydia needs us."

Her heart sank. Brandon must be desperate, he had tracked her down—and that meant the worst: Lydia was in big trouble.

"Lydia? Who's Lydia?" Georgiana asked.

"*My* sister, another girl who fell for George Wickham's pretty lies."

"I wish that man was dead."

"He is, Georgiana. Someone beat us all to it."

••

TWENTY

This wasn't Elizabeth's first trip to the 8th Precinct on 3rd Street, not by a long shot. In fact, almost all the boys in blue at that police station knew her, but none gave her the respect that Brandon had. Most tried to obstruct her investigations, resenting the fact that she was a female private dick. So it wasn't a surprise when she felt the burn of stares upon her when she entered the big house with Darcy on her arm. The smoke-filled precinct was a hive of activity of disorderly conduct: drunks, angry criminals, smart-mouthed prostitutes, and the uniformed officers who fought with them all.

It seemed as though everyone fell silent when Darcy's hand touched the small of her back to lead her ahead of him down the hallway. Maybe it was her choice of apparel causing the astonishment. She couldn't be sure. Mink didn't suit her, and Lord knows none of the flatfoots present had seen her in anything so glamorous. But it was cold out and her flimsy trench coat wasn't going to cut the mustard for the trip downtown in the Darcy family limousine. Thank God her future sister-in-law was her size—and a moneybags. Of course, sporting the huge piece of ice on her finger made her look like one, too. Maybe it was Darcy causing the stares. She heard one B-girl say, "Come to mamma." Yeah. His blue eyes and scrumptious kisser, even that confident swagger of his, was enough to curl any woman's toes.

"Well, well, Eli. I see you finally managed to get down here. Took you long enough, toots." Brandon said with a crooked smile as they approached the front desk. "But I can see why. You look like a million smackers."

"Thanks, pally."

He nodded, eyes raking over her appreciatively. "Yep. You're looking mighty uptown. What happened—you finally got Jackson Heights outta your system?"

"Darling, you know that place has been out of my system well over a year now."

Brandon held out his hand to Darcy for a shake. "Welcome to the 8th, Mr. Darcy. I'm glad to finally meet the fella who had enough moxie to go after my girl's heart."

"Your girl?"

"Don't worry, sir. Nothin' like that. She's my partner in crime only, a real smart cookie and a talented gumshoe."

She could feel the jealousy roll off Darcy. One hour ago he was a real grouch and now he was all territorial. Getting accustomed to his vacillating moods was going to take some real dancing. "Don't you remember, Darcy? I told you about Chris. Similar to my friend Oscar, he helps me when the doors get slammed in my face. He's a real stellar guy without the funny business or the *overt* leering."

"That's good to hear. Pleasure to meet you, detective. Thanks for tracking us down."

"Well, it didn't take much searching given the way Eli here stonewalled me when I asked about you. When I couldn't get her on the horn last night, I assumed she finally made her way downtown to the Dakota to break the news about that photograph of your sister. It doesn't take a detective to figure out that you two were meant for each other."

All business, back on the case, Elizabeth scanned the precinct; her tone grew serious. "Where is she?"

"She's on ice in the interrogation room, and about as tight-lipped as you were when you didn't spill that she was your sister and the moll of your dead grifter." He raised an eyebrow.

"Sorry about that. I was shocked to see her at the Kit Kat and had to get her out of there, back home. You know, she's only seventeen and I was afraid she'd be busted for working as a juvie."

"Yeah. I know all about that. I paid a visit to your parents. I'm not saying that they were boozehounds, but I was the only sober one answering the questions on 'What's My Line'."

She ignored that comment and stayed on point. "Hmm ...What did you haul Lydia in for?"

"Trespassing and attempted robbery of that poor slob Wickham's apartment in the Bronx, but she says she has a story to tell and only wants to tell you. Oh, and Mr. Darcy, too. And another thing, she says she knows who killed the Commie at the Kit Kat, but we already know that, too. The fingerprints came back late last night."

"And?" Elizabeth asked.

"Again, Wickham. His prints were identical to another murder weapon down in Baltimore from four years ago, and the Feds telephoned this morning with the news that the mugg's fingerprints matched Naval records. They were finally able to put their mouth into this investigation with something I didn't already know."

She looked to Darcy, their eyes meeting. "I guess Wickham wasn't too happy when he didn't get his payment from the Red at the club," she said.

"Payment for what?" Brandon asked.

Darcy chuckled wryly. "Long story, but the short of it is that we think we have some information as it relates to Wickham's murder."

"Is that your way of tellin' me that you didn't pull that trigger? Where were you when he was kil—?"

"Darcy was with me, Chris," she interrupted, placing her hand on Darcy's bicep to silence him before he objected to Brandon's presumption and her obstruction to an investigation "We had lunch together ... at his place ... alone."

Brandon raised an eyebrow. "Like I said, Eli, I'll take your word. You're not the type of dame to kiss and tell unless it's called for. I'll accept his alibi then." He scrutinized them both, narrowing his eyes before adding, "Follow me, Mr. Darcy. I'd like to take your statement, so we can get 'Dixie' off the hot seat, too."

"Oh! You don't ... she's not also a murder suspect is she? Tell me no!" She clutched Darcy's arm, needing his support.

"Well, I caught her holding a bag of dough, but maybe she'll do some confessing to her sister. She tossed her cookies a couple of times, so I'm thinking she's scared about something."

"Did you ... did you find the derringer? Because we may have another lead. It might have been that Commie after all, just like I suspected."

"No sign of Wickham's murder weapon, but we are also investigating some other avenues. Turns out your bad hat had a long string of dames on the side. Lydia wasn't his only girl."

"No surprise there. Lord knows he played around with almost all the girls in Jackson Heights."

"What did you call him?"

"Slick Wick," Darcy said.

"Yuppers. That about sums him and his libido up. A real skirt-chaser, that one. We're trying to get an i.d. on a particular chippie that he met with on a regular basis several months ago. Maybe she knows something."

They walked down another long hallway until they stopped in front of a door with a frosted glass pane stenciled "Interrogation" in ominous black lettering.

"She wants to spill to you first, Mr. Darcy."

"Me? She doesn't know me. I think Elizabeth needs to see her sister first. If for no other reason than to calm the both of them. This can't be easy for the girl."

"I know, but she made me give her my word and a homicide detective never goes back on his word."

Darcy pushed his hat back slightly before entering the room then winked at Elizabeth. She rewarded him with a tender smile as he closed the door.

He turned, eyes fixing on the pretty girl before him. She looked so young, like a bobby-soxer, and it saddened him to think of her stripping in that seedy joint, and then remembered seeing her that night at El Barrio. She was the dame Wickham took back to his apartment.

Dissimilar from Elizabeth, the girl was blonde and plump, but she had Elizabeth's soulful expression and amber eyes, which were now bloodshot. She looked up at him, her complexion wane in the dimly-lit room, illuminated by only a small window that faced the brick façade of the building next door. Rain pelted the glass in teaming beats. It was obvious that Lydia was ill; the small space stunk like a sewer on a hot afternoon in Gotham.

"Who are you?" she groaned, her hand supporting her head at the rickety wood table.

"Hello, Lydia. I'm Fitzwilliam Darcy."

"You're the brother of that society girl George took to Cuba?"

He slid out a chair and sat cattycorner to her, gently asking, "Yes. Are you ill? We can get you some help."

"There ain't no cure for what ails me. He did this to me."

"I see." Yeah. He did see, but wasn't about to ask, wondering if Wickham had knocked her up—or worse—given her venereal disease. "Your sister is just outside the door. Would you like for me to get her?"

"Not yet. I gotta talk to you. There's something you should know."

Darcy reached into his inside coat pocket then withdrew a handkerchief, holding it out to her. "Here take this; you're breaking out in a cold sweat."

"Thanks. You're not so bad, not like George said you were."

"I'm sure he said a lot of things about me, many of which aren't true."

She took a drink from the water glass in the center of the table then said, "I know something about you, and I figure that if they're gonna pin his murder on me then I'm not going up the river with this on my conscience."

"Did you kill Wickham?"

"I ain't talkin' about that. I'm talkin' about something *you* did—not me."

His body stiffened. "I'm listening."

Lydia swiped the handkerchief across her forehead then looked away, obviously embarrassed to make eye contact with him. "Well first, I'm sorry about what happened to your sister. I only went along with the scheme because ... well ... he said he loved me and although he didn't know why, I needed the dough, which he promised to share with me. He read about your sister and your politics in the paper and then told his buddies at the club. They contacted their friends in Havana. The Commies were gonna pay him big money afterwards and we were gonna leave town, but when he came back ..."

Her eyes filled with tears and he reached out, resting his fingers on her wrist. "Thanks to you and the information you provided Elizabeth, Georgiana is safe, so don't worry about that. It's over."

"Good. She was lucky if you ask me."

"I'm sorry that George hurt you."

"Yeah. Me, too. He played me a fool, just like he did Lizzy and all the rest—including your sister."

"He did. He was a very bad man. Now tell me what is it you think you know about me?"

"It's about that Marine. You know ... in the war."

He abruptly stood.

"Wait! Don't go!"

"I'm not going anywhere. I promise."

Opening the door, he spoke more brusquely than he meant, but in that moment he was panicked. "Elizabeth. You need to be in here."

Brandon's head snapped up from where he leaned against the wall, smoking a cigarette, and Elizabeth furrowed her brow but did not question his command.

"No! I don't want her to hear this, Mr. Darcy. It's between you and me."

"It's okay, Lydia," Elizabeth said, her voice soft and supportive as she entered the room. "Mr. Darcy and I are going to be married. We have no secrets between us."

"No, we don't." He held the third chair out for his girl then took his seat. Leaning, once again, toward Lydia, his right hand held onto Elizabeth's resting upon the table.

"Married? You're marrying this moneybags?"

"That's right. I'm crazy about your sister."

"Did you give her that mink?"

He smiled, "No, that's my sister's coat, but if Elizabeth wants one of her own, she can have one or two. So could you."

"Hmm. Well, if you say so, okay then." She took a deep breath then began. "The night you threatened to kill Wickham, you know, at El Barrio last week, I met up with George after my performance at the Kit Kat." She blushed, twisting the linen still in her hands. "He was lit up, and told me stuff, some I didn't want to hear, but there was something about you in a bar fight in the South Pacific back in '43. Said you clocked someone because he cheated at cards."

"Perhaps," he vaguely admitted, feeling the mortifying shame and the guilt that went with it wash over him, once again.

Elizabeth squeezed his hand tighter, trying to calm him and for her benefit he attempted to keep his expression expressionless. His heart raced. What could Lydia know about Nouméa?

"Go on Lydia. Tell us everything," Elizabeth prompted. "Whatever you tell us, won't leave this room."

Lydia gazed up into Darcy's eyes, making sure he was paying attention to every word she said. "I don't want anyone thinking that I killed George, and no one, especially you, should think that you killed that Marine. He told me that you didn't do it. He only wanted you to *think* you did—that way he could manipulate you. It was him—he did it when he went back that night, followed him on his way to his ship then snapped his neck. The only one who thinks you killed that Marine was you, and that was just what George wanted."

Stunned silent, Darcy sat back in the chair, arms outstretched with hands on the table. Darcy's expression of shock matched Elizabeth's.

His heart stopped for a mille-second, his thoughts blank until they came forward in a rush. *I didn't kill him! My God!*

Their eyes met and she bit her lip, again. He was sure his tough girl would cry.

"Are you sure about this, Lydia?" he asked in astonishment.

"I ain't lyin' about this. It's just like he told me. He laughed about what he did to you, laughed about going to Cuba with your sister, and I didn't like that. I knew then that I had to make a back-up plan—just in case."

"Darcy, you didn't do it!" Elizabeth cried.

"Thank you, Lydia! Thank you. My God, all these years! All this guilt! You're sure? Positive?"

"I'm sure."

He tugged Elizabeth closer to him and they embraced at the small table, neither caring that they weren't alone, and he sure as hell didn't give a damn if either woman saw his tough façade strip away with tears. "Baby, I'm free!"

"I told you that he lied. I told you that you didn't do it."

"My God."

Suddenly Lydia gagged, covering her mouth with the handkerchief.

"Lydia?" Elizabeth asked, pulling back from Darcy's embrace. "Are you okay? Are you going to be sick?"

"It'll pass. Can you go now, Mr. Darcy? I gotta talk to my sister, alone."

"Yeah. Sure, kid." He stood, gazing down at her. "Whatever you need, Lydia, just come to me. I'll move heaven and hell to take care of you. I owe you and I keep my word. We'll get you outta this mess you're in."

The poor girl attempted a smile before she gagged again.

As soon as the door closed, Elizabeth slid a chair beside her sister. "You did good, Sister. I'm proud of you and like Darcy, I'm here to help you."

"You promise?"

"Of course I do. I told you that the other night." She reached up, petting Lydia's short hair. "I love you. Now tell me, what's all this business about you burglarizing George's apartment? Detective Brandon said he found you with a bag full of money."

"That's the dough Viktor gave him last week at the club. I knew George hid it when he told me that he lost it all in a card game. I was gonna use it to get outta town."

"Darcy and I will help you do that, but tell me why. Is there something else I need to know before I talk to the detective so he can drop the charges?"

Shocked, Lydia set back from her sister, examining her face. "You'd lie for me?

"Yes. I'd lie for you."

There was only one person she had told—and that person was now dead. Lydia leaned forward and whispered into Elizabeth's ear. "I'm gonna have George's baby."

"Oh no! Lydia."

"Yeah. I'm four months."

"There's more, something I suspected but he confirmed it when he was in the sauce before he left for Cuba."

"Go on."

"I don't think I should tell you. Kitty sent me at letter last week and made me promise not to tell what she saw before leaving for France, but then George blabbed about what he did at the beginning of the year."

She leaned in again and whispered. Elizabeth's jaw dropped, her eyes widened and then she sniggered. *Well, well, well. Guess Janie ain't so prim and proper after all.*

••

TWENTY-ONE

Jane Bingley's cool blue eyes could not leave Elizabeth's left ring finger. It seemed to be permanently affixed to every movement the many diamond facets made when the chandelier hit the stone just right, and that reaction was what Elizabeth had hoped for.

Three miles from the Long Island Sound, Netherfield Hall may have been lovely to some, but it wasn't to Elizabeth's liking. Perhaps because it was Jane's home, resembling another easy won victory between two competing sisters. A triumph to Jane, and where Charlie was concerned, a conquest her sister had never ceased gloating over. Perched on a gold velvet arm chair, the lady of the house looked prim and proper, even in her ninth month of pregnancy. But Elizabeth knew that all of this suburban housewife affluence and high society was a veneer.

Her short, blonde waves and pearl earrings accented the Peter Pan collar of the custom-made maternity blouse of drab brown. All of which she modeled as a sort of another victory—along with the new strand of pearls that her husband had just come home with in honor of the impending birth of the future President of the United States, they referred to as "Junior."

Seated beside Darcy in the sitting room, surrounded by her family, Elizabeth realized that something had changed inside her: she was feeling content for the first time in her adult life. Sure, that sense of satisfaction that her sister was green with envy over the size of her engagement ring was nice, but that knowledge didn't make her as smugly giddy as she had thought it would. To her, the size of the ring didn't matter, only the quality of the man who offered it. It didn't matter the vast amount of wealth and society that she was marrying into, only that she was accepted and loved—not to mention respected—by the Darcy family. And it sure as hell didn't matter that her sister was having a child so soon into her marriage. One day, when the time was right, she and Darcy would have a brood—and not because 3.7 children was society's acceptable norm, or that it would appease her cuckoo mother, but because their children—no matter how many—would be an extension of her and her husband's love.

On this Thanksgiving Day, 1952, she finally awoke to the fact that she had spades over her vain, mercenary—and deceitful—sister whose ankles had swelled to be the size of tree trunks, derriere spread the width of a dirigible, and face puffed like a melon. And had it not been for George Wickham choosing her over Jane, using her followed by Mary and her disappearance, then she never would have met the man of her dreams—Darcy.

"So when is the society wedding between you two love birds?" Charlie's sister, Caroline, asked, the sneer to her coral tinted lips almost mocking as she scanned her unexpected and unwelcome opponent for Darcy's affections up and down.

"We'll be having a small wedding, something intimate, maybe even at City Hall." Gone was Elizabeth's desire for a big church wedding. None of that mattered any more, not after having survived their dangerous trip to Havana. "We'll be honeymooning in Niagr—"

"Lydia," Jane interrupted, toying with her pearl necklace. "Mother tells me that you've been working as a hat check girl? Is that a respectable job for a young woman of only seventeen? Are you even allowed to work in a nightclub?"

"I quit that joint after saving up enough money to become a nurse." She looked at Darcy and that made Elizabeth's heart swell, especially when he gave her youngest sister a wink on the sly. School would come, but for right now, it provided an alibi to await the birth of her baby.

"A nurse? Don't you need to go to school for that? You must think more reasonably about your future?"

"I have. There's a good school in upstate New York and I'm leavin' next week."

"Upshtate?" their mother slurred.

"Yeah. I'm leavin' Queens, and I might not be back."

"I don't think that's a wise decision, Lydia. Who is going to care for Mom and Pop?"

"You are. It's about time you helped them out. You got the dough; use it. I'm tired of being their bankroll. Like Lizzy, I got a career ahead of me."

"Well I think that deserves a toast!" Charlie said, standing with his glass of scotch. Poor man, his happy demeanor and love for Jane made him appear a boob.

"To the Bennet sisters: May this coming year be blessed with a wedding, a baby, and a nurse!"

Again, Jane's eyes bore into Elizabeth's ring twinkling when the water-filled crystal glass rose to her lips. The jealous creature opposite her held out an arm to inspect her own measly two-carat stone. "How big is your diamond, Lizzy?"

"Jeepers, I don't know! It was Darcy's mother's." Gazing down at the ring, she held out her hand to admire it. "It really is stunning. Isn't it? Darcy how big *is* it?"

"It's seven carats," he said, his lips twitching slightly. "Only the best for my girl."

Obviously enjoying this verbal boxing match whereby Jane was taking a pummeling, he squeezed her free hand. Her man may have been the pugilist champion aboard the USS *Stevens*. But he was holding back from throwing punches himself tonight. This was her fight and one that was long overdue—even if it was Thanksgiving Day.

After an awkward silence, Jane glanced down at her ring again then back up to Elizabeth's. "It looks so uncomfortable on your short fingers. Hands like yours can't carry off something so magnificent—so expensive. May I try it on?" Jane asked.

"I don't think so. Given the size of your fat fingers—from the pregnancy, of course—you may not get it off, but I assure you, my engagement ring fits me like a glove—perfectly." She paused, making sure that she caught her sister's eye, and then added with a smile from the heart, "Just like the man who gave it to me."

The smile remained, beaming when she looked up to Darcy; he did the unthinkable—the unimaginable—he deposited a tender kiss to her lips for all to see.

Jane gasped.

Lydia snorted.

Georgiana smiled, and Caroline, huffed, stood, then wobbled to the window where she braced herself to keep from falling to the floor in a jealous heap of tears.

"And how did the two of you meet?" Jane continued in her interrogation, her hand smoothing over her large belly.

"Oh, didn't I tell you, Janie? Lizzy came to Darcy's office to invest some money. I happened to be there setting up the trust for Junior and introduced them."

"*You* introduced them, Charlie? But you never said."

He shrugged. "Your sister has a head for figures and with Darcy being high finance, I knew right away that they were meant for each other. Had they met at our wedding, I am sure they would have hit it off. And now they're engaged!"

Jane snorted, "How much money could you possibly make as a bookkeeper at Macy's, Lizzy? Hardly enough to invest in any of Darcy's ventures, I'm sure."

"I do very well, thank you, but I suppose that's irrelevant now." *God that felt good!*

Their father shifted on the settee beside the fireplace, losening his tie when it constricted around his neck. All eyes turned to him as he mumbled something about some homicide detective, which prompted a throat clearing from Darcy.

"Say, Darce, will you be driving back to the Dakota tonight? You may hit some traffic if you don't leave directly following dinner." Charlie laughed uncomfortably. "What am I saying? With that El Dorado of yours, you'll fly home."

"I hadn't planned on going back to Manhattan this evening. I thought we'd spend the night at Pemberley. It's been a while since I was out this way and with that ice storm last week, I'd like to check on the guest house. The roof had some issues and, although Crenshaw said he'd look after it, I'd like to give it a once over. Just to be sure, you know."

Elizabeth lit a cigarette, loving the direction of the conversation. Yeah, she knew where this was gonna go and now—yes, now—came that smug glee. She couldn't help herself.

"Right! Pemberley! Jolly good, that's a smashing idea!"

"Pemberley?" Jane asked, furrowing her brow. "What's that?"

"You know Pemberley, darling. Don't you remember? It's that estate we drove past last summer when I took you on a tour of the North Shore. The Darcy home is that stone castle overlooking the Sound on Sands Point."

Jane's chin dropped. "Th ... that's your mansion?"

Surprisingly, it was Georgiana who answered, obviously unhappy by Jane's condescending tone to both her new friend, Lydia, and her future sister-in-law. "Well, Jane, it's not really a *mansion,* per se. I think the society pages would refer to it as an estate because it has six outbuildings on 243 acres. Netherfield is defined as a mansion, though —and an impressive one in its own right!"

No matter how hard Jane had tried to pass herself off as born and bred, old money of best society, her upbringing and ignorance would always show through. The woman's eyes narrowed at Elizabeth. Yeah, green—her moneybags fiancé was greater than the Bingley fortune.

"We'll be neighbors soon, Jane ..." Georgiana placed her soda water on the coaster. "... since I just inherited Matlock Hall only two miles from here. It was my uncle's mansion, put in trust for me when his two sons were killed in the war."

"How nice... and ... and how many rooms did you say Pemberley has?" Jane swallowed.

"What did you tell me earlier, sweetheart? Thirteen bedrooms, 10 bathrooms?" Resisting a giggle, Elizabeth squeezed Darcy's hand resting on her lap.

"That's about the sum of it. A measly fifty thousand square feet when you consider the size of some of the Rockefeller and Vanderbilt estates."

God she loved her man; he was playing right along with her, vindicating her to a sibling who always made her feel less. Poor Charlie, so happy-go-lucky that he had no conception of what lay below the conversation. Darcy meant no offense to him—just to Jane. Nothing had been kept from him; he was mad as blazes at her.

"Oh. So, you're not as wealthy as Rockefeller then?" Jane asked.

"No. Not that wealthy. On par with, maybe, Howard Hughes but not the Rockefellers."

A slight whimper left Caroline's lips at the window.

Then silence. It was so quiet you could hear a pin drop until Thomas snored in the corner, breaking the tension between sisters.

Placing her hand on her lower back, Jane struggled to stand, her belly jutting out. "Lizzy can I refill your drink, fill your plate with more canapés?"

"Sure, Jane. You're such a wonderful hostess, but let me help you. I'm not a lady of leisure yet." She extinguished the cigarette before rising. "Darcy, can I get you anything?"

"No, baby, but thank you." He winked again in support of what she was about to do.

Together the sisters strolled toward the padded bar at the far end of the parlor. Examining Jane's profile and contorted expression of discomfort, Elizabeth suddenly felt guilty for her gross grandstanding of wealth, but ignored the urge to apologize, squashing the Lizzy of old who would kowtow in deference and insecurity to her perfect sister. "Are you feeling well, Jane?"

"Yes." She suddenly stopped, then turned to face her. "I'm just shocked."

"Really? About what?"

"You and Mr. Darcy."

"What could be so shocking? He's a good catch, a top-notch fella."

"And obviously convinced that you are, too, in spite of your living alone in Manhattan and being a career girl. Does he know about your past relationships?"

"If you mean George, yes he knows about my bad judgment. Darcy and I keep nothing from each other. We have an *honest* relationship." *And a passionate one.*

"Hmm. I suppose you lucked out."

"That's the first thing we can agree on. Sure, I'm a lucky woman, but I'd like to think I have qualities that he's attracted to. I didn't do too bad for a once insecure girl labeled 'an ugly duckling, someone whose own boyfriend married another because she was so worthless'. None of those things you found so objectionable about me matter to Darcy. He's not superficial; he knows my worth—and, further, so do I."

Jane furrowed her penciled eyebrows but said nothing, dismissively turning to face the bar. She placed a selection of mini Velveeta sandwiches, deviled eggs, and crabmeat stuffed celery stalks onto a bone china plate. "Is that a Dior dress?"

"It is. Darcy purchased it for me in Havana."

"Havana? Whatever were you doing there?"

"On holiday."

"Before marriage?"

"Yes, before marriage."

"That's a silly question. Once a floozy, always a floozy."

Now that crossed the line. "Tell me, Jane, does Charlie know about George? How you once pined for him, fought me for him? How you stalked Mary and that scoundrel even after Charlie came on the scene?"

"Of course he doesn't know about George."

"Then he doesn't know about that night in the garage?" She filled a glass with wine, needing something stronger than soda water for her final set down.

"What night?"

"You know the night. The one when you told your fiancé that you were going to the movies, but actually rendezvoused with George in the office after closing time? It was the night before he skipped town."

A little gasp escaped her sister's lips; her hand trembled slightly. The woman was all figure eights and Elizabeth smiled.

"I ... I ... don't know what you're talking about."

"Sure you do. Unfortunately for you, you didn't expect Kitty to spy on the act, but in typical Jane fashion, you got lucky. She left for Paris before blabbing." Elizabeth took a drink, enjoying the slow delivery of torture to her sister and watching her overload the plate in anxiety.

"But your luck turned, Jane. Lydia received a letter from Kitty last week with all the sordid details of the 'Oh Georgie, thrill me' on Pop's desk."

Jane blanched. "Stop it! I don't want to hear this!"

"I suppose the final nail in your coffin was when, days later George, deep in his cups, flapped his lips about a few other things about the two of you to someone. I wonder ... if I should be the one to tell Charlie."

"You wouldn't!"

"Maybe I will ... maybe I won't. Maybe Darcy will put his mouth into the conversation in some man to man talk."

Again, Jane's eyes flashed, narrowing. "It's none of his business."

"Oh, trust me, it is."

Elizabeth paused, drinking deeply from her glass, feeling even more brazen then before. "Say, did you hear that George is dead? He was murdered last week, a bullet to his brain."

Jane dropped the plate she held, the hors d'oeuvres scattering across the bar top.

A glance over her shoulder showed that Darcy held Charlie's attention, talking finance. Elizabeth leaned closer and whispered. "They haven't found his murderer yet, but they did find out that at the beginning of the year, he'd been frequenting a seedy motel with a blonde a few miles from here."

Shaking fingers flew to her sister's round belly. She lovingly caressed the baby within, her eyes filling with tears.

"Yeah. That's what I thought. Darcy and I will *consider* not telling your husband about how those pinochle games at the country club were actually rolls in the hay with another man. Charlie is too good a fellow to have his heart broken by an adulterous wife. Good natured as he is, he's no dope; he'll figure you out eventually."

Eyes locked, staring each other down before Jane turned away, her lip trembling.

"But the redeeming thing to do is to be honest with him before he puts two and two together. He, and your marriage, the love he has for you deserve that, even if you are a shrew."

"What do you know about marriage? What George and I had was special. He loved me before ... before that other woman came along."

Elizabeth mockingly laughed. "Yeah. That seemed to be his practice and standard end to his affairs with all his past conquests. Poor Jane, just another in his long line of *floozies*."

She walked away, leaving her sister at the bar with her perfect hors d'oeuvres, not so perfect life, and George Wickham "Junior."

Dinner was going to be an interesting show to watch.

••

Twenty-two

Elizabeth sat drinking coffee at the counter of her favorite haunt, Ruby's Diner, across the street from the Darcy Private Investigation Agency. Inwardly she grinned; her heart leaped in joy; her little corner of Gotham was now infused with light, more brilliant than a Times Square billboard. Yeah. She was one happy dame on this perfect early April afternoon.

The workers had finally finished remodeling her former three-room apartment, turning the entire space into a top-notch, classy office right there in Hell's Kitchen. She had even hired two other tough gumshoes and the phone hadn't stopped ringing off the hook with new clients. Now all they needed was a Girl Friday. And the cream on the cake was that she had just closed the book on the Carter adultery case, exonerating Mr. Carter. The man might have been unhappy, but he wasn't cheating, just needing to be away from his wife.

Bright afternoon sun streamed into the plate-glass window of the diner spotlighting the New York cheesecake in the dessert case. The colorful music jukebox played the Theresa Brewer Billboard hit, "Til I Waltz Again With You." She sighed contentedly breathing in the familiar aroma of Ruby's famed cinnamon crumb cake. It was a perfect day. Nineteen fifty-three was a great year so far.

After turning the page of the latest issue of *Variety,* Elizabeth scanned the gossip column, her thoughts, again, drifting to the absolute euphoria she felt at this moment. Having just received exciting news, she couldn't wait to share it with the man she was absolutely head-over-heels, positively lulu in love with: her husband of three months. She expected him at any minute to join her for coffee and cake after his meeting with the City Council about financing a park and memorial statue to veterans of foreign war.

Sipping her coffee, the delightful jingle above the diner door caught her ear, and she swiveled on the counter stool, beaming a welcome. It wasn't him. A uniformed soldier entered, removing his cap, and he took a seat in a booth at Ruby's welcoming invitation.

"Sit anywhere you like; coffee's on the house for all G.Is."

"Can you believe it? We're still in this wacky war," Ruby said to Elizabeth.

"Truman called it a police action, but my husband says it may be over soon. Now that Stalin is dead, peace talks with the Chinese and North Koreans may continue," she noted, humored how she was becoming more politically minded each day, thanks to Darcy.

Ruby harrumphed. "Police action? That's government mumbo jumbo. Tell that to Josie on the night shift. It's a war alright. Her nephew ain't going back to Hoboken ..." As she walked to the soldier, with coffee pot clutched in hand, she added over her shoulder, "... not now, not ever."

Elizabeth frowned. She hoped war would end soon, along with the Red scare and the threat of an atomic attack. No, she wouldn't think on those things today. Today she had blissful news to share with her husband. Damn politics always tried to suck the joy out of her, but she focused on the jukebox music, letting herself get lost in the lyrics and more pleasant musings as she waited for Darcy.

"Say, you're looking like a class act, Eli," Ruby noted coming back to the counter, her quirky tiara-shaped hat tilted to one side. "A real lady with all those fancy clothes of yours."

"Thanks, Ruby. Well, I have to look the part, right? High society wife and respectable lady dick all in one." She snorted, "Who would've believed that a girl from Jackson Heights would marry a beefcake moneybags who'd let her remain a career-girl. Go figure."

"Is that ensemble one of them Paris designers I read about in *Life* magazine?" Ruby filled the empty coffee cup then leaned upon the pink Formica counter, one palm supporting her shifted weight.

"Hattie Carnegie, I'm told. Charlotte says she's high fashion." She ran her hand down the waist of her Wedgwood blue suit jacket.

"What does Mr. Darcy say?"

She chuckled. "That I look like a million bucks ... baby ..."

"I love when he calls you baby. Does this old girl's heart good to hear how much he adores you, dotes on you like every girl should be. A good man's hard to find and you got yourself a real keeper in that gee. Easy on the eyes, too."

"Yeah. I'll keep him." She leaned closer with a smile that wanted to burst into a grin, "I love him, too."

"Soon you'll be off to Washington with him, and I'll lose my favorite regular customers."

"Didn't I tell you? We're not going anywhere. The agency is here to stay and so is my man. No politics for this Darcy family."

"Not even with that Ike takin' up residence in the White House?"

"Nope. Darcy and I are staying put. We'll have other things to concentrate on."

The bell jingled again, several loud times, and Elizabeth glanced up to see a dark-haired woman wearing a yellow, floral print dress, struggling with a cumbersome baby carriage as she attempted to enter the diner. Her back pushed against the glass, fighting to get the pram wheels over the metal threshold.

"Here, let me help!" Elizabeth offered, jumping up at the same time as the G.I. to hold open the door. He got there first with a gentlemanly smile and an "Allow me."

"Thank you!" The mother exclaimed, her body bending forward to check on her child after the jostling.

On this lovely spring day, the woman's happy spirit was another burst of sunshine into the pink and white décor of the diner. The little circle hat she wore concealed her face from that angle, her coos of comfort to the little one sounded melodic—familiar.

Finally she looked up, turning to enter with the bulky carriage. Her gaze met Elizabeth's astounded gape.

Shocked, Elizabeth's heart seized. She could barely form the words. "M ... Mary King?"

The woman beamed. "It's me! Yes, Lizzy, it's me!"

"It is you! I thought you were dead!" she cried, running to her long-lost friend then hugging her tightly, eyes filling with tears. "My God! You're alive!"

Mary laughed. "You always did jump to outlandish conclusions. I wasn't dead, although, trust me, at the time of my departure, I had wished I was." Their embrace ended and she reached for the carriage handle, gently rocking it when the infant fussed. "This little man was unexpected, definitely unwelcome, but now I can't imagine life without him."

"You left because ... you were pregnant?" Elizabeth whispered.
"Yes."
"By George Wickham?"
"Yes."

Elizabeth gazed in wonderment at the beautiful baby bundled in a sky-blue layette set in the carriage. "Oh, Mary, he's beautiful! What's his name?"

"Robert, after my grandfather."

Wrapping her arm around her best friend, together they strolled to a vacant booth. "Ruby, can you bring us some coffee and crumb cake?"

"Sure thing, doll."

"Sit, tell me everything! Oh, how I've missed you. I never gave up; I never stopped searching." Elizabeth said, reaching for Mary's white-gloved hand.

"Thank you. I'm so sorry, but I had to go. I truly didn't want to ruin my family by being an unwed mother, especially by a chiseler who never had any intentions to begin with."

"But I would have helped you."

Mary smiled. "You would have and then your mother would have found out and told my mother. No, it was best that I left, even if it meant that you, my dearest friend, and my parents thought me kidnapped or dead. Pop never would have understood. He would have kicked me out had he known I got knocked up."

"You know they hired me to find you?"

"Really? Maybe I'll consider going home for a visit. Not now, but one day."

She stood and lifted Robert from the carriage, righting his little crocheted hat.

"He has your eyes," Elizabeth admired in amazement.

"Thank goodness for that!"

They laughed and Mary sat back in the booth, arm firmly wrapped around the babe.

"He must be ..."

"Just over a year now."

Elizabeth reached for the baby's eager fingers, grasping his tiny hand. "Amazing, Mary. You're a mother!"

"I know ... I'm a long way from that starry-eyed, foolish girl in Jackson Heights, aren't I? And look at you ... you're no longer that slighted, insecure girl I left on the library steps before I quit town. I mean, look at that diamond! I'm almost blinded."

Laughing, she admired her engagement ring. "This and a mushy proposal were hard won, I tell ya'."

"You sure have come far, Lizzy ..."

"You have no idea ... I'm so happy ... And just this morning ... well, I just found out that I'm going to be a mother, too."

Mary laughed. "That's wonderful! Congratulations!"

"Thank you. I was waiting for my husband to arrive so I could tell him. You're the first to know."

Robert squealed and Elizabeth squeezed his hand, laughing with him, unable to contain her joy as Ruby arrived balancing a tray, placing two cups and two pie plates on the table. A brief introduction was made, but that was all Elizabeth could manage. A ghost had just appeared and she had hundreds of questions. Today was turning out to be the happiest day of her life.

The lady dick in her asked in wonderment, "Mary? Where did you go? I looked everywhere. I put a tail on that man hoping he'd lead me to answers."

"Oh! There was a home for unwed mothers in Westchester County. They took me in. Lizzy, I had to leave Queens."

"Because of your reputation?"

"In part, but also because George threatened me. He said if I told a soul that he was the father, he'd find me and kill me and my baby."

Elizabeth gasped.

"I was afraid." Mary smiled wistfully. "But not anymore."

"You never need to fear again."

"I had even considered putting Robert up for adoption, but I just couldn't do it. So I remained living there in hiding until I could get settled and get on my feet. Then your Mr. Darcy found me and moved me into a lovely sunny apartment in Murray Hill. He's been so kind, paying for everything, even hired a nanny so I could look for a job. I changed my name and as far as anyone knows, my make-believe husband, Bill Collins, an army chaplain, was killed in Korea."

"Did you say ... my ... Mr. Darcy?"

"None other. He'd been searching the different homes for me for about a month. He's the one who told me you'd be here today."

Well that knocked her for another loop. "He ... my husband ... Fitzwilliam Darcy ... found you?"

"Yes he did. Lizzy, you are one lucky girl. He's positively dreamy, a real gentleman, and deserving of you!"

Elizabeth threw her head back in laughter. *He did this for her! All for her.*

"I have to agree with you there. He surprises me at every turn. I've never met a man more suited to me. We respect each other; we are of the same mind in so many ways, but mostly, he is a good man, an honorable one in this city of corruption and crime."

"Is he a private eye, too?"

"No. I guess I wore off on him. But he's a Philip Marlowe addict."

"After I got settled, he broke the news to me about George, too. Was his murderer ever caught?"

"Not really. There was a flimsy sort of confession down in Havana, but no hard evidence. At any rate, that Cuban Commie thug is dead, too..." her voice trailed recalling the night of Georgiana's rescue. "Anyway, that's one case I don't care to investigate further. Good-bye, good riddance, I say."

"You know, I'm torn. On one hand, I'd like to thank the bad hat who shot him. On the other hand—without George—I wouldn't have

Robert. I guess, in the end, I'm glad that he's gone so that he can't take advantage of other girls like he did you and me."

"And Lydia ..." *and Jane.*

"Oh no! Your sister, too?"

"Yeah. He led her on a pretty dance, just like he did us. Her baby will be born any day now. That jerk told her to take a hike the minute she said that she was in the family way. Told her he had another chippie waiting in the wings to go off to Rio with."

"He said the same thing to me. Well, not the Rio part, but said he didn't want any ball and chain and no brat. That was for sure. Where is Lydia now?"

"With Mary's religious order in Baltimore. My Mr. Darcy gave the nuns a substantial donation to care for her and see that the baby gets adopted into a good home. Mary keeps an eye on her between prayers."

"Poor girl. She's lucky she has a sister who cares so much. It's a tough road when you have to go it alone."

"Yeah, but you did good, real good. You know, Mary, for so long I had hung a red light on that man, believing he kidnapped and murdered you. It feels odd now, knowing that I wrongfully accused Slick Wick."

"Do you feel guilty?"

"No. He did kill someone ..." her thoughts trailed off to the poor fella in the South Pacific and she had to snap herself from the morose knowledge that a Marine died by George's hands. She sipped her coffee and tried to focus on the here and now. "Say, Mary, can you type?"

"A little. Why?"

"How'd you like to come work for the detective agency? I'm looking for a Gal Friday."

Mary's face lit up. "Really?"

"Sure! I'll pay you top dollar, too. You can start next week, even bring the baby if you like."

"Gee, Lizzy! That'll be swell!"

The bell rang for a third time and Elizabeth glanced up to see Darcy standing at the threshold. He looked so dashing in that gray sport coat and navy trousers, his fedora tilted just right. He had a twinkle in those indigo eyes, and he wore a mischievous grin that made her heart do wacky flips.

"And here's my incredible husband now," she effused, rising as fast as she could after tossing her napkin on the table.

What more could a girl want in life when every day and night was filled with Mr. Darcy?

"Are you happy, sweetheart?" he asked.

He laughed at her replying expression when she seamlessly molded into his hard body, then boldly kissing him as his arms wrapped around her.

"Darling," she purred. "Since you are obviously a skilled gumshoe now, I'd like to make you a bona fide offer to come work for the Darcy Detective Agency? My figures, digits, and skills are going to be out of commission for the next seven months or so."

Darcy raised an eyebrow. "Seven months? What are you up to, vixen?"

"Our greatest case yet ... Daddy."

••

Swollen feet and body waddled through the one-hundred-year-old convent as Lydia made her way to the vegetable garden for her daily gathering. She groaned, her back hurting, her belly low, ready to give birth any day. It could have been worse; she could be on her own—alone and ruined. Besides, the nuns were nice, even if they didn't speak much. Heck, her own blood, Sister Mary Magdalena of the Cross barely conversed with her. But they were cloistered and had devoted their lives to prayer. What was she to expect? Girl talk and "I Love Lucy" on the television? There was no television or even a radio in the convent. Like now, all she had was the nuns' prayerful singing four times a day. It was at those times that she explored her place of sanctuary—or captivity—depending upon a day's perspective and how violently the baby was kicking. For five months the Sisters of Mercy convent had been her home, and for all those months she'd been saddled with kitchen duty as if she was in the Army. She supposed this was their punishment for her "sinful" ways, even if they always treated her kindly.

With each footstep along the stone floor, her hand braced against the wall as she neared the heavy wood door; her other hand held tightly to a basket and its contents.

Today was an important day and she sniggered at the thought.

Exiting into the tranquil setting, she took a deep breath. Everything was green and bursting with life in the center of this busy city so far from Jackson Heights. Here, she was unknown to the world, protected from hurts and memories, safe from investigation and speculation. And when it was all over, her dreamboat brother-in-law promised to help her get on her feet, pay for nursing school so she could be a career girl just like Lizzy. She had hopes and dreams for her future; maybe one day meet a real nice guy. Thanks to Darcy, she was getting a second chance at life.

He and Lizzy wanted to do more than her parents had ever offered in her entire life. Sorry pie-eyed lot that they were had only said, "Come back to see us and don't forget to bring the rum," when she left, suitcase in hand. Did they even love her, she wondered often, or did they just love the incoming money she had made at the Kit Kat?

The heavenly aroma of roses mixed with fresh vegetables tickled her senses as she walked to the edge of the garden where a small statue of an angel perched on a pedestal overlooked the bounty that sustained the sisters.

She released the basket from her grasp and with straining energy, managed to lift the angel, bending to place it at her feet. The baby kicked as if knowing what she was about.

A shove to the pedestal, shifted it in the dirt.

As big as she was, the next task required kneeling and it took all she had in her to get down on hands and knees. Perspiration glistened upon her forehead and upper lip; her hand trembled as she reached into the basket to remove the spade shovel resting beside the pruning shears.

Digging the hole seemed effortless at first; the soil here was soft, amiable under the violation of metal. She was focused on the task; she still had gardening to attend to.

She dug deeper, her back straining from the position of her body hunched over the task. One hand held her tummy at the bottom of the maternity blouse she wore, keeping it from interfering and becoming soiled with each heave to scoop the soil.

Finally.

Lydia sat back on her heels, gazing down at the 12-inch ditch. She laughed aloud and dropped the spade.

From the basket she removed a cloth-wrapped item, opened the folds of fabric and admired the pretty content: A lady's .41 caliber Remington derringer, purchased from that pawn shop a block from El Barrio Steakhouse. Just like Oscar had told her, the owner of the shop wasn't going to be flapping his lips to anyone—not even to her nosy, albeit fabulous, sister.

The sun hit the shiny metal, followed by a final fingerprint-removing buff to the 3-inch barrel and the rose image on the handle. She felt satisfied that, here, hidden under the angel in a cloistered nunnery's garden all the way in Maryland, no one would ever put the finger on her for killing the man who knocked her up and threw her away like day-old bread. The lying, cheating, no-good double-crossing

George Wickham would never hurt another girl thanks to her and Oscar.

Lucky for her, the owner of El Barrio liked revenge, too, and right before she left the bar, he said, "Consider it my gift to Eli in payback for what that thug did to her."

She didn't know who Eli was but she was damn glad Oscar was real cream.

The End.

•••

Glossary

AWOL = Absent Without Leave

Bad hat = con man, criminal

Blue ice = sapphires

Chiseler = low-life, someone who cons money from others

Chippie = woman, girlfriend

Commie = communist

Cream puff = pushover, softie

Femme = slang for feminine lesbian, not butch

Femme Fatale = seductive, dangerous woman

Figure Eights = nervous wreck

Flatfoot = police officer

Gams = legs

Gee = guy, man

Grifter = con artist / swindler

Gumshoe = private investigator

Gunsel = hired gunman

Hackie = taxi driver

Hard-boiled = emotionally tough

Hecho en Cubana =made in Cuba

Lady dick = female private investigator

Lovemaking = pre-1960s definition: sweet words, flirting

Lollipop = weak, naïve person

Lo Siento = I am sorry

Moll = a ganster's girlfriend

Mug = face

Mugg = guy, man

Newshawk = tenacious reporter

Nickel dropped = the other shoe drops

Piece of beef = good-looking man

Pinko = Someone with Communist leanings

Por Favor = please

Private dick = private investigator

Pro skirt = prostitute

Put a blanket on = covered up, kept quiet

Real cream = good person

Rod = gun

Shoot cookies = vomit

Stiff = dead person

Stool-pigeon = informant

Acknowledgements

This novel could never have happened without my dear friend and publishing partner's challenge for me to write a difficult genre that hasn't been done in JAFF before: an Austenesque Noir/Crime Fiction Romance. Thank you, Pamela, for your support in everything, not just my historical fiction endeavors. Special thanks to my BFF Sheryl whose encouragement helps me hold it together when I have my doubts! I love you, girlfriend, and greatly appreciate your eye for detail. Kristi, thank you so much for expertise and going above and beyond in the editing of a genre (Noir) wholly unfamiliar to you. You're the best! Thank you, sweet friend and talented author, Zoe Burton, for your enthusiasm as you patiently waited for each chapter to cold read. And, a very special thank you to Jack, one of the toughest, hard-boiled detectives of the former Central Investigation Bureau of the New York City Police Department.
As always, thank you to Bill, the man who owns my heart and mom whose love holds me up as I try to reach for the stars!

About the Author

Cat Gardiner loves romance and happy endings, history, comedy and Jane Austen. A member of National League of American Pen Women, Romance Writers of America, and her local chapter TARA, she enjoys writing across the spectrum of *Pride and Prejudice* inspired romance novels. From the comedic Christmas, Chick Lit *Lucky 13,* and bad boy biker Darcy in the sultry adventure *Denial of Conscience,* to the romantic comedy *Villa Fortuna,* these contemporary novels will appeal to many Mr. Darcy lovers.

Her greatest love is writing 20th Century Historical Fiction, WWII–era Romance. Her debut novel, *A Moment Forever* will release in late spring 2016 with *The Song is You* following.

Married 23 years to her best friend, they are the proud parents of the smartest honor student in the world—their orange tabby, Ollie. Although they live in Florida, they will always be proud native New Yorkers.

Connect with Cat here:
Catgardiner.blogspot.com / facebook.com/cat.t.gardiner
vanityandpridepress.com / twitter.com/VPPressNovels
cgardiner1940s.com / twitter.com/40sexperience

Other Austen-inspired books
published by Vanity & Pride Press

Lucky 13

by Cat Gardiner

•Austenesque Reviews Favorite Modern Adaptation for 2014

"What a phenomenal read!! The attention to detail and the clever way the author immersed her audience in the story was such a terrific experience!"

A contemporary Austen-inspired, *Pride and Prejudice* novel.

Denial of Conscience

by Cat Gardiner

• One of Austenesque Reviews Top 10 Favorite Austenesque novels for 2015

• Margie Must Reads & More Agreeably Engaged Favorite Modern JAFF for 2015

"Denial of Conscience smolders with action, adventure, and romance. Darcy and Liz are hot together! I'd beat down Jane Austen herself for this Darcy!"

A fast-paced contemporary, Austen-inspired *Pride and Prejudice* novel.

Villa Fortuna
by Cat Gardiner
• Voted Just Jane 1813's Favorite Modern Adaptation for 2015
"Romeo and Juliet meets Pride and Prejudice in this hilarious, sweet, and oh so sexy modern adaptation."
Inspired by Jane Austen's *Pride and Prejudice* characters, a contemporary romantic comedy.

Dearest Friends
by Pamela Lynne
• Bronze Medalist 2016 IPPY Award in Romance
"Dearest Friends is one of those rare stories that quickly grabs hold of the reader and never lets go; it is a thrilling ride filled with danger, seduction, romance, and humor. I never wanted it to end."
A heartwarming, *Pride and Prejudice* Regency variation.

Sketching Character
by Pamela Lynne
• One of Austenesque Reviews Top 10 Favorite Austenesque novels for 2015
• Margie Must Reads Favorite Original JAFF for 2015
• More Agreeably Engaged Favorite Variations for 2015
"Such a book, the kind you don't want to stop reading until the end. It was fantastic! I must say I was pleasantly surprised. I laughed, I cried and so much more."
A romantic Regency *Pride and Prejudice* what-if variation.

Made in the USA
Coppell, TX
15 April 2025

48337194R00144